A FRONTIER CHRISTMAS

Four captivating Christmas love stories by today's leading historical romance authors at their heartwarming, passionate best!

LOVING SARAH
Madeline Baker

"Madeline Baker is synonymous with tender Western romances!"

—Romantic Times

A CHRISTMAS ANGEL
Robin Lee Hatcher

"Tenderness and passion are Ms. Hatcher's hallmarks!"

—Romantic Times

THE HOMECOMING
Norah Hess

Norah Hess's historical romances are "treasures for those who savor frontier love stories!"

—Romantic Times

THE GREATEST GIFT OF ALL
Connie Mason

Connie Mason writes "the stuff that fantasies are made of!"

—Romantic Times

Other Holiday Specials from *Leisure Books*
and *Love Spell:*
THEIR FIRST NOEL
CHRISTMAS ANGELS
AN OLD-FASHIONED SOUTHERN
  CHRISTMAS
CHRISTMAS CAROL
A WILDERNESS CHRISTMAS
A TIME-TRAVEL CHRISTMAS

A FRONTIER CHRISTMAS

MADELINE BAKER **NORAH HESS**

ROBIN LEE HATCHER **CONNIE MASON**

LEISURE BOOKS **NEW YORK CITY**

A LEISURE BOOK®

December 1995

Published by

Dorchester Publishing Co., Inc.
276 Fifth Avenue
New York, NY 10001

MADELINE BAKER
Loving Sarah

Happy Holidays to Bill, Bill Jr., John, David, Julie, Marian, Ashley, Amanda and Wade— who make every day seem like Christmas.

Chapter One

New Mexico, 1869

It was there again, a large oak basket filled with fresh meat and wild vegetables. Sarah Andrews stared at the basket for a long moment, as if it might tell her where it had come from. There were no other white people in the immediate area, and she was certain the Indians were not in the habit of providing for their enemies. It seemed to be a riddle without an answer.

Her heart filled with gratitude, Sarah carried the basket into the kitchen, quietly blessing the unknown giver who had put fresh food on her table once again.

As she sliced the venison, Sarah wondered anew who it was that brought her food several times each week. Without her unknown provider, she would have died of starvation long ago, for there

weren't enough vegetables left in the garden behind the cabin to sustain life, and she'd long ago
eaten all of the dried and tinned food Vern had
brought from town. All she had left was a sack
of dried apples, a little sugar and flour.

In the beginning, she'd considered trying to
walk to Pepper Tree Creek, but the thought of
crossing over fifty miles of the desert alone and
on foot, defenseless against snakes and predators,
frightened her almost as much as the very real
possibility of encountering Indians along the way
and she always changed her mind.

Sarah quietly cursed the savages who had killed
her husband and kidnapped her son. The Indians
had burned the barn, stolen their horses and cattle, taken Vern's rifle and all their supplies. To
this day, Sarah didn't know why her life had been
spared.

She'd been in the root cellar when the attack had
occurred. She had heard gunshots, a bloodcur-
dling war whoop. And then she'd heard Danny's
terrified scream, the same scream that haunted
her dreams. *"Mommy! Mommy, help me!"* Filled
with dread, she'd hurried toward the stairs only
to find an Indian blocking her path, a war club
adorned with feathers and what looked suspiciously like a scalp clutched in his hand.

Terror had frozen her in mid-stride. She had
stared at the Indian, repulsed by the weapon in
his hand, by the hideous war paint that covered
every inch of his face, distorting his features so
that he looked like a demon from hell. In that

instant, she'd known she was looking death in the face.

But nothing had happened. The Indian had looked at her as if he were seeing a ghost and then, to her surprise, he had scrambled up the ladder and disappeared.

By the time Sarah made her way outside, the attack was over, the Indians were gone. She had found her husband's body sprawled face down in the dirt, a single arrow protruding from his back. Her six-year-old son, Danny, was nowhere to be found. She had searched for him for over an hour, refusing to believe what she knew to be true. The Indians had taken her child, her only child.

Resolutely, she had set out after them, but a late summer shower washed out the tracks, forcing her to give up the chase, and she'd returned to the cabin to bury her husband along with her dreams. . . .

Sarah fried the venison and boiled the vegetables, grateful to have something to do. Sitting at the small raw plank table in the narrow kitchen, she ate without tasting the food, automatically lifting the fork to her mouth until her plate was empty.

Occasionally she thought of not eating, of just curling up in bed, closing her eyes, and waiting for death, but she didn't have the willpower to starve herself when food was available, and she didn't have the courage to slit her wrists. She'd never had any courage at all. And now all she had to sustain her was hope. Hope that the cavalry would find her next time they made a sweep through the area. Hope that they'd find the savages who had taken Danny.

After dinner, she put the basket outside the front door, knowing that tomorrow or the next day it would be gone and the following morning it would be there again, filled with food.

She hadn't expected it to be refilled the first time she set it out on the porch. She'd emptied the basket and put it outside simply to get it out of the way. It had been gone the next day. For a little while, the mystery of the basket had helped take her mind off her troubles. She'd wondered who had left it in the first place, and who had taken it. Two days later, it had appeared on her doorstep again, filled with food.

For a time, Sarah stood at the front window, staring at the charred ruins that had once been the barn. It was a blackened shell now, cold and empty, like her life. She lifted her gaze toward the sky, watching the late summer sun set in a riotous blaze of crimson that reminded her of blood . . . Vern's blood.

Turning away from the window, she went to the homemade calendar that hung beside the fireplace and crossed off another day. Three months, she thought. Three months without Vern, without Danny. Three months of no one to talk to, no one to care for. Three months of solitude. How long would it take before she went mad? How long before the Indians came back?

Going into her bedroom, she gazed at the small tintype of her son that stood on the narrow table beside her bed. Danny, her baby, at the mercy of godless savages. How frightened he must be! Did anyone comfort him when he cried? Was he getting enough to eat?

Thoughts of her only child being ridiculed and abused brought quick tears to her eyes. He had never known anything but kindness and love in his short life, never been away from her for more than a few hours. If only she could see him for a moment, assure herself that he was all right, that he was still alive. She'd heard stories of children being raised by Indians. It sickened her to think that her son might be forced to become a warrior, to ride against his own people, to commit the terrible atrocities she'd read about in the newspapers back home. She thought of her son, her own flesh and blood, taking a scalp. . . .

"No!" She shook the horrible thought from her mind, refusing to dwell on it any further. Surely a merciful God would not allow such a thing to happen.

Later, kneeling at her bedside, she prayed for the soul of her husband, comforted by her belief in an afterlife and her conviction that Vern had been a good man who would be welcomed into heaven. Poor Vern. Theirs had been a marriage of convenience. He had wanted a wife and she had wanted a way out of her father's house. When Vern proposed, she had accepted, so eager to get away from home she'd never stopped to think what it would be like to be married to a man almost old enough to be her father, a man she didn't love.

During the eight years of their marriage, she had developed a genuine fondness for her husband. Vern had been a kind and gentle man, thoughtful of her needs, her likes and dislikes. When she took a liking to a high-backed sofa she saw in a mail-order catalog, he had ordered it for her, even though they couldn't really afford it at the time. In the good times, he had surprised her with gifts: a fancy blue bonnet she had no occasion to wear, a pretty apron, a hand-painted fan. In the bad times, he had promised her that things would get better. And he had given her a son. . . .

She was sorry now that she had never loved Vern. He had deserved so much more than she had given him. She had tried to love him, but she'd never been able to give him the heartfelt devotion and affection a man deserved from his wife. The fact that he'd never complained only made her feel more guilty.

Blinking back tears of sorrow and regret, she prayed fervently for a miracle that would return Danny to her arms. And then, as she had every night since the attack, she asked God to forgive her for hating the heathen savages who had ridden out of the foothills early one summer morning and taken away everything she'd ever loved.

Chapter Two

Toklanni squatted on his heels, his hands resting on his knees, as he watched the white woman. She was washing her clothes in a big wooden bucket, scrubbing them on a board, then rinsing them in another bucket filled with clean water. When she finished washing the last garment, she stood up and began hanging them on a line strung between two trees.

She was a pretty woman. Her hair was as yellow as the sun, bright and shiny. She wore it in a knot at the nape of her neck. Her eyes were a vibrant shade of blue, like the sky in midsummer. Her features were dainty and well-shaped, from the delicately arched brows to her finely sculpted lips.

When she finished with the wash, she began chopping wood. He wondered how such a small woman could lift the heavy ax, and even as he watched, he knew she would be exhausted before

15

she managed to cut enough wood for a single fire.

His mouth curled into a wry smile of admiration as she kept at it, worrying the log like a puppy worrying a bone, until finally the ax sliced through the log and she had a good-sized chunk of firewood.

Wiping her hands on her apron, she picked up the wood and carried it into the house.

When she didn't come outside again, Toklanni stood up, one hand massaging the back of his neck. He had watched the woman every day for the last three months, seen her grow thinner, more pale, seen the lines of pain and fatigue deepen around her mouth and eyes. Sometimes she spent the day sitting at her husband's grave. Sometimes she talked to him as if he could hear her. Sometimes she put flowers at the base of a small wooden cross.

He did not understand her need to be near her deceased husband. The Apache buried their dead as soon as possible, never speaking the names of the deceased lest they arouse or anger the ghost of the departed, never returning to the grave site. The wickiup of the deceased was burned, along with everything the departed had worn or come into close contact with before he died. The surviving family members immediately moved out of the area and built a new wickiup. Those who had buried the body also burned the clothing they wore at the time, and then purified themselves with the smoke of the sagebrush.

But the woman carried flowers to her husband and spoke to him.

She was very brave, he mused, or perhaps just crazy.

But he could not stay away from her.

He was baffled by the hold she had on him. Was it because she looked so much like his mother, the same wheat-colored hair, the same vibrant blue eyes? Or was it because he'd failed to do his part when the Apache raided the homestead? He was to have killed the white woman and burned her house. Instead, he had let her live. He brought her food. He camped nearby to make sure no harm came to her.

With a grunt of self-disgust, Toklanni made his way to the foot of the hill and quenched his thirst in the narrow stream that watered the white woman's land. Soon it would be dark. He would take the basket and go home.

He told himself that he would go back to the village in the morning. She was a white woman, the enemy. Whether she lived or died was of no consequence.

But he was lying to himself, and he knew it.

He would continue to prowl around her house like a wolf protecting its den because she was alone and helpless and he felt responsible. Tomorrow or the next day he would refill the basket with fresh meat and vegetables. And to ease his conscience, he would throw in the colorful skirt that had been part of the spoils from their last raid against the Mexicans.

It was the least he could do for her, he thought bitterly, since it was his brother who had killed her husband and taken her child.

17

Chapter Three

Sarah woke with a start, not knowing what had awakened her. Slipping out of bed, she drew on her wrapper and padded into the parlor, her gaze searching the dark corners of the room. It was times like these, when she was scared without knowing why, that she missed Vern the most.

Going to the window, she peered outside, and gasped as she saw a dark shape walking quietly toward the door. Fear coiled around her insides, stealing the strength from her legs so that she sank down into the rough-hewn chair in front of the window, her gaze riveted on the dark figure approaching the cabin.

A scream rose in her throat, but sheer terror choked it off, and then she saw the basket in the man's hand and her fear left her. He hadn't hurt her in the last three months, she thought, please God, don't let him start tonight.

She stared at the Indian as he drew closer. In the dark, all she could see was that he was tall and broad-shouldered and his hair fell to his waist.

The Indian gazed at the house for a long moment before he placed the basket on the porch, then turned and walked away. She couldn't help staring after him. He walked with an odd kind of grace, his strides long and effortless, as silent as the sunrise.

With a start, Sarah jumped to her feet and ran to the door. What a goose she was, sitting there staring after him. He was the only soul she'd seen in months. Maybe he could tell her where the Apache camp was, maybe he'd take her into town.

Flinging open the door, she ran into the yard. "Mister! Hey, there, wait!"

At the sound of her voice, the man darted to the left and disappeared from sight behind a stand of scrub brush.

Tears of frustration welled in Sarah's eyes. Why had he run away? She was so tired of being alone, of feeling helpless. If she only knew where the Indian camp was, she'd go there and beg them for Danny.

She turned back toward the house, staring at the basket beside the door. Why did an Apache warrior bring her food? Why wouldn't he speak to her? How could she go on accepting his charity knowing that Indians had killed her husband? How could she refuse?

With a sigh, she carried the basket inside. She had to keep her strength up, had to go on living for Danny. She had to go on believing that she would see him again.

In the morning, Sarah went through the contents, surprised when she found a multicolored skirt wrapped in a piece of doeskin.

She held it at arm's length, her gaze moving over the vibrant colors—red and green, bright blue and yellow. It should have been gaudy, ugly even, and yet it appealed to her as nothing had before.

But she couldn't wear it. Taking food from an Indian was one thing; taking a gift of clothing was something else entirely.

She would have to give it back. She picked up the skirt, intending to refold it and place it in the basket. Instead, she went into the bedroom, removed her nightgown, and stepped into the skirt.

"Just to see how it fits," she told her reflection in the mirror.

It fit as though it had been made for her. She took a few steps, then twirled around, delighting in the way the full skirt swirled around her ankles. Rummaging through her meager belongings, she found a white shirtwaist with short puffed sleeves, the perfect compliment to the multicolored skirt.

Sarah found herself humming that afternoon as she carried water from the stream to her garden, hoping to infuse some life into the last of the vegetables. Humming, and her husband hardly cold in his grave! She should be ashamed. She knew her cheery mood was because of the skirt swishing around her ankles, because it was new, because it made her feel different somehow. Her dresses were all drab—dark blues and greens and browns—but the skirt, just seeing the brilliant colors had brightened the day.

She glanced up at the sky, noting for the first time in months how blue it was. There were flowers on the hillside, scattered clusters of pink and purple and white. And she had no one to share them with.

She felt her happiness slip away, like water through a sieve. What difference did it make if she had a new skirt? Who was there to see it? What difference did it make if her garden lived or died, if she lived or died? No one knew she was here. No one cared that her husband was dead and her child had been kidnapped by savages. She was alone, more alone than she'd ever been in her life.

With a strangled sob, she sank down to the ground and buried her face in her hands, crying as she had not cried since the day of the attack, weeping because she was alone and afraid.

Toklanni sat on top of the hill overlooking the white woman's house, his brow furrowed as he watched her cry. It was the first time he had seen her weep, and it did odd things to his heart. For a moment, he was tempted to go to her, to take her in his arms and comfort her, but he quickly shook the notion aside. His appearance would only frighten her, and not just because of who he was.

Hardly aware of what he was doing, he lifted a

21

hand to his left cheek, letting his fingers slide over the scar that ran from his cheekbone to his jaw. With a grunt, he let his hand fall to his shoulder. The scar didn't end at his jaw, it continued down the side of his neck, then slanted across his chest and belly to end at his right hip. It was a long, thin scar, souvenir of a knife fight with a Mexican soldier. When it was new, the women of the village had turned away, unable to look at him. But they were used to it now and no one spoke of it anymore.

He leaned forward as the woman stood up, her face streaked with tears, her eyes red and swollen. As she turned toward the house, he noticed that she was wearing the skirt he'd brought her. It swirled around her ankles as she walked, the movement of the skirt and the unconscious sway of her hips decidedly feminine, decidedly alluring.

He could take her, he thought. It would be so easy to ride down the hill and grab her, but he knew his mother would not have approved of such a thing. And if he took the woman to the village, everyone would know that he had not killed her.

Sarah walked slowly back to the house, her shoulders slumped, her earlier good mood gone. She was alone, so alone. She almost wished the Indians would come back and finish what they'd started. Vern was dead and Danny was gone and she had no reason to go on living. Every day was the same. She was tired of being alone, tired of her own dreary company.

She stopped in mid-stride, a chill snaking down her spine. She was being watched. She knew it. She whirled around, her gaze moving from the side of the house to the stream and back again, but there was no one there. And then she felt her gaze being drawn toward the low hill a short distance away.

Slowly she lifted her gaze to the top of the rise and there, silhouetted against the midday sun, she saw an Indian astride a big gray horse.

Sarah swallowed past the lump in her throat, wondering if it was her Good Samaritan. Squinting, she tried to get a better look at him, but the sun was in her eyes and all she could see was a dark-skinned man wearing a loose-fitting buckskin shirt and moccasins that reached to mid-calf. Even as she watched, he reined his horse in a tight, rearing turn and disappeared from her sight.

She thought about him all the rest of the day, unable to suppress the little shiver of fear that rippled through her as she remembered the Indian she'd come face to face with in the root cellar the day Vern had been killed. It was as close to an Indian as she'd ever been, as close as she ever hoped to be, and it had frightened her to the very depths of her soul. The red and black paint smeared over his face and across his chest had made him seem like something out of a nightmare. There had been a necklace of what looked like animal teeth at his throat, a feather in his long black hair. To this day, she still wondered why he hadn't killed her.

That evening, she sat at the window gazing at the setting sun, wondering who the Indian was and why he watched her.

She put the basket on the porch before she went to bed, smiling faintly as she imagined how surprised her benefactor would be when he found the apple tarts she'd made from the last of the dried apples. She hoped he'd realize it was her way of saying thank you for the skirt. Perhaps, if she could win his trust, he'd help her find Danny.

Chapter Four

Toklanni frowned at the sweet scent rising from within the basket. Lifting the cloth, he stared at the fragrant-smelling tarts lying in the bottom of the basket, and then he smiled, realizing they were a gift from the white woman. Her way of saying thank you for the skirt, he supposed. His mouth watered in anticipation as he selected one of the pastries. Taking a big bite, he closed his eyes as his mouth filled with the taste of apples and sugar. It had been years since he'd tasted anything so good.

That afternoon, he went into the hills and cut an armload of wood, which he left beside the basket the following night. A thank you for a thank you.

Sarah blinked back tears as she saw the wood piled at her door. How had her Good Samaritan known she was out of firewood?

She stared at the blisters on the palms of her hands, souvenirs of her last attempt at cutting wood. The ax had grown dull in the months since Vern's death and she didn't know how to sharpen it properly.

She didn't know anything, she thought bleakly. It had seemed like such an adventure when Vern told her they were moving west. He'd talked her into selling their dry goods store and buying a little spread in New Mexico. It had plenty of water and grass, and they were going to raise cattle and get rich. Vern and Danny had been so excited at the prospect of leaving Providence that she'd pretended to be excited, too. Why hadn't they realized sooner that they all lacked the skills necessary to survive in a harsh, untamed land? Having grown up in a city, Vern didn't know anything about raising cattle, and she didn't know anything about planting a vegetable garden, or making her own soap. She was only an adequate cook, at best, and a poor seamstress.

But there was no point in dwelling on the past, no point in wishing they'd stayed back east where they belonged.

With a sigh, she carried the wood inside and stacked it beside the hearth, then returned for the basket. There were two rabbits inside, already skinned and gutted, as well as an assortment of wild onions, turnips, and squaw cabbage.

That night, as she prepared her dinner, Sarah pretended that the food had been left by a knight of the realm who had secretly loved her from afar and was only waiting for her broken heart to mend before he came forward and declared his love. She would fall in love with him the moment she saw his handsome face, and he would carry her off on his white charger and they would live happily ever after.

The images lingered in her mind as she ate her solitary meal, washed the dishes and put them away, got ready for bed. Happily ever after, she mused. If only real life were as rewarding as fairy tales.

Toklanni sat on his heels on the far side of the stream, hidden from view by a tangled mass of scrub brush and cottonwoods, his dark eyes intense as he watched the woman walk down toward the water. She stopped when she came to a large flat-topped rock. Sitting down, she removed her shoes and stockings; then, lifting her skirts to keep them dry, she made her way down to the stream, squealing a little as the cold water covered her feet and ankles. She walked back and forth in the purling water, smiling faintly. Once she stopped to pick up a small round stone which she examined a moment before tossing it back into the stream.

He liked looking at her, liked the way she moved, graceful as a willow in the wind. Her hair caught the light of sun, and the water that clung to her legs glistened like dew drops. Sometimes when he looked at her, he saw a woman full grown, ripe and desirable. Her features were clean and well-defined, her waist was narrow, her neck slender. And sometimes he saw a curious little girl, her eyes filled with wonder.

Now was one of those times. Her blue eyes were bright with interest as she bent to study a flower, stopped beneath a cottonwood tree to watch a bird feed its young, paused to watch a squirrel scamper across a sunlit patch of ground.

He felt a quickening in his heart, a tightening in his groin as his footsteps paralleled the woman's. He could take her. The thought was always there in the back of his mind, had been there since the first time he saw her in the root cellar, her face pale, her eyes wide with fear. He grimaced as he imagined her reaction to his scars. Almost, he could see the revulsion in her eyes, hear her scream of horror as he reached out to touch her.

He did not want to take her by force. He wanted her warm and willing, her lips parted in a smile of welcome, her blue eyes glowing with desire.

He made a sound of disgust low in his throat. She would never be his, and the sooner he stopped thinking of her day and night, the better.

But he did not leave his hiding place among the cottonwoods.

Sarah made her way out of the stream and retraced her steps to where she'd left her shoes and stockings. For a time, she sat on the sun-warmed rock, her legs stretched out in front of her. It was pleasant, sitting there in the sunlight. For a while she had forgotten her troubles, forgotten everything but the simple joy of being alive on a beautiful afternoon.

She was reaching for her stockings when she paused, the hair along the back of her neck prickling. She was being watched again.

Eyes narrowed, she stared at the foliage across the stream, and gradually she made out the shape of a tall man clad in buckskins, the color of his skin and clothing blending almost perfectly into the surrounding shadows.

Picking up her skirts, she hurried to the edge of the stream and began wading across the water, wanting to get a better look at him, wanting to know who he was once and for all, certain that he was the same man who brought her food. A voice in the back of her mind warned her she might be asking for trouble, but she shook the niggling fear aside. He might know where Danny was, and no risk was too great if it would help her discover her son's whereabouts. Besides, if the Indian meant to do her harm, he'd surely have done it by now.

She glanced down to check her footing when she neared the far bank, and when she looked up again, he was gone.

Toklanni sat with a group of young warriors, listening as they boasted of their exploits in battle, bragging of the white men they had killed, of horses stolen, homes burned, women and children taken captive.

He glanced up as his brother, Noche, perhaps the biggest braggart of all, began to speak, telling of the raid on the white man's house and how he had killed the white man and taken his son.

Toklanni grimaced. Noche made it sound like a big battle when, in fact, there had been only four warriors on the raid and it had been over in a matter of minutes.

He shook his head as the man next to him prodded him in the ribs, urging him to tell of his daring in battle. He was in no mood to strut around while the others looked on. More than anything, he wanted to be alone in his wickiup with a woman in his arms. A white woman with hair like sunshine and eyes the color of a warm summer sky.

Rising, he left the circle of wickiups and walked downriver. He had returned to the village for a change of clothes and to pick up some supplies. No one had questioned his absence. It was his way, to come and go as he pleased. He'd always been a man apart, had always felt that he didn't quite belong.

Leaning against a tree, he gazed up at the starlit sky, remembering his childhood. . . .

He couldn't remember how old he was the first time he knew he was different, but one day he had looked at his mother, at the color of her hair, and realized she wasn't like the other women of the tribe. That night he had asked his father why his mother's hair wasn't black. He would never forget that night, or the shock of learning that his mother was a white woman who had once been called Christine Talavera.

Soon after that, his mother had taken him away from the rancheria. She was taking him home, she said, back to her people so he could learn

to live the white man's way. He had not wanted
to go. He had begged his father to let him stay,
but his father said he must go, and so it was
that he went to Santa Fe to live with his white
grandparents. It was a bad time. People stared
at his mother, at the blue tattoo on her forehead.
They talked about her behind her back, saying
cruel things that he didn't fully understand at
the time, things that made her cry in the night.
Though he was only nine, he soon learned that
"squaw" was a dirty word when a white man
said it.

It had been there in Santa Fe that he heard
the word "half-breed" for the first time, heard
the derision that accompanied the term, the suspicion, the hatred. Half-breed. Half Indian, half
white.

After six months, his mother packed up their
belongings and they went back to the rancheria.
You were right, he heard his mother tell his father,
and she never spoke of going home again.

He'd been much older, and his mother long
dead, when he heard the story of how his mother
came to be with the People from his half-brother,
Noche. He would never forget his shock at learning that his father had captured his mother during an attack on a stagecoach and made her his
woman against her will. When he had confronted
his father with this knowledge, Uncas had admitted it was true.

And then you were born, Uncas had said. *By
then, I loved her with all my heart, and when she
asked to go back to her people, I could not refuse.*

Though he was fully accepted by the people by the time he was a warrior, Toklanni never forgot who he was, never forgot the childish taunts that had followed him when he walked down the streets of Santa Fe, never forgot the suspicious looks, the hatred, the sense of being different. . . .

He pushed away from the tree, disgusted with himself for dwelling on what had happened so long ago.

In the morning, he bridled the gray and rode away from the village. He would find more wood for the white woman. It would give him something to do besides think of the past.

It was late afternoon when he reached a stand of timber. Dismounting, he tethered the gray nearby and began to gather an armful of fallen branches. When he had a good-sized bundle, he bound it together with a strip of rawhide, then began picking up more branches.

"Woman's work," he muttered under his breath, and grimaced as he imagined what Noche would say if he knew his brother was looking after the white woman.

Deep in his heart, he knew he didn't care what Noche would say. The white woman had become important to him in a way he dared not examine too closely. He could not put her from his mind, could not stop thinking of her, living alone in the house. Could not stop thinking of the color of her hair, wondering what it would feel like in his hands.

Too late, he heard the muffled sound of footsteps. He was reaching for his rifle when they attacked him, three white men reeking of cheap whiskey. Surrounding him, they used their rifles like clubs, crowing with delight as they hit him again and again.

The first blow glanced off his right shoulder, the second drove him to his knees, the third smashed into his right side, the fourth sent him down into a world of swirling blackness. . . .

When he regained consciousness, the moon was low in the sky. For a moment he lay still, afraid to breathe, reluctant to embrace the increased pain that any movement was sure to arouse. He moved his head slowly, staring right and left. His horse was gone, his rifle also.

Gritting his teeth, he sat up, wrapping one arm protectively around his ribcage. The pain was worse than he'd imagined, and he closed his eyes, fighting the nausea that churned in his stomach.

When the world stopped spinning, he lifted a hand to the back of his head and felt the blood matted in his hair. The distant cry of a wolf and the sudden splatter of raindrops warned him that he couldn't stay where he was. Tilting his head back, he opened his mouth and let the raindrops trickle down his throat while he debated which way to go.

For a moment he thought of going home, but the urge to see the white woman again was too strong. He would be taking a big risk, going to her for help. She had no reason to help him, and more than likely would slit his throat. He was an Indian, after all, and she had little reason to feel anything but hatred for his people. But he had to see her one more time.

Jaw clenched with determination, he struggled to his feet and began walking, each slow step rekindling the pain in his head and side.

But it didn't matter. Nothing mattered but his sudden inexplicable need to see her one last time before he surrendered to the darkness that hovered all around him.

Chapter Five

Sarah sat in front of the fireplace, a blanket draped over her shoulders as she stared, unseeing, at the Bible in her lap. She'd been reading from the book of Job. His troubles had far outweighed her own, she mused, yet that thought gave little comfort as she listened to the soft patter of the rain on the roof.

She leafed through the pages of the Bible until she came to the 25th Psalm, and felt tears well in her eyes as she read,

"Consider mine enemies; for they are many; and they hate me with a cruel hatred. O keep my soul, and deliver me; let me not be ashamed, for I put my trust in thee . . ."

She had put her trust in God, she thought as she read the verses a second time. She had no one else, only a mysterious stranger who disappeared whenever she got too close.

Rising, she went into the kitchen and filled the coffee pot with water, thinking that she'd make do with a cup of sassafras tea and the last of the apple tarts for breakfast.

Waiting for the tea to steep, she went to the window and gazed out at the dawn, then gasped as she saw a man crumpled in the mud.

Throwing her cloak around her shoulders, Sarah hurried outside and felt her breath catch in her throat as she realized the man was an Indian. Somehow she knew it was the Indian who had been watching her. For a moment she stood there, afraid to get too close, and then, seeing that he was unarmed, she dismissed her fears and knelt beside him.

His stillness alarmed her, and she shook his shoulder. "Don't be dead," she murmured. He couldn't be dead. He was her only contact with humanity, her only chance, however slim, of discovering Danny's whereabouts.

When there was no response, she shook him again, harder. "Please don't be dead."

Toklanni's eyelids fluttered open at the sound of her voice. Though he had not spoken the language of the white man in years, it came readily to his tongue. "Not . . . dead," he gasped.

Sarah reared back in astonishment. "You speak English," she exclaimed, realizing it was a perfectly ridiculous thing to say.

The Indian grunted in reply.

"Can you stand up?" Sarah asked.

He grunted again, and she hovered over him as he got his feet under him. He swayed unsteadily and she slid her arm around his waist to keep him from falling. Step by slow step, they made their way into the house, and then, as if the effort had cost him whatever strength he had left, he collapsed on the floor in front of the fireplace.

Closing the door, Sarah yanked off her cloak and covered him with it, then stood staring down at him, wondering whatever had possessed her to bring a mud-covered stranger, an Indian, into her house. She looked at him closely, a little apprehensive at his nearness, though he hardly seemed to be in any condition to do her harm. Still, one couldn't be too careful.

A cursory examination revealed a deep gash on the back of his head. She was glad to see that the bleeding had stopped. She eyed him speculatively. The logical part of her mind told her it would be necessary to wash away the mud that covered him from head to foot before she could effectively examine him further. The squeamish part of her mind balked at the mere idea.

But it had to be done. Going into the kitchen, she filled a basin with hot water, found a rag to use as a washcloth, pulled a clean towel and a bottle of salve from the cupboard, then tucked a roll of bandages under her arm.

Returning to the wounded man, she saw that he was asleep, or perhaps unconscious. It was just as well, she thought. It would be easier, and much less embarrassing, to look after him if he wasn't watching her.

Working quickly but carefully, she washed the dried blood from the back of his head and cov-

37

ered the ugly red wound with salve. Next she removed his hard-soled moccasins, then began to wash the mud from his chest. There was no blood beneath the layers of mud and leaves, only firm, copper-hued flesh. The area near his ribcage was swollen and badly bruised, as if he'd been hit with a club.

Sarah was not unfamiliar with the male form. She'd been married for eight years, she had a son, but she couldn't help admiring the stranger. His body was long and whipcord lean, perfect except for the grotesque scar that cut across his cheek, down his neck, and across his chest to his thigh. She felt the bile rise in her throat as she stared at the hideous scar, wondering how he had survived such an awful wound.

It took all her strength to lift him enough so that she could bandage his ribs, which were badly bruised but didn't seem to be broken. He had a large bump on the left side of his head, and more bruises near his shoulders.

It was near midday when she finished. For a moment she stared at the Indian lying on the floor in front of the fireplace. There was no way she could carry him into the bedroom and lift him onto the bed. Instead, she covered him with a couple of spare blankets and put Vern's pillow beneath his head. Then, after a silent battle of modesty versus cleanliness, she reached beneath the blanket and removed his clout. Taking it into the kitchen, she dropped the mud-stained garment in a pail of water.

Returning to the parlor, she added some wood

to the dwindling fire in the hearth. Though it was the middle of the day, she was exhausted, and with a last look at the stranger, she went into her bedroom and crawled into bed, fully clothed.

There was an Indian in the house. Was it possible he was the answer to her prayers? She smiled. Of course, she would take care of his wounds, and he would accompany her into town so she could get help to find Danny.

She fell asleep with that thought in mind.

Toklanni awoke slowly, immediately aware of the dull ache in his head. He lay still for a long moment, feigning sleep while he listened for some sound that would tell him where he was, but he heard only the crackling of flames.

Satisfied that he was alone, he opened his eyes and looked around, surprised to find himself in the white woman's house. How had he gotten there? Vaguely he remembered stumbling down the hill, crawling toward her house. After that, he didn't remember anything.

He started to sit up and knew immediately that it was a mistake. Pain slashed through his right side, and his head began to pound like old Nana's war drum, throbbing relentlessly, mercilessly.

Lying back, he closed his eyes and surrendered to the darkness that beckoned to him once more.

Sarah sat up, stretching. For a moment she felt disoriented, and then she remembered the Indian in the other room.

Slipping out of bed, she hurried toward the

parlor, pausing in the doorway as she saw that he was still sleeping. No doubt he'd be hungry when he woke up, she mused, and went into the kitchen to see what she could do with the last of the rabbit and wild vegetables.

Toklanni's stomach rumbled as the rich aroma of stewing meat reached his nostrils. Eyes closed, he inhaled the smell and felt his mouth water at the prospect of a hot meal. And then another scent reached out to him. The scent of woman.

He opened his eyes to find the white woman standing beside him. She was even more beautiful close up, he thought. Her hair was as gold as the metal the white men craved, her eyes a deep clear blue, her skin smooth and unblemished.

Sarah stared at him for a moment, wondering if she'd done the right thing in bringing him inside. Just because he hadn't hurt her before didn't mean she was safe now. He was a savage, untamed and unpredictable, for all that he spoke English. And then she thought about Danny. This man was her only hope of getting to town for help.

"How do you feel?" she asked, speaking slowly and distinctly.

"Like I was kicked by a buffalo."

Sarah smiled. "That's how you look, too," she remarked, and then, staring at his scarred face, she flushed in horror at what she'd said. "I didn't mean . . ." She raised her hand and let it fall, helpless to explain that she hadn't been referring to the scar but to the awful bruises that marred his right side, back, and shoulders.

Toklanni shrugged. He had expected her to be repulsed by his scarred face and body. Everyone was. Why should she be different?

"Are you hungry?" she asked.

"Yes."

He watched her walk out of the room, wondering what she'd say if she knew his brother had killed her husband and taken her child, wondering what she'd do if she knew he was the man who had almost attacked her in the root cellar.

The woman returned minutes later carrying a large bowl of fragrant stew and a cup of hot tea. She placed them on the hearth, then knelt beside him and helped him sit up, his back braced against the fireplace.

Sarah picked up the bowl of stew. "Shall I . . . can you . . . ?" Sarah stumbled over the words. Vern had liked being coddled occasionally, but the look in the stranger's deep brown eyes told her that he would not take kindly to being mothered. And she was right.

"I can do it," the warrior said tersely. He took the bowl from her hands, and bit back a groan as every muscle in his body protested the simple movement.

"Are you sure?" Sarah asked doubtfully. "That stew's hot . . ."

Toklanni grimaced, readily understanding what she'd left unsaid. If he dropped the bowl, he'd be sore in a whole new place.

"Maybe you'd better do it," he allowed, though he hated to acknowledge he was too weak to feed

41

himself. The Apache had little tolerance for weakness in themselves or anyone else.

Sarah took the bowl from his hand and offered him a spoonful of broth. She looked away while he swallowed it, sensing that he was embarrassed to have her wait on him.

Toklanni ate slowly, savoring the taste of the stew, sipping the tea, letting its warmth spread through him.

"You're the one, aren't you?" Sarah asked. "The one who's been bringing me food all this time."

It was in his mind to deny it, but then he nodded.

"Why have you befriended me in such a way?"

"You're alone."

"I wouldn't be alone if Indians hadn't killed my husband and taken my son," she retorted bitterly.

Guilt sliced through Toklanni, as sharp as an Apache skinning knife, but he kept his face impassive as he said, "This is Apache land."

"We weren't hurting anyone."

He had no answer to that, nothing he could say that would comfort her, or excuse what Noche had done. He was relieved that it didn't occur to her to ask how he knew she was alone.

Sarah felt a twinge of regret as she saw the weariness in the Indian's eyes. What was the matter with her, browbeating the man who had put food on her table for the last four months? She had no business blaming him for what someone else had done.

"Would you like some more?" Sarah asked when the bowl was empty.

Toklanni shook his head. The mere act of eating had drained him of what little energy he had and he wanted only to sleep, to escape from the pain of his injuries. Every movement, every breath, was an effort.

He was about to ask her to help him lie down again when a new need made itself known. Gritting his teeth, he looked at the door. Though it was only a few feet away, it seemed like a mile.

Seeing that her patient intended to get up, Sarah laid a restraining hand on his shoulder. "Where do you think you're going?"

"I need to . . . to go outside."

Sarah stared at him blankly for a moment, and then blushed as she understood what he was saying. "I don't think you should get up," she said firmly. "I'll get the . . ." She looked away as she felt the heat climb into her cheeks. "I'll be right back."

Toklanni stared at the white enamel pot the woman offered him when she returned, then looked up at the woman, a question in his eyes.

"You use it instead of going outside," she explained, and fled the room.

Sarah's cheeks were still flushed when she returned ten minutes later. She told herself it was silly to be embarrassed. After all, it was a perfectly natural act, but it was one thing to handle such matters when the man involved was your husband, and quite another when he was a complete stranger, and a heathen to boot!

Eyes averted, she picked up the chamber pot and carried it outside.

43

She stayed outside longer than necessary, letting the night air cool her cheeks, taking deep breaths to calm her rapid heartbeat.

Returning to the house, she left the chamber pot within his reach, then went into the kitchen to eat her own dinner and wash the dishes.

When she went into the parlor again, the Indian was asleep. She stared at the horrible scar that marred an otherwise handsome face. He had long arms ridged with muscle, large hands with long, strong-looking fingers. No matter that he was an Indian, she was glad for his company, appreciative of the bounty he had provided for her in the past. But, more than that, she had hope for the first time in months. Hope that the Indian would take her to Pepper Tree Creek. Hope that the Army would be able to hunt down the Indians who had kidnapped Danny. Hope that her son would soon be returned to her.

"Soon, Danny," she whispered. "We'll be together soon, I promise."

That night, as she said her prayers, she prayed that the Indian would be all right.

It was the first time she'd ever asked the Lord to bless an Indian with anything less than the ten plagues of Egypt.

Chapter Six

He woke to the sound of singing. The words were somehow familiar, and then he realized it was a song his mother used to sing, a song he'd heard in the big white church where she'd taken him on Sundays. He hadn't liked the white man's religion, or the grim-faced man clad in black who spoke of hell and damnation. He hadn't liked anything about living with the whites.

He sat up slowly, one arm wrapped protectively around his ribs, as the white woman entered the room. She wore a dress of dark blue. It had a high collar, long sleeves, and a full skirt, yet it clearly defined every curve.

She smiled as she handed him a cup of tea. "I'm sorry, I don't have anything else to offer you," she said, making a gesture of apology. "I'm out of food."

Toklanni grunted softly. Lifting the cup, he

45

sipped the tea. It was hot and bitter, but it took the edge off his hunger.

When he'd drained the cup, the woman placed it on the hearth, then bent to examine the wound on the back of his head.

"Does it hurt very much?" she asked.

"Enough."

"You're not seeing two of me, are you?"

"No."

"No spots in front of your eyes, or anything?"

"No."

"Good. I'd like to ask you a favor."

"Ask."

"I want you to take me to town," she said, speaking rapidly. "I need to get someone to help me find my son. Will you help me?"

"Perhaps, when I am stronger. It is a long walk, and I have no horse."

Sarah smiled, relieved that he hadn't refused, and then frowned as he started to get up. "Where are you going?"

"We need food."

"You shouldn't get up yet," she admonished, wondering at the warm glow that spread through her when he said "we," as if they were more than strangers. "Your ribs are badly bruised."

"If I don't get something to eat, I won't live long enough for them to heal."

Sarah grinned, unable to argue with his logic. She put out her hand, intending to help him to his feet, when she suddenly remembered he was naked beneath the blankets.

"Don't move!" she cried, and hurrying into the

kitchen, she grabbed his breechclout from the back of the chair where she'd left it to dry.

Toklanni grinned as the woman thrust his clout into his hand, then quickly turned her back so he could put it on. She had bathed him and treated his wounds, but now she was afraid to look upon him. It was very strange. Such modesty was unknown among the Apache.

Her cheeks were flushed when she turned to face him again. "Let me help you up."

It was in Toklanni's mind to refuse, but every movement sent bright shafts of pain darting through him. Mouth drawn in a tight line, he took hold of her arm and let her help him to his feet.

"How will you find food?" Sarah asked, then smiled. "There's fish in the stream. I tried making a fishing pole, but I never had much luck. Maybe you'll do better."

"Apaches do not eat fish."

She looked at him a moment, wondering if it had been Apaches who had killed Vern and taken Danny. Of course, it could have been Comanches. She didn't know one tribe from another. She started to ask and then she changed her mind. Instead, she said, "Why not?"

"My people do not eat anything that lives in the water."

"Well, you can't hunt. You don't have a gun."

"There are ways to catch game without shooting it."

Sarah watched him walk slowly toward the door, his left arm wrapped around his middle.

47

He shouldn't be up yet, she thought ruefully, then moved ahead of him to open the door.

"Look!" she exclaimed.

Toklanni peered over her shoulder, then grinned as he saw his big gray stallion trotting toward the house. The rope around the horse's neck had been chewed in half.

"I guess he's yours," Sarah remarked as the horse nuzzled the Indian's shoulder.

"Yes."

"Now we can go to town!" Sarah exclaimed.

Toklanni backed away from the joy in her eyes. He could not take her to town to find help. If the Army got word that the Apache had kidnapped a white child, there was sure to be a battle. People would be killed on both sides.

"I am in no condition to make such a ride," he said. "And we have no weapons."

"But—"

"When I am stronger," he said firmly.

She wanted to argue, to say that she'd take the horse and go by herself, but the harsh look in his eyes stilled her tongue.

Turning his back to the woman, Toklanni removed the rope from the gray's neck, deftly fashioned a hackamore, and slipped it over the horse's head. Briefly, he contemplated trying to swing onto the horse's bare back, but the mere thought of putting any undue strain on his bruised ribs was enough to make him break out in a sweat. Instead, he swallowed his pride and asked the woman for help.

Sarah obligingly locked her hands together and

gave him a leg up. He sat there for a moment, his eyes closed, his face pale, and then he was riding out of the yard, his body rigid with pain.

She wondered where he was going, and if she'd ever see him again.

He was gone so long Sarah was certain he wasn't coming back. She lost track of the times she went to the window and looked out, hoping to see the stranger riding into the yard.

Resting her head against the sill, she closed her eyes. She didn't understand her eagerness to see him again. After all, he was a stranger, an Indian, a heathen. Was she so hungry for companionship that she could overlook the fact that it had been an Indian who killed Vern, an Indian who had kidnapped Danny? Yet it was also an Indian who had kept her alive all this time.

She opened her eyes and stared out the window again. She wished the Indian would come back. The Indian, she mused. She didn't even know his name, but it didn't matter. She was lonely, so lonely. It had been months since she'd had someone to talk to, someone to care for. She'd slept the night through for the first time, and all because there was someone else in the house. No, she thought, not someone else, a man. Though he was injured, he'd made her feel safe somehow, protected.

She gazed into the yard and pictured his face in her mind, wondering again how he'd gotten those awful scars, wondering why they didn't repel her. Instead, she felt angry because such masculine beauty had been ravaged, and with that anger she felt a rush of sympathy for the pain he must have suffered, both physically and emotionally.

It was late afternoon when she turned away from the window. Shoulders sagging, her stomach growling loudly, she accepted the fact that she'd never see him again.

Choking back a sob, she sat down on the sofa, then buried her face in her hands and let the tears flow unchecked.

"White woman, why do you weep?"

Sarah looked up, startled to find him standing before her. She hadn't even heard him enter the room. "You came back!"

He frowned at her as if she'd said something incredibly stupid. "Did I not say I would return?"

"Yes, but . . . you were gone so long, I . . . I thought . . ."

"Can you help me?"

"Of course."

With a curt nod, he turned and went outside. Sarah stared after him for a moment, wondering what kind of help he needed, and then followed him outside, only to come to an abrupt halt when she saw the two heavily laden horses.

"Oh, my," she murmured, her mouth watering as she saw the deer slung over the withers of the gray stallion. A buffalo robe, a rifle, and two chickens were tied behind the Apache-style saddle. A second horse carried two bulging packs.

Sarah looked at him suspiciously. "Where did you get all this stuff?"

He looked at her for a long moment, one thick

black brow raised in mild amusement. The chickens and the food in the saddlebags had been looted from a Mexican household; he'd killed the deer, and had the devil's own time hoisting it onto the back of the stallion.

"Well?" Sarah said

"You don't want to know."

She started to argue, then thought better of it. He was right; if she expected to eat any of this, it might be better if she didn't know where it came from.

She removed the saddlebags from the pack horse, collected the chickens, and carried them into the house, leaving the Indian to skin the deer. As she unpacked, Sarah discovered a variety of dried meat, small cakes made from ground acorns and mesquite beans, a sack of nuts, another of dried berries. There were several sacks of flour and sugar, as well as sacks of red beans and cornmeal and coffee.

She hummed softly as she put things away, thinking that her cupboards hadn't been so full in months. She hadn't hummed in months, either, she thought, not until the Indian entered her life.

When she'd put the last of the food away and plucked the chickens, she went outside. She watched the Indian work awhile, noting the perspiration that glistened on his skin, the lines of pain around his mouth and eyes.

"Here, let me finish that," she said, taking the knife from his hand.

"Can you?"

Sarah nodded. An Indian scout had shown Vern

how to skin a deer and Vern had taught her, though she had been loath to learn. The blood and the smell made her gag.

Toklanni was in no condition to argue. Raiding the Mexican's place and getting the deer onto the stallion's back had sapped his strength. He'd been skinning the buck on will power alone.

Walking behind the carcass, he found a shady place beside the house. When an Apache skinned a deer, he always laid the head facing east and thereafter he did not walk in front of it or step over it. The bones were not cast aside, but neatly piled so that the spirit of the deer would not think a part of its body was being thrown away.

With a weary sigh, Toklanni eased down on the ground and watched the woman. She had no love for the task at hand, that much was obvious from the expression on her face, but she worked with stubborn determination, pausing now and then to wipe the sweat from her face with the hem of her apron.

His thoughts were troubled as he watched her. He felt a certain sense of pride that she had volunteered to skin the deer when he knew she'd rather not, and with that pride he felt a renewed sense of guilt for being a party to the raid that had killed her husband. Perversely, he was glad her husband was dead, and that made him feel guilty all over again, because no matter how much he cared for the woman, she could never be his.

It was near dark when she'd finished skinning the deer. With a sigh, Toklanni stood up. Securing a rope around the deer's neck, he hung the carcass from a tree well away from the house, high enough so the coyotes couldn't reach it.

The woman filled a bucket with water and they washed side by side.

Sarah could not keep her gaze from the Indian. Water glistened on his broad chest, running in little rivulets down his torso, down the length of his arms. Wordlessly she handed him a towel, and when his hand brushed hers, she felt the shock of it hiss through her veins like a bolt of lightning.

Toklanni was aware of the woman's gaze. Indeed, he found himself staring at her, helpless to look away. Tendrils of hair curled around her face, drops of water clung lovingly to her skin, her face was flushed from her labors, making her eyes seem bluer, brighter.

Washing up took the last of his energy. Tossing the towel aside, he followed the woman into the house. Spreading the buffalo robe he had brought with him on the floor before the hearth, he eased himself down on the robe, and was asleep as soon as he closed his eyes.

Stepping into the parlor a few moments later, Sarah saw the Indian asleep in front of the fireplace. She gazed at him for a long while before she went into the kitchen to prepare dinner. It took her several minutes to decide what to fix. It had been a long time since she had a choice.

It was dark when he woke up. For a moment he lay there, content to be warm and alive. Gradually he became aware of the scent of roasting meat, and his stomach rumbled loudly, reminding him he hadn't eaten all day.

Rising, he padded barefoot into the kitchen, pausing in the doorway to gaze at the woman. As if sensing his presence, she turned around to face him. She had changed her dress and brushed her hair, and he thought again how beautiful she was. Her hair was the color of the sun, bright enough to light the room, and he longed to take it in his hands and discover if the strands were filled with light and warmth.

Sarah smiled at him uncertainly. His presence dwarfed her small kitchen. He was tall and muscular and very male, easily the most virile man she'd ever seen. It still surprised her that she wasn't afraid of him. He was an Indian, after all, the enemy, yet she knew instinctively that he would never harm her.

"Are you hungry?" she asked, wondering at the sudden quiver in her voice.

His gaze lingered on her face. "Yes," he replied quietly, only hungry didn't begin to describe what he was feeling.

"Dinner's ready." She gestured at the table. "Won't you sit down?"

It felt strange to sit in a chair again. Toklanni stared at the clean linen cloth, at the plate, at the knife and fork. It had been over twenty years since he sat at a cloth-covered table.

The woman carried several platters to the table, then sat down across from him. Bowing her head and folding her hands, she blessed the food, thanking the white man's God for his goodness and mercy.

"Help yourself," Sarah said, then bit down on

her lower lip. Should she have served him? Would he know how to use a knife and fork? Did he even know what a napkin was for?

Toklanni filled his plate with chicken and dumplings, and then, feeling awkward, he picked up his fork and began to eat.

It was the most pleasant meal Sarah had eaten in months. Although they didn't have much to say to each other, it was a treat for Sarah just to have company at the table, to have a man to cook for again, even if that man was a savage. Yet he didn't seem like a savage, this man who brought her food, this man who was becoming her friend.

When dinner was over, Sarah started to rise, but he placed his hand over hers. "Wait."

His touch sent a little shiver up her arm. "What is it?"

"I would like to know your name."

He wanted to know her name. Why did that please her so much? "It's Sarah. Sarah Andrews."

"Sarah." He repeated her name slowly, thinking it sounded like a sigh. It had been a long time since he'd heard any but Apache names.

"Would you tell me yours?"

"Toklanni."

"Toklanni." It sounded musical. "Do you have a white name?"

"Yes, Devlin."

"Would you mind if I called you Devlin?"

"If you like, though I may not answer."

"Where did you learn to speak English?"

"From the woman who was my mother."

"Oh?"

"She was a white woman," he explained. "My father kidnapped her from a stagecoach and made her his woman."

"How awful!" Sarah exclaimed in horror, and then blushed. "I'm sorry."

"No need to apologize. I guess it was awful for her, at first, but later . . ." He shrugged.

"Later?" Sarah prompted. She was intrigued by the fact that his mother had been white, intrigued and pleased. Somehow, it made him less threatening.

"They fell in love and got married."

"And she was happy, living with the Apache?"

"You find that hard to believe?"

"A little."

"She left my father when I was nine or ten. We went to Santa Fe, to live with her parents. Her people scorned her because she'd had a child by an Apache warrior. After six months, we went back to my father."

"It must have been hard for you," Sarah said sympathetically.

"Not as hard as it was for her. I vented my anger and frustration with my fists, proving that I was a savage, just like everybody said. But it hurt my mother deeply, the way her people treated her, as if she were unclean. She tried not to let it show, but I often heard her weeping in the night."

"Do you live near here?"

"My village is a two-hour ride to the south."

The thought that Indians were so close sent a

shiver of apprehension down Sarah's spine. She bit down on her lip, wondering again if his people were the ones who had killed Vern and kidnapped Danny.

"Are there any other white women in your village?"

"No."

"Are there . . . any children? Any white children?"

Toklanni heard the hope in her voice. The hope, and the fear. "A few."

"Were they kidnapped?" Sarah asked.

His nod was curt. "My people don't usually make war on children, but they often take them captive to be raised as Apache."

His words chilled her soul. It was the thing she had dreaded most, that her sweet little boy would be raised to be a savage.

"Have you seen my son? He's six, with blond hair and blue eyes. He was wearing brown pants and a blue plaid shirt when the Indians took him."

Slowly Toklanni shook his head. He did not want to lie to her, but he wasn't yet ready to tell her that his people were the ones who had raided her farm, that it was his brother who had killed her husband and taken her son, but mostly he was afraid she'd beg him to take her to the village, and that was something he could not do.

"Do not worry about your son," Toklanni said, hoping to ease her mind. "Indian children are rarely punished, and children of any color are prized among my people."

57

Sarah nodded. His words allayed some of her fears, but not all. "You'll still take me to town when you're feeling better, won't you?" she asked. So much time had passed since Danny was taken. With each day, she felt her chances of getting him back dwindle a little more.

Toklanni let out a long sigh. He could not tell Sarah the truth about her son's whereabouts, nor could he let her go on thinking he would take her into town. Such a thing would only cause more trouble.

"Won't you?" Sarah asked.

"No. Wait, hear me out. If you tell the soldiers that your son has been kidnapped, they'll have to search for him. They'll search every village they find. The Indians will fight. And there's a chance that the Indians who took your son will kill him rather than be caught with a white captive. Are you willing to take that chance?"

Sarah listened to his words with growing horror, unwilling to believe he was telling her the truth. Now she shook her head. "They wouldn't."

"It's been done before." He saw the revulsion in her eyes, heard the anguish in her voice. Perhaps it would be better if he left this place before he caused her more pain. "Do you wish me to go?"

"No," she said quickly. Even if he wouldn't take her into town for help, she might be able to persuade him to look for Danny on his own. There was something reassuring about Devlin, a quiet strength that soothed her fears. His eyes were a deep brown, almost black, his nose was straight, his lips full and finely shaped. Even the scar didn't diminish the fact that he was a strong and handsome man.

A muscle twitched in Toklanni's jaw as Sarah's gaze moved over his face. He had a sudden urge to look away, to hide the scar beneath his hand. He thought he'd grown used to it, being stared at, but for the first time in years he felt the humiliation of being disfigured, of having people look at him with pity or revulsion.

But it wasn't pity or revulsion he read in the depths of the woman's eyes, and that confused him more than anything else.

Sarah felt her cheeks flush as she realized she'd been staring at him. "I'm sorry, I . . . I mean, I . . ."

"It's all right," he said with a shrug. "Everybody stares at first."

"How did it happen?"

"In battle."

"You're lucky to be alive," Sarah remarked.

"Yes," he replied bitterly. "Lucky."

"I wasn't staring because it's ugly," Sarah began, then wished she'd never said anything. How could she tell him she thought he was the most handsome man she'd ever seen, scar or no scar? And what right did she have to be noticing such a thing? Her husband had been dead less than six months. "I mean, I . . ."

Toklanni watched the color rise in her cheeks and slowly shook his head. Was it possible she wasn't repulsed by his appearance?

Sarah stood up and began clearing the table. She couldn't sit there any longer, couldn't endure the force of his gaze for fear he'd somehow see into her heart and mind. She was a white woman, and no matter how attractive he might be, he was still an Indian. It didn't really matter that he was half white, after all. He had obviously turned his back on that part of his heritage long ago. He was a savage now, a heathen. He couldn't live in her world, and she couldn't live in his.

"Why don't you go lie down?" Sarah suggested. "You need the rest. I'll bring you a cup of coffee after I've done the dishes."

Toklanni nodded, wondering at the abrupt change in her attitude, the sudden lack of warmth in her voice.

Leaving the kitchen, he went into the parlor and stretched out on the buffalo robe. Eyes closed, he listened to Sarah as she moved about the kitchen. He had never thought of going back to the white man's world, but now, with Sarah Andrews humming softly in the next room, he wondered what it would be like to settle down in this place with this woman.

He swore softly, startled at the turn of his thoughts. Never before had be contemplated marriage, and marriage to a white woman would be impossible, even if she'd have him. He had spent too many years with the Apache to make the kind of husband Sarah would want.

If he was smart, he would put her on a horse and take her to Pepper Tree Creek and leave her there. Someone would take her in.

If he was smart, he would take her there tomorrow.

But sometimes he just wasn't smart.

Chapter Seven

Toklanni spent the next few days resting, feeling guilty for staying in the woman's house and accepting her hospitality when he had lied to her about her son's whereabouts.

At night he often heard the sound of weeping from her room, and it was like a knife twisting in his gut. He knew Sarah wept for her husband and for her son, and though he was not personally responsible for her loss, he was guilty just the same. He knew he should tell her that her son was well, but he didn't want to spoil the tenuous friendship between them, didn't want to see the growing affection in her eyes turn to loathing when she realized that he had been with the raiding party that day. He didn't want to admit to himself that if her hair hadn't been as yellow as new corn he might have killed her.

In all the years he'd been with the Apache, the

only whites he'd killed had been soldiers, and that only in self-defense. And Noche knew it, had taunted him about it on more than one occasion. That was why his brother had sent him to kill the woman, to test Toklanni's loyalty, to see if he still felt bound to his mother's people, or if he had at last become totally Apache in mind and heart.

A muscle twitched in Toklanni's jaw as he tried to imagine what he would have done if Sarah hadn't reminded him of his mother. Would he really have killed her? Could he kill a woman in cold blood? He didn't want to think so, and yet it happened all the time, on both sides. He'd seen white women riddled with arrows. He'd seen Apache women brutally slaughtered. Children, too, on both sides. Who was to say who was right and who was wrong?

In the days that followed, he made excuses for not telling Sarah who he was, lying to himself, telling himself it was to protect her feelings when all the time he knew it was to protect himself from her scorn, her hatred, because he was falling in love with her.

As his ribs healed, he began to do little things around the cabin. He repaired the corral fence, sharpened the ax, cut enough firewood to last the winter. His hands blistered and his side ached, and he relished the pain because he deserved it for being such a coward. Each night before he went to bed he swore he'd tell her the truth in the morning, and each morning he put it off again, wanting to be near her one more day, see her smile, touch her hand, listen to the soft, slightly husky sound of her voice as she read from the Bible each evening.

Tonight she was reading from 1 Corinthians, Chapter 11. "For the man is not of the woman, but the woman of the man. Neither was the man created for the woman, but the woman for the man . . . Nevertheless, neither is the man without the woman, neither the woman without the man, in the Lord. . . ."

Neither is the man without the woman . . . How had he fallen in love so quickly, he who had vowed never to love at all?

He thought of her son, living in Noche's lodge. Noche had not taken the boy as an act of vengeance or to replace a child who had been lost. To the contrary, Noche had taken the child because he thought both of its parents were dead and he did not wish to leave it behind. But both parents weren't dead.

Toklanni gazed at Sarah. She was sitting in front of the hearth with the Bible in her lap. The lamplight danced in her hair, turning the yellow to gold. Should he tell her where her son was? Would she find comfort in knowing he was well, or would it cause her more pain to know her son was nearby when she could not go to him?

He thought about it all that night and the next day, wondering what to do.

The following evening after dinner, he went into the parlor and laid a fire in the hearth, then sat on the sofa, staring into the flames. He had heard her weeping again last night and he knew he had to tell her that he knew where her son was, that the boy was being well cared for. He couldn't spend another night listening to her sobs.

He glanced up as Sarah entered the room, her full skirt making a soft swishing sound.

"How are you feeling?" she asked.

"Better every day, thanks to you."

She smiled, her cheeks flushing a becoming shade of pink. Taking up her mending basket, she sat on the other end of the sofa.

Toklanni watched her thread her needle. He had come to enjoy the evenings they spent together. Often there were long silences between them, but they were not uncomfortable silences.

He listened to the crackle of the flames, to the rush of the wind as it swept across the land. Winter was coming and he had to make a decision, whether to stay here with Sarah or return to the rancheria. He had been gone too long already. Noche might already be looking for him.

"Sarah."

She looked up at him and smiled expectantly.

"Sarah, I . . ."

"Yes?"

"I know where your son is." He spoke the words in a rush, afraid he'd change his mind if he didn't blurt it out and be done with it.

She sat up, her body suddenly tense, her gaze riveted on his face. "You know where Danny is? Is he all right? Why didn't you tell me before?" She lurched to her feet, the dress she'd been mending falling unnoticed to the floor. "Where is he? Can you take me to him?"

"He's fine. He's at my village. With my brother."

Sarah stared at Toklanni. His village. His brother. That meant . . . "It was your people who attacked us. Why? We never did anything to you."

"You're on Apache land," he said defensively, inadequately.

"We never bothered your people, yet they killed Vern and took Danny." Eyes narrowed suspiciously, Sarah jabbed an accusing finger in his direction. "You were there."

"Yes."

"Did you kill Vern?"

Slowly Toklanni shook his head. "I was sent to burn the house."

"You! It was you in the cellar, wasn't it?"

Toklanni nodded. He could feel her withdrawing from him, feel her friendship turning to disgust.

"How could you? You're white."

"Half white."

She stood with her hands on her hips, her expression fierce with anger. "Half, whole, what's the difference? How can you go around killing your own people?"

"The Apache are my people."

"I want to see my son."

"No."

"Why not?"

Why not? How could he explain it to her? How could he explain it to himself?

"Please, Devlin." There was no anger in her voice now, only a soft note of entreaty.

He winced at her use of his white name. "Sarah,

my people think you're dead. That day in the cellar, I was supposed to kill you."

She remembered that day vividly, the awful fear, the certainty that she'd been looking death in the face. "Why didn't you?"

He couldn't sit still any longer. Gaining his feet, Toklanni walked to the window and looked out at the night. His voice was low when he spoke to her.

"I might have killed you if you didn't look so much like my mother." He turned to face Sarah again. Like his mother, Sarah Andrews had fine bones and delicate features and a way of looking at a man that made him feel he was invincible.

Toklanni gestured at her hair. "My mother's hair was blonde, like yours. You look like her in other ways, too." He shook his head. "Anyway, I couldn't do it. I burned the barn instead so the other warriors would see the smoke and think it was the house."

Sarah wrapped her arms around her waist, chilled in spite of the heat from the fireplace. Would she be dead now if her hair had been brown?

She gazed at him through the dark fringe of her lashes. "What would happen if your people found out I wasn't dead?"

"I don't know. My people are still angry. A few days before we raided this place, our village was attacked. Several warriors were killed and Noche's wife was badly wounded. The young men are eager for bloodshed." They'd been on the war path for the last five months, Toklanni mused, and each victory seemed sweeter than the last. Only the coming of winter would put an end to their raiding.

"I want my son back. I'm willing to take the chance."

He crossed the room, silent and graceful as a cat on the prowl, until he was standing in front of her. "I'm not."

The tone of his voice touched her like a caress, telling her without words that he wasn't willing to put her life in danger. She gazed into the depths of his eyes and saw her own loneliness, her own longing, mirrored there.

"Please, Devlin. I miss him so much. He's just a little boy. He needs me." Two large tears welled in her eyes and slid down her cheeks. "And I need him."

"Sarah." Wanting to comfort her, he drew her into his arms. And knew immediately that it was a mistake. The warmth of her body, the soft feminine curves pressed against his chest, drove everything from his mind, everything but the aching desire he'd been holding in check since the day he first saw her.

Sarah had not been prepared for tenderness, or for the sense of belonging, of peace, that filled her heart as Toklanni's arms closed around her. With a sob, she buried her face in the hollow of his shoulder, crying for Danny, for her own loneliness, for fear that the affection she felt for Toklanni was turning into love. But she couldn't love him. It was wrong, so wrong.

And yet being in his arms felt so right, and as

67

her tears subsided, she grew increasingly aware of the strength of the arms that held her, of the rapid beating of her own heart, of the telltale evidence of Toklanni's rising desire.

"I'm sorry," she stammered, trying to disengage herself from his embrace. "I don't know what got into me."

"Sarah."

His arms held her loosely, a welcome prison from which she had no desire to escape. "Please." She kept her head lowered so she wouldn't have to see the longing in his eyes, so he couldn't see the hunger in her own.

"Please what?" he asked, his voice low and husky.

"I can't," she whispered. "I'm still in mourning for my husband, and you're . . . I'm . . . please, Devlin, I can't."

"I haven't asked you for anything."

"You're asking me now. I can hear it in your voice, feel it in the way your arms tremble."

"Sarah, look at me."

Hesitantly she lifted her gaze to his.

"You say you can't. I believe you, but tell me the truth. Is it because you're in mourning, or because I'm Indian?" He lifted a hand to his scarred cheek. "Or because of this?"

She looked at him, stricken by the hurt in his voice, by the anger that blazed in his eyes.

"I . . ." She shook her head, searching for the right words. How had they gotten onto this subject anyway? All she'd wanted was to see Danny.

Toklanni's arms dropped to his sides. "I guess I have my answer," he said, mistaking her confusion for revulsion. And pivoting on his heel, he stalked out of the house.

Chapter Eight

He was gone in the morning. Sarah wandered through the house, unable to concentrate on the simplest task. Was he gone for good? The thought that she might never see him again pierced her heart like a shard of broken glass, sharp and painful. And Danny. What about Danny? If Devlin was gone for good, how would she ever find her son?

Wrapping her shawl around her shoulders, she went outside and walked along the riverbank, oblivious to the cold. Winter was coming. Soon it would be Thanksgiving, and then Christmas.

How could she endure Christmas out here alone? She thought of the Christmases they'd known back east, the parties, the scent of pine and bayberry that filled the house. She wasn't much of a cook, but she loved baking pies and cookies, and it had always been such fun, with

Danny there to help roll out the crust and decorate the gingerbread men.

Even here in the West, Christmas had been a special time. They'd decorated the house with pine cones. She and Danny had made the usual treats, filling the cabin with the scent of fresh-baked cookies. And on Christmas Eve they'd gathered before the fireplace, just the three of them, while Vern read the Christmas story.

She had no appetite for dinner that night. After brewing a pot of tea, she sat in front of the window and stared into the darkness. The days were growing short, the nights long and cold. How would she endure the winter alone? There would be days when it would be too cold to leave the shelter of the cabin, days of heavy rain and snow. Thus far, she'd been able to endure the loneliness because she'd been able to keep busy, to go outside and wander along the riverbank. But to be trapped inside, alone . . . She shuddered at the thought. Maybe she should leave, try to walk to town. But it was so far, she knew she'd never make it on foot.

She couldn't sleep that night. With the covers tucked up to her chin, she stared at the white-washed ceiling, feeling more alone than she'd ever felt in her life. She missed Toklanni, missed him in ways she had never missed her husband. She remembered the desire she had seen in his eyes, the touch of his hands on her arms. He thought she was repelled by his scars, that she had spurned him because she was afraid of his touch, but it wasn't Toklanni that had frightened her, it was the depths of her own desire, the emergence of feelings and passions she had never known existed. And now he was gone, perhaps for good.

Slipping out of bed, Sarah dropped to her knees and buried her face in her hands, imploring a kind Heavenly Father to be merciful, to return her son to her arms. She felt a twinge of guilt as she prayed that Toklanni would come back. She had no business even thinking of another man so soon after Vern's death, especially a man who was an Indian, but she couldn't forget the sense of belonging she'd felt in Toklanni's arms, the peace and joy that his touch had aroused in her. Right or wrong, she was in love with him.

Toklanni sat outside Lupan's lodge, his arms folded across his chest as he listened to the old medicine men tell the story of how light came into the world.

"In the beginning," the shaman said, "there was only darkness in the world. There was no sun. There were no stars. No night sun. Only the thick black of darkness. Back then, there were all manner of feathered and four-footed creatures. There were hideous monsters and dragons and all manner of creeping things. The People did not prosper at this time because the beasts and serpents ate the young."

Toklanni watched Danny's face as Lupan paused to take a breath. Sarah's son was leaning forward, his elbows on his knees, his expression one of concentration as he tried to follow the story.

"At this time, all creatures could talk and think," the medicine man went on. "There were two tribes of creatures, the Birds and the Beasts. The Bird People were led by an Eagle.

"As time went on, the Birds wished to have light in the world, but the Beasts refused, and after a time the Birds made war upon the Beasts. The four-footed Beasts were armed with clubs, but the Eagle had taught the feathered beings to use bows and arrows. The Birds had to be careful who they killed, for when they killed a bear, more bears rose up in his place; the dragons could not be killed at all.

"After many days, the Birds won the battle, and that is how light came into the world."

Toklanni watched Sarah's son as he went off with some of the other boys. Though Danny had been among the Apache for only a few months, it was easy to see that he had already absorbed much of the Indian language, and Toklanni thought he had probably understood most, if not all, of the simple story the aged shaman had told.

Later he watched Noche trying to teach Danny how to use a bow and arrow. Sarah's son was a good-looking boy with light blond hair, fair skin, and deep blue eyes. He'd been living in Noche's lodge for over four months now. He no longer cried in the night, or begged to go home, and he was learning to speak Apache. Just now, his brow was furrowed with concentration as he drew back the bowstring.

Toklanni watched the lesson with interest. Danny had a keen eye, and on the fourth try his arrow hit the outer edge of the target. Danny flushed with pleasure as Noche gave him a pat on the back and a broad smile of approval.

In time, Toklanni knew the boy would accept the Apache way of life completely. He'd already made a place for himself with the other boys, he was quick to learn and quick to obey Noche. As he grew older, he would learn that the Apache way of life was hard and well-disciplined. Anyone who was not Apache was considered the enemy, and the Apache displayed no pity where an enemy was concerned. A true warrior excelled in battle and thievery, though he would never steal from his own. He was generous. He loved his family. Truth was a virtue held in high regard. Soon Danny would learn to hunt and to track. To fight. And to kill.

Toklanni took a deep breath, remembering how hard it had been for him, growing up as a mixed blood. Though he was accepted as an Apache, he'd known he was different from the other boys, and the difference had become more pronounced as he grew older. Now, watching as Danny continued to practice with the bow and arrow, he wondered how the boy would handle the situation when the time came.

Toklanni shook his head, knowing Sarah would be appalled at the direction of his thoughts, mortified if she knew the harsh lessons of life and death that awaited her son.

Sarah. He'd left because he wanted to make sure Danny was all right, and because he had to get away from her, because he couldn't think clearly when she was so close and he wanted her so badly. He realized now that he had pushed her too far, too fast. She needed time; time to mourn her dead, to face her own warring emotions, to come to terms with the ever-growing attraction between them.

Sarah. He had been away from her for two days and he missed her more than he'd thought possible. It was inexplicable, how rapidly he had grown to love her, how deeply ingrained she'd become in his life. He'd known her such a short time, yet he felt that he was missing a vital part of himself. He longed to hear her voice, see her smile, fill his nostrils with her sweet womanly scent.

He shook her image from his mind. She was not for him, no matter how much he desired her.

He waited until after the evening meal before he took Noche aside. It was time for truth, time to discover what his chances were of returning Danny to his mother.

"So, brother," Noche mused as they walked away from the village, "what is it that you have to say that must be said in secret?"

Toklanni took a deep breath, then plunged in head first. "I did not kill the white woman or burn her lodge."

Noche came to an abrupt halt. "She still lives?"

"Yes."

In the moonlight, Toklanni could see the contempt on his younger brother's face. "I should have known you were too weak to kill her. I should have done it myself. I *will* do it."

"No."

"You dare to tell me I cannot?"

"The woman is mine."

"You have scorned every maiden in our village, and now you take a white woman?" Noche shook his head in disgust. "It is as I have always said; in your heart you are not Apache. You are weak, like the white eyes."

"I am strong enough to keep what is mine," Toklanni retorted sharply. "And the woman is mine. To harm her is the same as harming my family."

"I hear you, brother," Noche said, sneering. "Will you leave us now and make your home in the woman's square house?"

"I don't know."

"You will not bring her here."

"You dare to tell me I cannot?" Toklanni challenged, flinging Noche's words back in his face.

"I tell you to think carefully. The blood of our dead is still warm. My woman's scars cry out to me for vengeance. I tell you our people will not accept a white woman in their midst." Noche took a step forward, his gaze intent. "And the boy is mine, *chickasay*. Do not forget that."

"My woman wants him back."

Noche shook his head. "The boy's place is in my lodge. Keep the paleface woman if you must. Plant another child in her belly to dry her tears, but do not think you can take the boy."

Toklanni nodded. There had been bad blood between himself and his brother ever since they were children. He had been a fool to think Noche would surrender Danny without a fight.

Toklanni studied his brother closely, wondering what the outcome of such a fight would be. As children, they had competed almost daily. It had all been in fun at first, but as they grew older, their games of skill and strength became more earnest until they weren't games at all.

Noche returned his gaze without blinking, the challenge in his dark eyes bold and clear.

But now was not the time. He had left Sarah alone for too long.

Turning away from the river, Toklanni returned to his lodge and packed enough supplies to last them through the winter. Catching up the gray, he rode out of the village, his heart growing lighter as he thought of seeing Sarah again.

In the spring he would take her to Pepper Tree Creek. She would be safe there, among her own people.

But first he was going to spend the winter with her. And then, somehow, he would tell her goodbye.

Chapter Nine

Hoofbeats. Had she imagined them? Throwing back the covers, Sarah slid out of bed and hurried to the window. Her heart leapt within her breast as she saw Toklanni ride into the yard.

She didn't stop to think, didn't stop to consider how inappropriate it was for a man to see her in her nightdress. Her feet were as light as air as she ran into the parlor, opened the door, and threw herself at Toklanni, her arms wrapping around his waist as if she would never let go.

She'd been afraid he might rebuff her after the way they had parted. Sarah breathed a sigh of relief as his arms locked around her, and she buried her face against his shoulder. He smelled of sweat and buckskin and horse. Closing her eyes, she drew a deep breath, filling her nostrils with his scent. Here in his strong embrace was where she belonged, where she yearned to be.

Toklanni held Sarah for a long moment, afraid to speak for fear of breaking the tenuous bond between them. He could feel her heart pounding against his chest, feel the tremor in her arms. It was only fear that made her so glad to see him, he thought glumly, fear of being alone. But he had no desire to let her go, not yet.

"You came back," Sarah murmured, her voice muffled against his chest. "I was afraid you were gone for good."

Toklanni shook his head. "I could not stay away."

"You were angry when you left," Sarah remarked, still not looking at him.

"I am not angry any longer. In the spring I will take you to Pepper Tree Creek. You will be safe there."

"No." She drew away from him, her face set in determined lines. "I'm not leaving here. I have to stay."

"Why?"

Because I'll never see you again, she thought. But she couldn't tell him that. "I have to stay," she repeated, more firmly this time. "I know if I just have faith enough, I'll get Danny back somehow." She had to believe that; it was all she had. She thought of the phrase in the Bible *Ask and ye shall receive. Knock and it shall be opened. Seek and ye shall find.* If she had faith enough, she knew God would answer her prayers.

"We will not speak of it now. I have brought enough supplies to last us through the winter."

"I'll help you unload the pack horse."

"I'll do it."

"All right," she said, puzzled by his curt manner. "Would you like something to eat?"

Toklanni nodded, his hands clenched at his sides as he looked at her. The sleeping gown she wore was of white cotton, ruffled at the throat and sleeves. The wind was blowing in her direction, molding the soft material to her figure so that every curve was clearly outlined.

"Go inside," he said and turned away before she could see the visible evidence of his desire.

Facing into the wind, he filled his lungs with cold air, cursing the weakness that had made him come back to her. How could he look at her, be near her every day, and not touch her?

It would be torture, sweet agonizing torture. But it was a torment he would willingly bear because he knew the memories of this one short winter would have to last him a lifetime.

Winter came in earnest a few days later. The wind howled like a banshee, battering the doors and windows, screaming down the chimney. Thunder shook the earth, lightning sizzled across the heavens, while the rain pummeled the roof like angry fists. Toklanni went out twice each day to look after the horses. To pass the time, he often sat on his buffalo robe before the hearth, fashioning a bridle from horsehair or cleaning his weapons. Sometimes he just sat there, staring into the fire.

Sarah busied herself with housework, cooking, baking, dusting, washing and ironing, mending, sweeping the floor. When there was nothing else to do, she read from the Bible, or from the works of Shakespeare.

On this day she sat in a chair before the fire, knitting a scarf out of red wool. She smiled to herself. It was a Christmas present for Toklanni, but he didn't know that. Having someone to make a gift for filled a void in her. No matter what her circumstances might be, Christmas was a time for sharing, a time for rejoicing, for hope. She wondered if Danny realized it would soon be Christmas, and she prayed that the good times they had shared would bring him comfort, that he would remember the laughter and the joy of the season.

Christmas, she thought. The most beautiful time of the year. A time for miracles. She knew she would not have felt that way if she was alone, but she wasn't alone anymore. Toklanni was here.

She slid a glance in his direction. He was standing at the window staring out at the storm. Her gaze moved over him in a long caress. He had said he wasn't mad anymore, but he was. She could feel the force of his anger, the bitterness that festered in his soul. Several times she had tried to tell him that she wasn't repulsed by his scars, that she loved him, but somehow she could not bring herself to say the words, could not reach past his silent anger.

She hadn't been able to bring herself to ask about Danny, either, though she wasn't sure why. Perhaps it was because the last time they'd discussed Danny, Toklanni had left her. But he couldn't go now, not in this storm.

She dropped her knitting in the yarn basket and went to stand beside Toklanni. For a moment she stared out at the rain and then, taking a deep breath for courage, she asked about her son.

"Did you see him?"

"Yes."

"Is he well?"

Toklanni nodded. "He has adapted to our ways very well. He has made friends with some of the boys. He has his own pony. And Noche has taught him to use a bow and arrow."

Sarah felt a twinge of pain. Didn't Danny miss her at all? "Does he ever ask about me?"

"I don't know."

"Does he seem happy?"

Toklanni shrugged. "He does not smile much. I have not heard him laugh, but he does not seem unhappy."

"Did you . . . did you ask your brother if I could have Danny back?"

"He said no."

"Oh. Isn't there some way . . . couldn't you . . . steal Danny back?"

It was the question he had been dreading, a question for which he had no clear answer.

"Please, Devlin."

Slowly, he shook his head. "The Apache are my people. To do what you ask would be to make war against my own brother, my own family."

Sarah nodded. She couldn't blame him, not really, though she wanted to scream that she didn't care if he had to fight the whole world if it would get Danny back.

Though her heart ached with longing for her son, she was relieved to hear that he was well, that he was making a life for himself, such as it was. She would not want him to give up hope, to turn his back on life, no matter what kind of life it might be. And she would not give up, either. She would continue to hope, to pray, to believe that her prayers would be answered.

Toklanni saw the sadness in Sarah's eyes, heard it in her voice. She seemed to shrink before him, as if her spirit were shriveling before his eyes.

He felt his own bitterness dissolve as he took her in his arms. He had been foolish to be angry with her because she had not melted in his arms the night before he left. Could be really blame her? She had reacted no differently than any other woman. But he had never really cared before. That was the difference, he mused. He wanted Sarah to see past his scars, past his mixed blood. He wanted her to see into his heart and accept him as he was.

He felt her shudder as she fought back her tears and he drew her closer, pressing her length against his. "Do not weep, Sarah," he murmured. *Somehow,* he vowed, *somehow he would find a way to bring Danny home even if it cost him his life*.

He started to draw away from her, but she held him tight, refusing to let him go. He was all the comfort she had in the world.

"Sarah . . ."

"Don't go."

His senses were alive, filled with her nearness. She smelled of soap and starch. Her skin was warm and smooth beneath his hand, her hair soft against his cheek. He could feel each breath she took, feel her breasts pressed against his chest.

"Sarah." His voice was thick with desire.

She looked up at him then, her heart quickening at the longing she read in the depths of his eyes. Slowly she lifted her hand to caress his scarred cheek.

"Don't." He caught her hand in his before she could touch him.

"I want to."

"Why?"

"To prove to you that it doesn't matter."

"Doesn't it?" he asked, and she heard the bitterness in his voice, the fear of being rejected.

"I love you, Devlin," she said quietly. "The scars don't matter."

"I'm not Devlin. I'm Toklanni. I'm not a white man, I'm a half-breed. Can you accept that?"

"Can you?"

"What do you mean?"

"You're Indian and white. Why do you accept your father's people and not your mother's?"

"Because my father's people have accepted me, and my mother's people haven't." There was no bitterness in his voice; it was merely a statement of fact.

"Can't we forget about red and white and just be a man and a woman?"

"No. My people will not accept you, and your

people will not accept me. A fish may love a rabbit, but where would they live?"

"Are you saying you love me?"

It was in his mind to lie, but he could not deny his feelings for her, not when she was looking at him like that, her beautiful blue eyes filled with hope, her lips slightly parted in invitation.

He was still holding her hand in his. He watched her face carefully as he pressed her hand to his scarred cheek, certain she would draw back rather than touch him, certain her revulsion would be mirrored in her eyes. But Sarah's expression did not change, and as her unblemished hand gently caressed him, Toklanni felt as if she'd pulled a dagger from his heart.

"Sarah, do you know what you do to me?"

"Tell me."

He shook his head, unable to put his feelings into words. She touched him and he felt whole again. She looked at him and he felt there was hope for the future.

She whispered his name, and he drew her into his arms again, murmuring that he loved her, that he would never let her go.

He kissed her then, knowing he would be Devlin, or Toklanni, or whoever she wished him to be so long as he could see the love in her eyes each day, hold her in his arms every night.

Sarah surrendered to the touch of his lips, her eyelids fluttering down as his kiss deepened, telling her more eloquently than words that he loved her.

And she loved him. When they drew apart, she

gazed into his face and she didn't see his scars, she didn't see a man who was a half-breed, all she saw was the man who had spared her life and renewed her hope in the future. The man she loved with all her heart.

"Sarah." His hands moved along her ribcage, slid down her thigh and back up again.

"I love you."

"Do you?"

"Yes."

He groaned low in his throat, wondering if he shouldn't turn tail and run before it was too late. Loving Sarah would mean leaving his people, going back to the white man's world. And yet, what other choice did he have?

Sarah leaned back, her gaze searching his face. "Is something wrong?"

"I've never been in love before," Toklanni said, his voice husky and uncertain. "Among my people, when a man desires to take a wife, his father or brother makes his wishes known to the girl's parents. When that is done, he takes horses to her wickiup. If the girl feeds and waters the horses, it means she accepts his proposal and there is a wedding feast which lasts three days. During this time the couple do not speak, but on the third night they slip away. When they return a week later, they are considered married."

Toklanni shrugged. "You have no parents, and I have no one to speak for me."

"Are you asking me to marry you?"

"So it would seem." He let out a deep sigh. "I have nothing to offer you but two horses and my weapons. I have no gifts, no home we can share, no family to welcome you."

"Do you love me?" Sarah asked.

"Yes."

"That's all I want." She smiled up at him, her eyes luminous. "Although I would like to hear you say it."

"I love you, Sarah." He traced the line of her jaw with his fingertips.

The words, softly and fervently spoken, made her feel as though she'd swallowed the sun. She caught his hand and pressed it to her lips. "We could go into town and be married," she suggested, certain he would hate the idea.

"Is that what you want?"

"Well, I would like someone to say the words over us. Would it bother you very much to have someone say the words?"

"Not if it's what you want."

Her smile seemed to light the room, and Toklanni knew that his life was about to change in ways he'd never imagined.

Chapter Ten

The storm blew itself out two days later; the following morning they started the journey to Pepper Tree Creek.

Toklanni wore a pair of buckskin pants, moccasins and a gray wool shirt and heavy sheepskin jacket that had belonged to Sarah's husband. The thought of wearing clothes that had belonged to a dead man filled him with a sense of unease. The Apache did not keep anything that had belonged to one who had died.

He glanced at Sarah. Clad in a dark blue riding habit, black boots, and a hooded cloak, she looked lovely, and when she smiled at him, it was like being kissed by the sun.

When they paused at midday, he warned Sarah not to say anything about the kidnapping while they were in town, reminding her that there was sure to be bloodshed on both sides if the Army got involved. He supposed it was a measure of her faith in him that she so readily agreed.

They camped on the trail that night. Sarah was sure she'd never be able to sleep, she was that excited at the prospect of becoming Devlin's wife. Not only that, but they were going to town.

Toklanni sat beside Sarah, staring into the glowing coals of their campfire. He didn't share her eagerness to go into town. Earlier, he had tried to warn her that people would likely shun her company when they discovered she was marrying a half-breed, but she refused to believe it. Whom she married was her business, she'd said, and if people didn't like it, that was their problem, not hers.

But later, lying beside her under the stars, he wondered if he was doing the right thing by marrying Sarah. He didn't need the approval of other people, he didn't care what they thought of him, but he wasn't sure that Sarah could withstand the blatant disapproval, the looks of contempt, the derision she was sure to encounter when the townspeople learned she had married a half-breed.

Almost, he told her he had changed his mind. But then he looked at her, sleeping peacefully beside him, and he knew that he could not let her go. Selfish though it might be, he needed her as he had never needed anyone. He would fight for her, die for her if necessary, but he could not let her go.

They reached Pepper Tree Creek just after noon the following day. The small town owed its existence to a number of outlying ranches, most of which were big enough to withstand occasional attacks by marauding Apaches.

Riding down the single street, Toklanni saw a number of small businesses that catered to the ranchers' wives. There was also a blacksmith shop, a marshal's office, a small hotel, and a barber shop. And at the far end of town was a square white building topped with a wooden cross.

Toklanni drew rein at the hotel, knowing that Sarah wished to bathe and change her clothes. She had packed her wedding dress, apologizing because she was marrying him in the same gown she'd worn to her first wedding, but Toklanni didn't care what she wore. He knew she'd also packed a change of clothes for him, and that did bother him, because the dark blue suit had belonged to her first husband.

Dismounting, Toklanni lifted Sarah from the back of her horse and removed their bag from behind his saddle. Then he took her by the hand and they entered the hotel.

The clerk blinked at them several times, his Adam's apple bobbing up and down as he tried to summon the courage to tell Toklanni he wasn't welcome at the hotel. But courage was apparently something the clerk lacked, and in the end he gave them the key to a room and promised to send up hot water for a bath.

"Well, I declare," Sarah had huffily. "What was that all about?"

Toklanni tossed the carpetbag onto the bed and

closed the door. "I'm afraid that's something you'd better get used to."

"What do you mean?"

"I mean that most folks aren't going to take kindly to your choice of a husband."

"That's ridiculous!"

Toklanni shrugged. "Don't say I didn't warn you."

"Are you trying to get out of marrying me?" Sarah asked. She injected a teasing note into her voice, but deep down she was afraid he was doing just that.

"No." Toklanni crossed the room and took her into his arms. "But that's what I *should* do. If I was any kind of man, I'd turn around and run like hell before I let you make the biggest mistake of your life."

"Is that what you think I'm doing?"

Toklanni nodded. "Yes, but I'm so glad you're doing it."

"I love you, Devlin. Have faith in that, if in nothing else."

He would have kissed her then, long and hard, if someone hadn't been pounding on the door.

Muttering an oath, Toklanni opened the door to find the hotel clerk standing in the hallway. Two boys stood behind him carrying buckets of hot water.

"Come on in," Toklanni said, and stepped out of the way.

When the tub was filled, he took up his rifle and left the room so that Sarah could bathe and change in private.

Leaving the hotel, he headed for the mercantile store where he bought a pair of black pants and a white shirt. The shopkeeper looked at him suspiciously, but took his money willingly enough. Toklanni hated spending Sarah's money on himself, but he'd be darned if he'd get married wearing her husband's clothes.

Taking up his package, he headed for the barber shop for a bath and a shave.

Sarah stared at her reflection in the mirror, trying to see herself as Devlin would see her. Her dress of ivory satin had a high ruffled neck, long fitted sleeves, and a full skirt. She was pleased that it still fit as well as it had the first time she'd worn it. She wished she had a new dress to wear for Devlin, something no one else had ever seen. She did have a new nightgown, one she'd made herself out of white muslin and a bit of leftover lace. She'd cut the neck daringly low and trimmed it with a bit of pink satin ribbon. The thought of wearing it for Devlin made her stomach curl with pleasure.

Minutes later Devlin was at the door, looking more handsome than ever in crisp black pants and a white shirt. He was freshly shaved; his hair, though still long, was neatly trimmed.

For a moment they stared at each other in silent admiration; then Toklanni cleared his throat.

"Are you ready?" he asked, his voice husky.

Sarah nodded, a warm glow spreading through her as Devlin took her arm.

People turned to stare at them as they walked

down the street toward the church. Toklanni knew that the looks were of derision, of contempt, but Sarah turned her brilliant smile on everyone they passed, friend and stranger alike, quietly bidding them all a good day, not stopping to talk to any of them, though several were openly curious about her escort.

Father deCristo was a tall, spare man with gray hair and eyes that had seen every facet of life. He smiled fondly at Sarah, shook hands with Toklanni. If he disapproved of the match between a half-breed and a lady of quality who had so recently been widowed, it didn't show on his face.

The words he spoke over them were soft and melodic as he admonished them to love and cherish one another, to be faithful to their vows, to be fruitful, to be mindful of God's law to multiply and replenish the earth. Lastly, he counseled them to invite God to be a part of their union.

There were tears in Sarah's eyes when the priest spoke the final words that made her Devlin Dennehy's wife. And then Devlin was kissing her, his touch gentle, filled with love and the promise of passion.

Father deCristo made the sign of the cross over them as he wished them a long and happy life, and then Devlin took Sarah's arm and they walked out of the small church into the sunlight.

"Mrs. Devlin Dennehy," Sarah murmured.

"What?"

"Nothing. I just wanted to say it out loud. Mrs. Devlin Dennehy. It has a nice ring to it."

Toklanni grunted softly, wondering if he'd ever get used to being called Devlin, trying to remember if she'd ever called him by his Apache name.

Sarah's cheeks were a becoming shade of pink when they reached the hotel, and Toklanni knew it had nothing to do with the walk or the kiss of the wind against her face. She was feeling suddenly shy, and so, he thought, was he. He had never made love to a woman. Oh, he had coupled with captives now and then; he was a man, after all. But that wasn't love, and he had never worried about what the woman thought or felt. But this was different. What if Sarah thought him a savage? What if his touch repelled her?

Alone in their hotel room, they stood mute, the silence ringing in their ears as they avoided looking at each other.

And then Toklanni crossed the short distance between them and took Sarah in his arms, holding her loosely against him.

"I'll try to make you happy, Sarah," he said with quiet conviction. "If I ever do anything to hurt you, just tell me. And if you ever feel you've made a mistake, I'll try and let you go."

"Devlin!" She placed her hand over his mouth, stunned by his words. "I love you. I'll never be sorry. How can you even think that?"

"I saw the looks people gave you when we left the church. The contempt on the faces of the women, the disrespect on the faces of the men. Even that pasty-faced clerk was looking down his nose at you, and it'll always be that way, Sarah, so long as you're my wife."

Sarah shook her head vigorously. She had no close friends in town, no one whose opinion mattered one whit. "I don't care. I love you and that's all that matters."

"You make me believe in miracles," he whispered, and then, unable to deny himself any longer, he kissed her hard and long, letting her feel the force of his desire, the depth of his need.

If he thought she would be repelled or disgusted by his touch, she quickly put his fears to rest. With a low moan, Sarah melted into his arms, her eyelids fluttering down as her arms curled around his waist, drawing him closer, tighter.

He gasped as he felt her tongue, silky and warm, slide across his lips, probing gently, felt a flame of heat dart through him as her tongue slid into his mouth.

Groaning softly, he lifted her into his arms and carried her to the bed, his mouth never leaving hers as his tongue began a gentle exploration of its own.

It had been a long time since he'd had a woman, a long time since she'd had a man. They undressed each other, their hands clumsy in their haste. She was silk and heat and soft warm curves. He was steel and fire and hard-muscled masculinity, and they flowed together like streams seeking the same ocean, rushing headlong into a raging whirlpool that carried them into ever deeper waters until, at last, the floodwaters broke, breaking over them in waves of pleasure that left them floating in a pool of blissful contentment.

Later, they made love again, slower this time, taking time to explore, to savor. Sarah was captivated by the sheer masculine beauty of his body. He seemed to be made of taut flesh drawn over hard muscle, and she delighted in looking at him, at running her fingertips over his chest and down his belly, pleased beyond words that her touch aroused him.

Toklanni wanted only to please her. Lacking the words to express how he felt, he tried to tell her with each kiss, each caress, that he loved her with all his heart, that she had turned his bitterness to hope and replaced his anger with passion. He could not stop looking at her. She was beautiful, so beautiful. Her skin was soft and smooth, constantly tempting his touch. Her hair spread across the pillow like liquid sunshine, flowing like silk in his hands.

He groaned low in his throat as they came together, flesh to flesh and heart to heart, two halves now whole, two souls made one for now and for always. . . .

Sarah nestled against Devlin, her head pillowed on his shoulder, one arm draped across his chest. She had never felt so cherished, so adored. He had not said much, and yet every stroke of his hand had been an affirmation of his love. Caught up in the magic of his touch, she had heard the words he could not say.

A small sigh escaped her lips. She had never been happier, she thought, never more at peace, and yet . . .

"What is it?" Toklanni asked, hearing her sigh.

"Nothing. I'm just so happy. Everything would be perfect if . . ."

"If Danny was here."

"Yes. I know you said he's all right, but I worry about him so."

Toklanni hugged her close, silently renewing his vow to return Danny to Sarah's arms or die trying.

They left the hotel early the following morning, traveling until nightfall with only a brief stop at noon. They were up the following morning before dawn. Toklanni rode with one eye on the dark clouds racing toward them, fearful that they might not reach the ranch in time, but luck was with them and they rode up to the house as the first drops of rain began to fall.

Toklanni sent Sarah into the house while he unsaddled the horses and turned them loose in the corral.

The smell of fresh-cooked coffee permeated the cabin when he stepped inside. Going into the kitchen, he found Sarah putting away the supplies they'd bought in town. For the first time, he wondered how he was going to support his new bride.

Toklanni frowned thoughtfully. If he could convince Noche to give up Danny without a fight, perhaps they could stay here on the ranch and raise horses or cattle. If Noche refused to let him have Danny, he would have to steal the child away from the village, in which case they would have to leave the territory.

Toklanni felt a twinge of regret at the thought. The rancheria was the only home he'd ever known. He had friends among the Apache, men he had grown up with, people he knew that he respected and admired, a life that suited him well.

Everything hinged on getting Danny back. Toklanni sighed heavily. Apaches had killed the boy's father. What would he think of having a half-breed Apache for a stepfather?

He put his thoughts aside as Sarah walked past him for the second time. Reaching out, he drew her into his arms and kissed her, amazed that she was his, that she found him desirable and worthy of her love. She kissed him passionately, holding nothing back, and he knew he would give up his old life without a qualm for the joy of loving Sarah.

Lifting her into his arms, he carried her into the bedroom, ignoring her half-hearted protests that it was midday. He undressed her slowly, his hands adoring her beauty, his desire rising like smoke from a forest fire as she returned the favor.

Lying beside her, he rained kisses on her cheek, her brow, the tip of her nose, one creamy white shoulder, the soft swell of her breast.

"Beautiful," he murmured. "So beautiful."

He made love to her gently, powerfully, his ardor kindling her own until Sarah thought she might die from the sheer pleasure of his touch.

Later, wrapped in his arms, she told him of her growing-up years in Providence, of marrying Vern, of moving west, of her anguish when Danny had been kidnapped by the Indians.

The tears in her eyes glittered like shards of broken glass, piercing his heart and soul, and he knew that he would not rest until he found a way to reunite Sarah with her son.

Chapter Eleven

Thanksgiving Day was cold and cloudy. Toklanni would not eat turkey, so they had a venison roast instead, with spice cake for desert.

For Sarah, it was a day of joy and sadness. Joy that she could share it with Toklanni, sorrow that Danny was not there. He'd been gone from her for almost five months and not a day went by that she didn't think of him, wondering if he was well, if he was happy, if the Indians were treating him all right.

If not for Toklanni, she knew she would have been mired in depression like a cow mired in a bog, but he refused to let her stay discouraged for long.

Indeed, life with Toklanni was everything she had ever dreamed of. He was a kind and gentle lover, even-tempered, tender-hearted. She read to him from the Bible each night, and when she learned he could not read or write, she set out to teach him. They spent many hours sitting before the fire while she taught him the alphabet, and how to read and write his name. It kept her mind occupied and her hands busy and left her with less time to brood about her son.

In mid-December Sarah began to prepare for Christmas. It was a holiday Toklanni had never celebrated, and she smiled each time she thought of the lovely red scarf she had made for him, of the blue wool shirt she'd bought in Pepper Tree Creek. She taught him Christmas carols and insisted he sing with her, delighted at the way their voices blended together.

In the evenings she read the chapters on Christ's birth from the New Testament. They were her favorite scriptures, and she wept as she read of Joseph and Mary making the long journey to Bethlehem, her heart going out to Mary who had to bring forth her firstborn son within the walls of a lowly stable.

Toklanni listened to the story with rapt attention, frowning as Sarah read the story of the Christ Child. The white man called the Apache cruel and heartless, and in some cases that was true, but no Apache would have turned away a pregnant woman in need of shelter.

He listened in fascination as she read of angels and shepherds, of wicked kings and wise men. It was a story that touched his heart and made him long to know more of the white man's God and His son.

When Sarah stopped reading, he urged her to

go on, caught up in the miracles of Jesus, in the love He had for people, all people. So much love that He died for their sins in a most horrible way.

"And you believe your God is the same as Usen?"

"Yes," Sarah said firmly. "There's only one God, and Jesus is His son."

Toklanni nodded. There were similarities between the story of the white man's Jesus and the Apache hero, Child of the Waters, who had been born of Usen and White Painted Lady.

He looked at Sarah, and saw that her thoughts had turned inward. She was thinking of her own son, he knew that without a doubt. She had adorned the cabin with her meager Christmas decorations, she had baked cookies and gingerbread men, she had made her son a pair of mittens and a new shirt, bought him a ball and a dozen toy soldiers in town. The presents were wrapped in bright paper beneath a small piñon tree that Toklanni had cut down for her.

In two days time it would be Christmas. He knew she had presents for him as well, and it grieved him that he had nothing to give her in return. He thought of how brave she had been in the last few weeks, smiling when he knew she wanted to cry, making plans for Christmas when he knew her heart wasn't in it. And he knew, with crystal clarity, that it was in his power to give her the greatest gift of all.

The next morning after breakfast, he told her he was going hunting.

"Hunting?" Sarah repeated. "Now?"

"I'm going to look for a turkey."

Sarah grinned at him. "Why? You won't eat it."
He had refused to have a turkey for Thanksgiving,
telling her it was another Apache taboo.

"I know you would like to have turkey, and
perhaps I will let my white half try it."

"How long will you be gone?"

Toklanni shrugged. "As long as it takes."

"Promise me you'll be careful." She wrapped
her arms around him, frightened by a sudden
sense of impending danger.

"A warrior is always careful."

"I know, I know," she teased. "An Apache warrior can travel over fifty miles in a day, and find
food off the land. He can disguise himself with
dirt and plants so as to be practically invisible."

Toklanni grinned down at her. "I think perhaps
I have been bragging too much."

"Perhaps. But you will be careful?"

He nodded. For a moment he held her close,
drinking in the scent of her, basking in her touch.
He kissed her then, a long hungry kiss, and then
kissed her again in farewell, wondering if he would
ever see her again.

His return to the village caused quite a stir.
Everyone knew there was bad blood between
Toklanni and his brother, though no one knew
the reason for it. Noche stayed in the background,
a speculative look on his face.

When the crowd dispersed, Toklanni approached Noche, keenly aware of the animosity in his
brother's gaze.

"Welcome home, brother," Noche said, his voice thick with sarcasm.

"Noche," Toklanni acknowledged tersely.

"Why have you come back?"

"This is my home."

"Is it?"

A shiver of apprehension skittered down Toklanni's spine. "What are you trying to say?"

"I have been to the white woman's house. I have seen your horse in the corral."

Toklanni nodded. "I told you before, she was my woman. Now I have made her my wife."

Noche snorted, his dark eyes filled with scorn. "So you have turned your back on the People."

"No. I am Apache. I will always be Apache. But the white woman is now my wife, and my first loyalty must be to her. I have come to tell you that we are going to live in her house, to tell you that my heart will always be good for my brother and the People."

"You have come for the boy," Noche said curtly, "and we both know it."

Toklanni did not deny it. "The woman is my wife. The child is now mine by right of marriage. I ask you to give him back to his mother."

"And if I refuse?"

"I will give you anything you wish in exchange for the boy."

"You have nothing that I desire, except maybe the great gray stallion."

Toklanni took a deep breath. He had raised the gray from a colt. It was the best horse he had ever owned, his most prized possession. "It is yours."

"It is not enough."

"I have nothing else to give you. Take the gray and let us part as brothers."

"If you want the boy, you must fight me for him. If you win, you may have the boy and I will take the horse."

"I do not want to fight you, Noche. It is not the Apache way."

"What do *you* know of the Apache way?" Noche said contemptuously. "I have spoken, and I do not change my words."

Toklanni eyed his brother speculatively. Noche was a few years younger, an inch or two shorter, several pounds heavier, but he was strong as an ox, fast and agile in his movements.

"Very well," Toklanni agreed. "It shall be as you say."

"Tomorrow morning," Noche said.

Word of the fight spread quickly through the village. In the morning, every man, most of the women, and a number of children had gathered to watch.

Danny Andrews stood at the edge of the crowd, his eyes wide as he watched the man who had captured him. Despite the cold, Noche stripped down to his breechclout, then paraded around the circle, flexing his arms and hands.

Moments later, a second man stepped into the circle created by the watching Indians. He, too, wore only a deerskin clout and moccasins.

They were fighting over him, Danny knew, though he did not know why. He knew only that he would belong to the winner, and he wondered why the tall, scar-faced stranger would want him, and what the warrior would do with him should he win.

Danny felt no love for Noche, but the man and his wife had been kind to him. What if the stranger was cruel? His eyes were dark and intense. The scar on his face made him seem ominous. What if the warrior took him far away? Danny blinked back his tears. He did not want to leave this place. He would never find his way back to his mother if the tall warrior took him away from the village. His mother . . . Danny tried not to think of her often, but now her image came clearly to mind, and a tear slid down his cheek as he recalled how much he loved her, how much she had loved him.

He looked at the two men who stood facing each other, their left wrists bound together by a short strip of rawhide. Each held a long-bladed knife in his right hand. It would not be a fight to the death; the loser would be the one who first asked for mercy.

Danny stared at them for a moment. Slightly crouched, they circled first to the left, then to the right. No one was watching him, and in that moment Danny knew what he was going to do. He was going to run away. He was going home. Nonchalantly he turned away from the crowd and strolled toward the edge of the camp.

Toklanni shut everything from his mind but the face of the man before him. Slowly, warily, they circled left and right, getting the feel of the knives, testing the distance between them.

Noche made the first move, lunging forward with the knife outstretched, slashing at Toklanni's side. Toklanni parried the blow, and the fight began in earnest. Noche was as fast as Toklanni remembered, agile as a cat, swift as a snake, but his anger and his hatred made him careless and Toklanni quickly slipped past his guard and drew first blood, opening a narrow gash in Noche's chest.

The early morning air rang with the sound of metal striking metal, of their harsh breathing, of the murmurs and cries of the crowd as both men drew blood again and again.

They drew back a moment to catch their breath, and Toklanni summoned Sarah's image to mind, reminding himself of what he hoped to gain. Renewed determination flowed through him. With a wild cry, he flung himself at Noche, pinning his brother to the ground as he held his knife at Noche's throat.

"Do you yield?" Toklanni demanded. "Will you give me the boy, or do I take your life?"

"Take the boy," Noche hissed between clenched teeth.

"I want your promise," Toklanni said, increasing the pressure of the blade at Noche's throat. "You will not try to take him back, or attack the white woman's place again."

Noche glared at him; then, as the edge of the knife pricked his skin, he muttered, "You have my word."

Toklanni nodded. Noche had given his promise grudgingly, but his honor would make him keep it.

Sitting back, Toklanni cut the strip of rawhide that bound him to his brother, then stood up, his sides heaving, his gaze scanning the crowd for Sarah's son. But there was no sign of the boy.

He let one of the women tend his wounds, then he slipped on his shirt and leggings and went to look for Danny. No one had seen the boy since the fight started, and a search of the village was begun. It soon became obvious that the boy had run away.

"Your prize has left the village," Noche said, his voice cold. "I suggest you do the same."

Toklanni turned away without a reply. Minutes later, mounted on his second-favorite horse, a big-boned bay mare, he circled the village, looking for sign.

It wasn't hard to find, a trail of small, moccasin-clad footprints heading north.

Thirty minutes later, Toklanni had the boy in sight.

Danny glanced over his shoulder at the sound of hoofbeats coming up behind him. When he saw who it was, he started running, his heart pounding with fear. The stranger had won the fight and now he'd come for him.

"Wait!"

Spurred by his fear, Danny kept running, though he felt his lungs would burst. And then the horse was beside him, so close he could feel the animal's warm breath on the back of his neck.

"Danny!"

He stopped at the sound of his name, too winded to go on. Turning, he stared up at the scar-faced stranger, wondering what awful fate awaited him.

"How do you know my name?" Danny asked suspiciously.

"Your mother told me."

"You know my mother?"

"Yes. I've come to take you to her."

"I don't believe you."

"It's true, *ciye*," he said, using the Apache word for son. "Won't you trust me?"

"What's my mother's name?"

"Sarah Andrews."

"What color's her hair?"

"Blonde. Her eyes are blue, like yours. And she misses you very much."

Danny swallowed hard. And then he walked toward the man, the need to see his mother overriding his fear of the tall warrior with the scarred face.

"I won't hurt you, *ciye*," Toklanni promised as he reached down and lifted the boy onto the mare. "Don't be afraid."

"You're really taking me home?" Danny asked. "You wouldn't lie to me?"

"I wouldn't lie to you, *ciye*. We'll be home before noon."

Chapter Twelve

It was Christmas morning. Sarah sat in front of the fireplace, a blanket across her lap. She'd been reading the Christmas Story again; now, as she closed the Bible, she wondered where Toklanni was. She hadn't expected him to be gone overnight, and though she told herself he was probably fine, she couldn't help but worry that he might have run afoul of Comanches or soldiers.

She was staring into the flames when, inexplicably, she felt compelled to go to the window. Rising, she drew the blanket around her shoulders and went to look out into the yard. A light snow was falling, frosting the trees and the fence posts with a layer of white.

Sarah stared at the scene for a moment, wondering what had prompted her to get up from her cozy place before the fire, and then she saw the horse and riders. She felt a quick shiver of apprehension when she saw that the horse was a bay, not Toklanni's big gray stallion. Who would be coming out here in the middle of nowhere?

She was about to turn away from the window to take up Toklanni's rifle when something stopped her in her tracks. Sarah leaned forward, her eyes narrowing as she sought to see more clearly through the falling snowflakes.

She felt a deep sense of relief as she recognized the tall rider as Toklanni. And the smaller one . . . no, it couldn't be. But it was.

"Danny!" She cried his name as she ran out the door, skimming across the snow-covered ground like a bird about to take flight. "Danny! Danny!"

"Mama!"

Toklanni reined the mare to a halt as Danny scrambled off the back of the horse and ran into his mother's outstretched arms.

Toklanni felt a catch in his heart as he watched Sarah embrace her son, tears of joy and happiness flooding her eyes as she hugged him close, kissing his cheek, the top of his head, the tip of his freckled nose. And all the while she murmured his name over and over again.

And Danny was crying, too, incoherent words of childish delight as he nestled against his mother's breast, holding onto her as if he would never let go.

After a long while, Sarah stood up, one arm hugging Danny close to her side. "Thank you, Devlin," she said, hardly able to speak for the flood of emotion that filled her heart.

111

Toklanni smiled down at her, his own throat thick with unshed tears.

"He came for me, Mama," Danny said, pointing at Toklanni. "He fought Noche for me, only I didn't stay to watch. I was afraid, and I ran away."

"You fought your own brother?" Sarah asked.

"With knives," Danny added, his blue eyes filled with awe.

"I'm all right," Toklanni assured Sarah, warmed by the concern he read in her gaze.

"Where's your stallion?"

"With Noche."

She knew without being told that he'd given his prized stallion in exchange for her son.

"What if you'd lost?"

"I guess I'd still have my favorite war horse." Toklanni's gaze moved from Sarah's face to Danny's and back again. "It was a fair trade. Come on, let's go inside."

Later, after Danny told his mother all about his stay with the Apache, and after they'd exchanged about a hundred more hugs, Sarah lit the candles on the tree, filling the little cabin with a soft warm glow.

Toklanni couldn't take his eyes from the woman who was his wife. Her blue eyes were filled with so much love and happiness it made his heart ache. Time and again, she reached out to touch Danny's arm, his shoulder, to ruffle his hair, as though to make sure he was really there.

Her face radiated joy as she watched her son open his presents. Danny was delighted with the mittens, thrilled by the wooden soldiers, pleased to have a new shirt, though he insisted on keeping the buckskin vest and moccasins Noche's wife had made for him.

"I wish I had something for you, Mama," Danny said.

"Oh, Danny, your being here is the only present I need."

Her words made Danny flush with embarrassed delight. "Really, Mama?"

"Really."

"Now it's your turn," Sarah said, and handed Toklanni a package tied with a big red bow. "This one first."

He unwrapped the package to find a blue wool shirt. It was his first Christmas present, his first gift of any kind. But it was the second present, a red scarf, that tugged at his heart, because Sarah had made it with her own hands, just for him. He smiled at her as he put it around his neck, the softness of the wool reminding him of the soft warmth of her hands.

They had turkey for dinner. Toklanni eyed it speculatively for a long moment before he took a bite. He chewed it carefully, and then grinned with pleasure.

"The Apache don't know what they're missing," he said solemnly, and Sarah and Danny both laughed.

The meal was a huge success and Sarah declared it was the best Christmas they'd ever had.

After dinner, Sarah and Danny sang Christmas carols, and then Danny asked his mother to read the Christmas Story. With a heart overflowing with love and gratitude, Sarah picked up the old family Bible and turned to the Book of Luke, Chapter 2.

" . . . And she brought forth her firstborn son, and wrapped him in swaddling clothes, and laid him in a manger, because there was no room for them in the inn."

Toklanni was watching Sarah's face as she read the words "firstborn son." He heard the catch in her voice and saw the two bright tears that sparkled in her eyes as she glanced up from the Bible to gaze lovingly at her own firstborn son.

" . . . And the angel said unto them, Fear not: for, behold, I bring you good tidings of great joy, which shall be to all people.

"For unto you is born this day in the city of David a Saviour, which is Christ the Lord."

Later that night, Toklanni and Sarah stood beside Danny's bed, their hands entwined as they gazed down at the sleeping child.

"I guess we'll have to leave here now, won't we?" Sarah asked.

"Only if you want to. I have Noche's promise that he won't bother you again."

"Do you want to leave?"

"No." This was home. It would always be home. He had been born here and his roots ran deep into the land. But he would willingly take Sarah anywhere she wanted to go. "Do you?"

Sarah shook her head. "It's funny. I've lived here for five years, and this is the first time it's ever felt like home."

"We'll stay then."

"I never thanked you for bringing Danny back to me," Sarah murmured. She wrapped her arms around Toklanni's waist and hugged him to her, her heart overflowing with love and gratitude for her husband. "Thank you with all my heart."

"I had to give you something for Christmas," Toklanni replied. "I knew you were making the scarf for me."

"How did you know?" Sarah demanded. "It could have been for me."

"No." He smiled down at her, his heart quickening at her nearness, at the love he read in the depths of her eyes. "I saw the look on your face while you worked on it, and I knew it was meant to be mine."

"A scarf seems like such a small thing when compared to the gift of my son."

"But I have you," Toklanni murmured.

And he silently thanked the gods, both red and white, for the gift of life, for the promise of a bright future in this life, and the hope of a life in the hereafter with the woman in his arms.

Sarah. She had given him hope and joy, wiped the bitterness from his soul, taught him what life and love and giving were all about.

Truly, loving Sarah and having her love in return was the greatest Christmas gift of all.

ROBIN LEE HATCHER
A Christmas Angel

To Micki's and Jennifer's little angels.
Welcome to the family.

Prologue

Idaho, 1892

Phoebe's eyes lit with excitement as she looked at the angel in the mail order catalog. She didn't think she'd ever seen anything more beautiful in all her life. And this was only an ink drawing. She could just imagine what the spun-gold hair, white satin gown, and gossamer-like wings *really* looked like.

The front door whistled open, and a cold blast of air whipped across the room as her father entered the house.

Phoebe glanced up. "Pa! Come look at this," she called, unable to hide the excitement in her voice.

"What've you got there?" Mick Gerrard smiled as he shrugged out of his wool coat and hung it on a hook near the door.

"Look at the angel, Pa. Wouldn't she be perfect on top of a Christmas tree?"

He crossed the kitchen in four strides. His hand alighted on Phoebe's shoulder as he bent forward, his gaze on the catalog. "Yes, she sure would, pet. She'd be perfect, all right."

Phoebe glanced up at her father. She'd heard the weariness in his voice, and she could see it in his face, too. She felt a stab of guilt for wanting something like the angel when she knew they couldn't afford it.

And it was all her fault. If she hadn't fallen out of the hayloft . . .

Mick ruffled his daughter's hair as he kissed her cheek. "We'll see what we can do."

"I didn't mean I wanted it, Pa," she lied. "I just thought she was pretty."

"Well, who knows? Maybe Saint Nicholas will decide to bring you one just like her."

She wrinkled her nose. "I'm too *old* to believe in Saint Nick," she replied, adding an emphatic *harrumph* for good measure.

Her father didn't say anything more. He simply nodded, then straightened and went into his bedroom.

Phoebe stared at the door to his room for a long time before returning her gaze to the angel in the catalog. Guilty or not, she *did* wish they could have it. She was certain a heavenly spirit like the golden-haired angel would bring good fortune to her father.

Maybe—if she'd still believed in Saint Nick—the jolly old elf would have brought her a Christmas angel, but ten years old was *too* old to believe in such nonsense.

Even so, she couldn't quite stop herself from closing her eyes and wishing for it, all the same.

Chapter One

Jennifer Whitmore sighed as she stared out the sooty window. The countryside, vast and snow-covered, rolled steadily past, the train carrying her farther and farther away from Chicago and all she'd ever known.

She tried her best not to think about what she was doing—leaving behind her comfortably familiar position at the Angel of Mercy Hospital, her comfortably familiar rooms at Mrs. Mulligan's Boarding House, her comfortably familiar courtship with Harry Reynolds.

"You can't be serious!" Harry had cried when she'd told him what she was going to do. "This is insane. What about me? Don't you care what I think of this? What if I tell you I don't want you to go?"

Perhaps Harry is right. Perhaps it is insane.

"What about you, Harry?" she'd asked. "Is there some reason for me to stay?"

His eyes had bulged slightly, as if someone had choked off his air supply. In the end, he'd stormed out of the house without saying another word.

What had she expected him to say? *I love you, Jennifer? Stay and marry me, Jennifer?*

No, she hadn't really expected him to say those things. Not then and not ever. Harry had always been content to see her on Tuesday and Thursday evenings, precisely at six o'clock. On Sundays, he'd never failed to walk her to and from the Methodist Church three blocks from the boarding house. He'd never shown any inclination to deviate from his accustomed routine, certainly not with such a drastic step as marriage.

In truth, she wasn't sure what she would have done if Harry had ever proposed. She supposed she was actually relieved that he hadn't. Whenever she'd tried to imagine herself as his wife, she'd failed. She'd known she wasn't in love with him. He wasn't the sort of man to send a woman's heart into flights of ecstasy. Solid and dependable. Safe and reliable. Comfortably familiar. Those were the words one would use to describe Harry Reynolds.

Just the right sort of man for a drab old maid— but even a drab old maid had a few dreams left.

Jennifer closed her eyes. When she did, it wasn't Harry's face that came to mind. It was a face from out of the past. A face she often remembered. A face she would be seeing again by this time tomorrow.

How much would Mick Gerrard have changed since she'd last seen him? she wondered. Would his hair still be the same honey-brown? Would it

123

still be thick and unruly, the way she remembered it? Would his eyes be the same intense shade of blue, like the sky on the clearest of winter days? Would he still stand head-above-the-crowd tall? Would he still have a crooked smile, one that reached his eyes while the right side of his mouth turned up higher than the left?

She opened her eyes and straightened, shaking her head to rid herself of Mick's image. It wasn't seemly of her to be thinking about him this way. After all, she wasn't a love-struck thirteen-year-old any longer. She was twenty-four and a nurse. And Mick Gerrard wasn't an eighteen-year-old clerk in her father's mercantile store. He was her stepsister's widower. His daughter was her niece—and Phoebe Gerrard was the sole reason Jennifer was headed for Idaho.

"We never should have let Phoebe stay out west after Christina died," Dorothea Whitmore had stated when her husband, David, had finished reading the letter from Mick.

The three of them had been sitting around the table when the letter from Idaho arrived. Jennifer had always come for dinner with her father and stepmother on Saturdays, and that day hadn't appeared to be any different from all the Saturdays that had gone before. Not until Mick's letter had been delivered.

"We should have demanded that *that man* bring our grandchild to us where she belonged. We should have known *he* couldn't take proper care of her. Now it's too late. She's crippled. What kind of father is he? And he has the *nerve* to ask us for help! We shall certainly *not* send him any money. Dear heavens, Christina's daughter a cripple. How will she ever find a husband now?"

"Phoebe is hardly old enough to have to worry about finding a husband," David had said without looking up from the slip of paper in his hand. "Besides, the letter doesn't say she won't get well. The doctor seems to have hope for recovery if she has the proper care."

Dorothea had dabbed at her misty eyes with her handkerchief, acting as if she hadn't heard him. "Oh, my poor Christina. When I think of what she had to suffer with *that man*. Oh, my poor, dear, dead Christina."

"Father?" Jennifer had interrupted softly. "May I see the letter, please?" She'd held out her hand, and he'd given it to her.

. . . Phoebe is in need of a nurse . . . no promise that she'll ever walk again, although the doctor has hope . . . all savings depleted . . . grateful for whatever you can do . . .

She'd read the few lines several times before she'd looked up again and stated simply, "I'll go to Idaho to care for Phoebe."

"Jennifer, are you sure?" her father had asked.

"Yes."

Why did I do it? she wondered now as she turned her gaze back on the wintry plains passing her window.

The steady rhythm of the train chugging along on its tracks lulled her into a dream-world, taking her thoughts further back in time. Back eleven years . . .

Mick carried a heavy box from the flatbed wagon into the stockroom at the back of the mercantile. When he set it down, he glanced toward Jennifer who was sitting on a pickle barrel.

"What're you reading now, Jen?" he asked as he wiped his hands on his trouser legs. He took the pamphlet from her hands. "*Suggestions for the Improvement of the Nursing Service for the Sick Poor* by Florence Nightingale." He cocked an eyebrow at her.

"I'm going to be a nurse some day."

He grinned, as if responding to a great joke. "*You?*"

"And why not?" She grabbed the pamphlet back from him. "I've always liked taking care of things. And I'm smart enough. Mrs. Ludden told me I am."

His teasing grin vanished immediately. "Never said you weren't smart enough. You'd have to be with all the books you've read. I reckon your teacher's right. You'll be able to do whatever you set your mind to." He smiled again, this time warmly.

Her whole stomach seemed chock full of butterflies as she looked up into his brilliant blue gaze. She didn't suppose anything could ever make her feel better than to have Mick looking at her like that, like he thought she was somebody special. She wished she could tell him how she felt about him. She wished she could let him know she loved him with all the love her thirteen-year-old heart possessed.

"What about you, Mick? You've never said what you want to do."

The teasing light was back in his eyes. "You mean when I grow up?"

"I'm serious. I know you don't want to just go on clerking in a store."

"And how do you know that, Jen?"

"Because I've seen that faraway look in your eyes, and I know it means you're thinking of someplace you'd rather be. Where is it?"

"You see a lot for a little girl."

She scowled at him.

He shrugged. "Okay, I guess it wouldn't hurt to tell you. I've always wanted to go out west. I'd like to own some land of my own, far away from Chicago and so many people. I'd like to see the mountains and be able to listen to the silence when I sit outside my own house at night. Someday, when I've got enough money put aside, that's what I'm going to do. I'm going to go west and have me a farm."

Jennifer closed her eyes and tried to imagine a place such as he'd described. She wondered if he'd build the house big enough for more than just himself. She wondered if he ever imagined her being there with him. She wondered if there was any call for nurses out west.

"Oh . . . *there* you are."

Jennifer felt her stomach plummet. She opened her eyes and watched her stepsister stop in the doorway to the storeroom.

Christina, clad in a bright-yellow gingham dress, didn't bother to look at the younger girl.

127

Her gaze was only for Mick. She leaned against the doorjamb, her head tilted slightly to one side, a small pout forcing her bottom lip forward.

Though only three years older than Jennifer, Christina was undeniably already a woman. She was turned just right to reveal the high, full curve of her breasts, the narrowness of her waist, and the soft rounding of her hips. Her curly burgundy hair tumbled freely down her back. As always, she was posed to be noticed.

And Mick certainly noticed, Jennifer thought irritably.

She glanced down at her own flat chest; at her plain brown dress, now wrinkled and covered with dust from the hours she'd sat reading in the back of the storeroom; at her nondescript blond hair that hung in two braids, one over each shoulder.

"Mick, can you spare me a moment, please? There's a box in my closet that I simply must get down, and it's far too heavy for me. Father isn't here or I would ask him." Christina smiled.

Jennifer felt her stomach drop again. Nobody could light up a room with a smile like Christina. Her flawless features made her the most sought after young woman in all Chicago. At least that's how it seemed to Jennifer.

She just wished Christina didn't have to go after Mick, too. It wasn't fair. She could have any one of six dozen young men, but she kept flirting with Mick Gerrard. Maybe Jennifer wouldn't have felt so bad if she thought Christina really and truly cared for him, but she didn't. Christina just liked

A Christmas Angel

to be the center of attention. She thought every man ought to be madly in love the moment he set eyes on her.

Trouble was, Jennifer thought, most men *did* fall madly in love the moment they saw her.

Nobody's ever going to feel that way about me. I might as well be part of the furniture.

"Sure. I'll be glad to help you," Mick said. "Just as soon as I've finished unloading the supplies from the wagon."

Christina straightened. "I'll be waiting for you upstairs. Thanks ever so much, Mick. You're so strong, I know you won't have a bit of trouble with it."

Jennifer felt like gagging. Couldn't Mick see what Christina was doing? Was he as blind as all the other village idiots who swarmed around the Whitmore family's store?

"I won't be long," he said, then turned toward the back door.

Jennifer glanced at her stepsister. Christina's smile disappeared the moment his back was turned. She stood there, biting her lower lip, lost in thought, and Jennifer had the distinct feeling that all was not right.

If only she'd known . . .

Jennifer blinked, cutting off the memories abruptly. She didn't want to think about Mick, but she couldn't seem to help herself. Not now, and not any time through the years. She supposed a woman always remembered her first love that way.

But that had been a silly, schoolgirl affection. She was a grown woman now. She was going west to help her brother-in-law and her niece in their time of trouble. She was going because she was a nurse.

Still, she wondered if he'd ever thought of her . . .

Why should he have thought of me? she reflected, disgusted with her continued mooning over the past. She'd been just a child when Mick and Christina had ridden away from the church, a man and his wife on their way west to fulfill a dream.

Chapter Two

Mick lifted Phoebe from the wheelchair and laid her on her bed, then pulled the blankets up snug beneath her chin.

"What's Aunt Jennifer like, Pa?"

It wasn't the first time she'd asked that question, and his answer wasn't much different from the ones he'd given before. "Don't know, pet. Last time I saw her, she was only a few years older than you. Still just a little girl. She used to hide in the storeroom and read. She did love her books. I remember her telling me that she wanted to be a nurse when she grew up."

"Is she going to be able to make my legs better?"

Mick pushed Phoebe's dark hair back from her face. It was difficult for him to answer around the lump in his throat. "I don't know." He leaned over and kissed her forehead. "Now you get some sleep."

"Can't I go with you tomorrow?"

"You know what Doc Jenkins said. You're not to go out in this cold weather. We don't need you takin' sick with pneumonia."

Phoebe let out an exaggerated sigh.

He smiled tolerantly. "Save it, pet."

She flashed a grin of her own. "You always say it never hurts to try."

When she smiled like that, he could see a little of Christina in her. Phoebe's hair was coal black and her eyes were umber with light flecks of gold around the darker irises—so different from Christina's burgundy-red hair and apple-green eyes—but she had her mother's perfect bone structure and ivory complexion. When Phoebe grew up, she would be even more beautiful than Christina had ever thought of being.

"Get some sleep, pet," he whispered, bending to kiss her one more time. He snuffed the lamp, then walked out of the child's bedroom, leaving the door slightly ajar so he could hear if she needed him in the night.

He crossed the room that served as both the kitchen and parlor of the small farmhouse. Reaching the window, he glanced outside. The blanket of snow that covered the earth sparkled in the moonlight, giving everything a peaceful, serene look.

This hadn't been a peaceful place in the early years. Christina had hated the farm and their solitary life even more than she'd hated him for bringing her to it. The house had more often served as a battleground than a home. More than once, Mick had considered giving up and going back to Chicago. It was difficult enough for a man to deal with the hardships that went hand-in-hand with farming—too little rain, too much rain, too hot, too cold, insects, blight—without having to contend with so much disharmony when the work day was done.

What's Aunt Jennifer like, Pa?

He wondered, too. Would she be anything like Christina—self-centered, vain, always wanting more than he could provide, more than he could give? Would she be like his mother-in-law, convinced that Mick was as incapable of taking care of Phoebe as he'd been incapable of making his wife happy? Had he made a mistake, writing to the Whitmores and asking for help?

Lord knew, it had been sheer desperation that drove him to write that letter, and he'd regretted mailing it many times. He'd known he was taking a risk. His mother-in-law had insisted more than once that Phoebe should be sent to live with her, so she could be raised "in Chicago, where she can meet people of quality and refinement." If Dorothea ever learned the truth, she just might be able to take Phoebe away from him, and that he couldn't bear.

But what had been left for him to do? Once spring came, he would be busy from dawn to dusk. He wouldn't be able to give his daughter the care she needed. He was only just managing to hold on to the farm as it was, and since Phoebe's accident, what little money he'd put aside was gone. It was clear that Phoebe needed a nurse, but he had no way to pay for one.

So he'd written to his in-laws and asked for help. It hadn't ever occurred to him that they would send Jennifer to care for her niece rather than loaning him some money. He'd forgotten until he'd received David Whitmore's reply that Jennifer had once told him she wanted to be a nurse when she grew up.

His jaw tightened. The day she'd told him was a day he'd just as soon forget . . .

Mick rapped on the door. "You in there, Christina?"

"Come in."

He opened the door and stepped into her bedroom. She was standing beside the bed. She was wearing a dark green wrapper now instead of the yellow gingham dress she'd had on earlier.

"It's that box on the top shelf," she said, pointing into the closet.

Mick nodded, then crossed the room.

"Do you need a chair or a stool or anything?" Christina asked from behind him.

"No." It was easy enough to reach the box. And when he did, he found it wasn't all that heavy. Even Christina should have been able to lift it.

He turned, box in hand, and then froze in place.

The green wrapper was lying on the floor. Christina stood before him—naked and pale and pink. His mouth went dry as he stared at perfection, from her firm, full breasts to a waist he could span with his hands, to the red curls at the apex of her thighs.

134

"Good Lord, Christina," he began, but the words were hardly more than a croak.

"Mick, hold me. Please hold me." She moved toward him. "Don't you know how I feel about you? I've wanted you forever."

"Christina . . ."

She took the box from his hands and tossed it aside before pressing herself against him.

It was like a torch being set against dry kindling. Mick was on fire with wanting. He forgot everything except the willing young woman in his arms. He kissed her with all the passion of an eighteen-year-old who had more lust than self-control and more zest than good sense.

Christina fell backward onto the bed, taking him with her. While her fingers pushed the suspenders off his shoulders, then worked to free his shirt from his trousers, he buried his face in her hair, breathing in the sweet fragrance of jasmine.

"Oh, Mick . . . Mick . . . Mick . . ."

Her skin was so soft, so smooth. Her breast filled his hand. Her lips were moist and tasted of peppermint.

"Christina darling. Chris . . ." A shriek split the air.

Mick scrambled off the bed. His body turned cold, warm blood replaced by something akin to ice water. He glanced from Christina's naked form to the horrified eyes of her mother, then back to Christina. The girl slowly drew the coverlet over her breasts, her cheeks blushing the most delicate shade of pink.

"Oh, dear. Oh, good heavens. What have you done? What have you done to my daughter? You fiend. You filthy . . ." Dorothea choked on her own words. She glared at Mick. "Get out of this room. Get out of my sight."

"Mother, please." Christina swept her curly hair behind her shoulder. "Don't get hysterical."

"Don't get . . . don't get *hysterical?*" Dorothea sank quickly onto a ladder-back chair.

"Yes. I'm sure he means to do the right thing by me." She looked up. "Don't you, Mick? You wouldn't allow me to be disgraced in front of my family, would you?"

Mick turned from the window and crossed to the cast iron stove. He plucked a tin cup off the shelf, then filled it from the blue-speckled pot. After simmering on the stove for the better part of the day, the coffee was strong and bitter. The taste seemed an appropriate match for his memories.

He sat down at the table, his gaze focusing on the catalog, still open to the page Phoebe had shown him earlier in the evening. He pulled the catalog toward him. *Dang,* he wished he could get the angel for her. The little mite never asked for much for herself.

How the dickens did Christina ever manage to give birth to such an unselfish child? he wondered.

There was very little about Phoebe that was like her mother, not in looks or in manner. He supposed she took after . . .

Mick's fingers tightened around the cup in his

hand. Unbidden, unwelcome, another unpleasant memory pushed its way into his thoughts. He remembered every moment of the day of Phoebe's birth—just six months after he'd married her mother. He remembered Christina's moaning and cursing. He remembered her yelling how much she hated him and the brat she'd carried in her womb for nine months. He remembered the harsh words she'd used to tell him how the baby's father had run off rather than marry her, and so she'd been forced to find another husband. Mick had been the first fool she could find.

He rose abruptly from the chair, feeling the old anger welling up in his chest. He preferred not to think about Christina, but as sour as those years had been, he would have lived through them all over again to have Phoebe. From the moment he'd first held her, the child had owned his heart. It hadn't mattered to him then and it didn't matter to him now that he hadn't actually sired her. She was his daughter, and no one could ever tell him any different.

Dorothea Whitmore might be sending Jennifer to Idaho to try to take Phoebe away, but it wasn't going to do her any good. Nobody could prove that Phoebe wasn't rightfully his. They could make as much noise as they wanted, but it wasn't going to do them any good. He wouldn't let them take his daughter away.

He glanced down at the catalog as a wave of despair hit him. He loved that child more than life itself. He would give up everything if he could undo the accident, if he could make her whole and healthy again. And yet he couldn't give her the smallest of requests, not even for Christmas. All she wanted was a simple ornament for the top of the tree, and he couldn't even give her that.

A taste more bitter than the coffee lay on his tongue as he turned toward his bedroom.

Chapter Three

Jennifer freshened herself as best she could in the passenger car's water closet, but she saw little improvement in the chipped mirror.

Her straight, pale hair was dull and badly in need of a good washing. Her aquamarine eyes had dark circles, evidence of her sleeplessness. Her gray shirtwaist was wrinkled and travel-stained. She looked like a woman who had been on a train for too many hours—which was exactly what she was.

She drew herself up straight and shot a determined glance at her reflection. *See here, Jennifer Whitmore,* she scolded silently, *it doesn't matter in the least what you look like. You're here to comfort an injured child. And that's all that matters.*

With her head held as high as she could get it, she opened the door and returned to her seat. She managed to maintain her prim, resolute posture until the conductor came through the car.

"Nampa station, next stop."

Her heart jumped into her throat. Her hands tightened in her lap. She felt the blood draining from her face, and she knew she must be as pale as a ghost. She forced herself to take several deep, steadying breaths. It wouldn't do for her to pass out from lack of oxygen at this precise moment.

Once again she mentally berated herself as she reached for her thick woolen cloak, not realizing until then how cold she had become without it on. She'd removed it before going to the water closet and had forgotten it upon her return. A fine thing it would be if she became ill because of her carelessness. Imagine coming all this way only to force Mick to take care of her.

Imagining it was just what she did, and she felt a blush stain her cheeks at the picture it brought to mind.

With a screech of iron wheels against iron tracks, the Oregon Short Line pulled into the Nampa station. As soon as the train came to a complete stop, Jennifer picked up her traveling case and her reticule, then rose from her seat. She drew in one more deep breath as she turned toward the exit at the rear of the car, and with a stomach full of battling alley cats, she walked down the aisle.

Mick waited with his back against the train depot's wall. A bitter December wind whipped small eddies of snow across the platform, stinging any exposed flesh it could find. From beneath the brim of his weathered felt hat, he watched the passengers disembark.

It wasn't as hard to find Jennifer as he'd feared it would be. Only three people got off the train, an older couple and a young woman. Clearly, the young woman had to be Jennifer.

But when he stepped forward and she turned to look at him, he knew that he couldn't have missed her even if there'd been a hundred other people around her. Jennifer Whitmore had scarcely changed from the girl he remembered sitting on a pickle barrel, her blond hair in braids, a book in her lap. She still had the same large eyes—not quite blue, not quite green—and a familiar, almost waiflike expression on her delicate face.

She smiled a little uncertainly. "Hello, Mick."

"Hello, Jennifer. Look at you. I think I was looking for a kid in pigtails, but you've grown up."

"That's what happens to a girl in eleven years." She glanced past his shoulder, then met his gaze again. "You came alone?"

"Phoebe's not supposed to be out in the cold." She shook her head. "Of course not."

He stepped closer, reaching to take her traveling case. It was large and heavy, and he wondered how she'd managed to carry it. Although she was tall for a woman, he figured she couldn't weigh more than a hundred and ten pounds. A strong gust of wind could have blown her away.

"Come on. Let's get you out of this weather." He took her arm and guided her toward the flatbed wagon sitting on runners.

He tossed her case into the back of the sleigh, then helped her onto the wagon seat. He hopped up beside her and handed her a lap robe.

141

"Tuck it around you good. We've got a ways to go, and it looks like we could get more snow before we get home."

They started off to the jingle of bells and the rattle of harness.

Mick had also changed in the past eleven years, and yet he was very much the same man she remembered. He was trim, although she had the feeling his arms, torso, and legs were well muscled beneath the thick layer of warm clothing. His face wasn't as smooth as it had been when he was eighteen. There were lines around his eyes and mouth and a few between his thick eyebrows that hadn't been there before. But his eyes were still the same intense shade of blue. She wondered if he had the same crooked smile that had always made her feel so silly inside. She hoped so.

Jennifer clenched her hands together in her lap beneath the blanket, her stomach acting crazy at just the thought of his smile. Afraid he might guess what she was thinking and feeling, she spoke quickly, saying the first thing that came to mind. "It's been a long time since I saw you, Mick."

"Yes."

She could see the shadow of his beard beneath his skin. It was strangely appealing. She wanted to reach out and touch his cheeks to see what the stubble felt like.

Her thoughts made her blush. Whatever had made her think such a thing? Nothing even remotely close to it had occurred to her when she'd been with Harry.

Jennifer felt the awkward silence stretching between them, and she wondered if he'd guessed what she'd been thinking, then mentally scolded herself for her foolishness. Of course he didn't know her thoughts.

And there was no reason for either of them to feel awkward, she told herself. No reason at all. They'd been friends once. He'd teased and laughed with her and even shared a few of his dreams. They could be friends again. It would just take some effort.

She decided to make the first move. "Was the farm everything you'd hoped it would be?"

He glanced at her.

"I remember how much you wanted to come west and have a place of your own," she said in a near whisper. "I just wondered if it turned out to be as wonderful as you'd imagined."

He nodded, then turned back toward the road. "It hasn't been easy."

I can tell.

"I guess it never will be," he continued. "That's the nature of farmin'. It's hard work, especially when a man's got no one to depend on but himself."

Jennifer looked away from him, her gaze set on the snow-covered countryside, dotted here and there with farmhouses and silos, barns and wooden fences. "I'm sorry about . . . about Christina."

When several minutes passed without a reply, she turned her head back in his direction. He was staring straight ahead, his mouth set in a tight line, his entire body warning that she was

143

treading on forbidden ground. It had been over three years since Mick had written to Christina's parents to inform them of her death, and yet it was clear from his attitude that time had done nothing to heal the wounds of his loss.

He must still love her very much, even after all this time.

She found the thought painful, too painful to dwell on in silence. "Tell me about Phoebe. What sort of little girl is she?"

The right side of his mouth curved upward. "The best."

Jennifer relaxed. "That's a father talking. Now tell me what she's really like."

He turned toward her, and she could see that his smile was unchanged. The left corner of his mouth still didn't turn up as far as the right. His blue eyes seemed to sparkle with a brightness from inside. "She's the best. You'll see."

She should have pressed him for information. She should have asked about the accident. She should have made him tell her everything the doctor had ever said or done for his patient. She should have behaved like the trained nurse she was. That was why she'd come out from Chicago, to take care of Phoebe, to try to make her well and whole again.

But she couldn't bear to take the smile away from him quite so soon. She wanted to enjoy it just a little longer.

So she smiled back at him and allowed them to continue on in a more comfortable silence.

Chapter Four

The white clapboard house was set back from the road about a quarter mile. It was small and, if not for the bright green shutters that framed the windows, would have been difficult to see against the snowy fields, barren now in the midst of winter. There was an unpainted outhouse about fifty feet off to the right. To the left was a barn, a hen house, and a corral for the horses.

Several large trees surrounded the house. Their limbs were bare now, but come spring, Jennifer knew that their leafy arms would provide plenty of cooling shade. Behind the barn she could see an orchard, the fruit trees planted in neat rows.

"Apples," Mick said, seeing where her gaze had traveled. "We make a mean cider."

"You truly do love it here, don't you?"

"That I do."

With sudden insight, Jennifer realized how it must have galled him to write to the Whitmores to ask for financial help. He was a proud man who had worked hard to get what he wanted. If not for Phoebe's accident, the Whitmores—and Jennifer through them—might never have heard from him again, even though Phoebe dutifully wrote to her grandmother several times a year.

Jennifer couldn't blame Mick for his unwillingness to contact his in-laws. Christina's mother had never tried to hide what she thought of Mick Gerrard. Of course, Jennifer secretly believed that Dorothea's periodic letters to Mick—demanding he send the child to live with them in Chicago—were more to pester and torment the man who had taken her daughter away than because she actually wanted to raise her granddaughter.

Mick drew the sleigh to a halt close to the front door, ending her musings as the bells on the harness fell silent. One of the horses snorted and bobbed his head, then turned to look at the occupants in the wagon.

"Let's get you inside, Jennifer, so I can unhitch the team before it starts to snow."

She glanced up and saw that the heavens had turned lead gray, the clouds thick and slung low to the earth. Somehow they looked different from the clouds that blew in over Chicago. She knew they weren't, but they did seem that way.

"Jen . . ."

She turned her head and found Mick standing beside the wagon. She stood up. Before she knew what he was doing, he'd placed his hands around her waist and lifted her to the ground. She felt heat rushing to her cheeks, but he didn't seem to notice as he released her and reached into the wagon bed to retrieve her traveling case.

"Follow me," he said.

She did so on unsteady legs.

Jennifer's eyes found Phoebe the instant she stepped inside the house. It would have been hard to miss the girl since she'd positioned her wheelchair only a few feet from the door, barely leaving room for her father and Jennifer to get inside.

While Mick helped her out of her cloak, the nurse and her patient studied each other.

The little girl wasn't anything like what Jennifer had pictured in her mind. She had envisioned a miniature version of the Christina she remembered, but instead, she saw a dark-eyed, black-haired pixie who resembled neither Mick nor her mother.

Suddenly Phoebe's face screwed up, as if in deep thought. "You don't look like what I expected. I thought you'd have red hair like my mother had."

"I always wanted hair like hers," Jennifer answered truthfully. "I thought it was lovely."

The little girl's mouth pursed as she tilted her head to one side before saying, "No. I think yours is pretty just like it is. It makes you look like an angel. Don't you think so, Pa?"

"What?"

"Don't you think Aunt Jennifer's hair makes her look like the angel? The one in the catalog?"

Jennifer turned toward him, feeling self-conscious as he looked her over with the same studiousness as his daughter had moments before.

"I think you're right, pet. She does look like the angel. Very pretty." Mick glanced at Phoebe. "You two get acquainted while I put the team in the barn. We've got a heck of a snow blowin' in from the west."

It was crazy how his words affected her.

He thought she was pretty. Jennifer Whitmore, pretty. She with her plain, straight, pale blond hair—hair she'd always hated because she'd thought Mick preferred unruly red curls. But Mick thought she was pretty.

As he turned toward the door, he winked at her, then disappeared out into the gathering storm.

It was *beyond* crazy how his wink affected her.

She felt rooted to the spot, and at the same time, she felt as though she were falling from a great height, falling so fast her breath was swept clean away.

"Aunt Jennifer?"

"What?" Snapped back from her paralyzed state, she spun around. She knew her cheeks had to be the color of ripe apples.

"You okay?"

She was surprised that she was able to think up an excuse for her odd behavior. "I . . . I'm afraid I've been on a train for so long, I can't seem to think straight. Perhaps you could show me to my room, Phoebe. We can talk while I get settled in."

"Sure. This way."

Jennifer noticed that all the furniture in the house had been pushed against the walls, leaving plenty of open space for Phoebe to get around in her wheelchair.

"This is really Pa's room, but he's going to sleep in the loft while you're with us." Phoebe pushed open the door and rolled her chair through the opening.

Jennifer allowed her gaze to move slowly over the room. It was sparsely furnished, like the rest of the house. There were no feminine touches that said a woman had ever stayed in this room. Not even any photographs of Christina on the chiffonier.

He must miss her terribly.

She felt a hollow ache inside and wished there were some way she could help him. She knew what it was like to remember someone, to long to see them years after they had gone away.

Her gaze stopped on the bed. Mick's bed. She would be sleeping in his bed while she was here. The realization made her heart race.

"I should be the one staying in the loft," she said quickly, turning her back to the bed.

"Pa wouldn't hear of it. There's no point in arguin' with him."

What was wrong with her? She'd come to Idaho to take care of Phoebe, to use her nursing skills to help a member of her own family, but instead, she was acting as if she had less common sense than her ten-year-old patient. It had to be because she was tired and, perhaps, a little overwrought. After all, she'd been nervous about seeing Mick again, nervous about meeting her niece, nervous about leaving Chicago and everything that was familiar. It was only natural that her emotions would be a bit unpredictable.

She took a deep breath. "Perhaps we could set up a cot for me in your room," she suggested.

The girl shook her head. "There's no room for a cot in there. It's too tiny." Her smile was totally disarming. "You might just as well quit tryin', 'cause Pa will tell you this is where you're gonna stay. Pa can be mighty stubborn when he has to be."

Jennifer nodded in defeat. Besides, what could it hurt? Once she had a good night's sleep, she would see how silly she was being about everything. Once she'd caught up on her rest, she would quit thinking about and reacting to Mick as if she were still thirteen. That's all she needed. Just a bit of sleep. Then she would be herself again.

"Well, then, I suppose I might as well unpack. Will you help me, Phoebe?"

Mick walked back to the house, wind-blown snow stinging his cheeks. He shrugged his coat up closer to his ears. If the past couple of weeks were any indication, it was going to be a long, cold winter. At least he had enough hay and grain to get his livestock through until spring. With luck and a bit of credit at the general store in town, he ought to be able to keep the three humans on the place fed as well.

Strange, the distrust and animosity he'd been harboring toward Jennifer Whitmore didn't seem as strong now as it had before she'd gotten off the train and turned to look at him with her large, blue-green eyes. In fact, he doubted there was any basis for those feelings at all. The moment he'd seen her, he'd been reminded of the times she'd sat and talked to him as he worked in the back of Whitmore Mercantile. She hadn't been anything like Christina or Dorothea back then. There was no reason to believe she might be so now. It seemed she truly had come to Idaho to help Phoebe get well, and he should be grateful for her assistance.

When he opened the door, he saw her sitting at the table, Phoebe's chair pulled close. The tops of their heads—darkest ebony and palest yellow— were nearly touching as they leaned toward each other. Jennifer was holding the mail order catalog in her lap while Phoebe pointed at items on the pages. The two of them looked up in unison, both smiling, traces of laughter lingering in their eyes.

Mick suddenly felt like the outsider, and he didn't care for the feeling. In a flash, his distrust returned.

Phoebe was *his* daughter, and no woman was going to come into his home and try to take her away from him. If that's what had motivated Jennifer Whitmore to come to Idaho, she'd better just pack up that carpetbag of hers and head back to Chicago right now.

Chapter Five

Jennifer awakened slowly. The first thing she noticed was the utter silence. It left her disoriented, unsure of her whereabouts. She half expected to feel the train start up again, to hear the constant chug-a-chug, to smell the smoke spewing from the engine's smokestack. But there was only silence.

Then she remembered. She'd arrived in Idaho yesterday afternoon. She was on Mick's farm. In fact, she was sleeping in Mick's bed.

Feeling rather reckless and a tad sinful, she nestled down further beneath the heavy quilt and blankets. She pressed her face against the pillow and breathed deeply. Her mind toyed with the idea of what it would be like to roll over and find Mick beside her, what it would be like if he should kiss her, if he should . . .

She felt her cheeks grow warm. She might still

be a virgin at twenty-four, but she was also a nurse. She'd studied all about the human reproductive system. She knew very well what it was a man and woman did in the privacy of their bedroom. Never once in the years she'd been seeing Harry had she imagined what it might be like to share such intimacies with him. Yet, only a few hours with Mick, and she was imagining it much too vividly for her own good.

Why did she react to him as if she were still thirteen? she wondered. She should have put her childish infatuation behind her by now. She was a grown woman, educated, a woman with a vocation. This wasn't like her, allowing such flights of fancy.

She thought of the moment yesterday when Mick had returned from the barn. Snow had dusted his thick, golden-brown hair and the shoulders of his wool coat. His nose and chin had been red from the cold. Jennifer had glanced up from the catalog Phoebe had been showing her, and for just a moment, she had felt the rightness of the three of them being together. For just a moment, she'd felt that she belonged, that this was her family.

The feeling hadn't lasted long. Mick's attitude toward her throughout the remainder of the evening could best be described as cool. At worst, it had seemed a bit hostile. It hadn't been hard for her to guess what had brought on his ill temper. Seeing her had reminded him of the wife he'd lost, and he'd taken out his pain on her. Jennifer had done her best not to show her own hurt.

If only she'd been a fiery beauty like Christina, maybe this *could* have been her family, she thought as she rolled onto her side and hugged a pillow against her chest. Maybe then Mick would have liked her enough to wait a few years. But she wasn't anything like her stepsister had been, not in looks or temperament or actions. It had been Christina who had come west with Mick to build his dream, Christina who had given birth to his daughter.

The pain she felt in her heart was all out of proportion to what she should have felt after so many years. She reminded herself again that she wasn't thirteen, but it didn't do any good. It was almost as if she still loved him, just as she had before he went away. But, of course, that wasn't possible. She couldn't still love a man she hadn't seen in eleven years. Besides, her feelings had been those of a child.

It simply wasn't possible that she loved him.

Was it?

Jennifer tossed the covers aside, ignoring the chilled air of the room as she rose from the bed and padded on bare feet over to the window. She pushed aside the curtains to reveal a wonderland of white.

Long icicles hung from the eaves of the house. Snow lay in deep drifts against the sides of the buildings, and tree limbs dipped low beneath the weight of the wintry blanket. Clear of storm clouds, the morning sky was the color of pewter in this predawn hour.

She shivered, hugging herself as she turned

from the window. Her glance fell on the bed, and she was tempted to scurry back into its waiting warmth. But she didn't want Mick to think she was a slugabed. She didn't want . . .

She drew her thoughts up short.

Listen to me, Jennifer Whitmore. You will not persist in these silly fantasies. You will concentrate on Phoebe. She is the sole reason you are here. Mick Gerrard is merely an old friend. He is your niece's father and no more. Now, get dressed and go see to your patient.

She had to break a thin coating of ice in the pitcher in order to pour water into the bowl on her dressing table. She performed only a perfunctory washing. To help control her chattering teeth, she tried to set her mind on something other than the frigid temperature.

Her thoughts returned once again to the previous evening, but this time they centered on her patient. At times, Phoebe had seemed far older than her ten years. She was unquestionably bright, and there was no doubting her love for her father. The two were closer than any father and daughter Jennifer had ever known. Certainly far closer than Jennifer was with David Whitmore, though she loved her father very much.

Perhaps Mick and Phoebe were *too* close. She thought about how he had fussed over the child all evening. There was hardly any reason for Phoebe to have a wheelchair, from what Jennifer had seen so far. The girl hadn't been given many chances to use it last night. Her father had been forever jumping up to get her this or bring her that. When

Phoebe's bedtime had come, Mick had lifted her up and carried her to her room.

Jennifer frowned as she donned her brown serge dress. It seemed she had more to do here than merely tend to the physical needs of her patient. Mick needed her, too.

She felt all fluttery inside at the thought of Mick needing her. She imagined him standing before her, looking down at her with his magnificent blue eyes. She could almost feel his hands closing around her arms. She could almost hear his voice as he spoke to her, telling her what he needed. She could almost . . .

A croak of frustration forced itself from her lips. She grabbed her hairbrush from the top of the bureau and furiously brushed her hair, intentionally slapping the bristles against her head, as if hoping to knock some sense into it before it was too late.

Phoebe. She was here for Phoebe.

Mick shoved more wood into the stove, then clamped the iron door shut as crackling sounds from the fire filled the kitchen. With movements guided by habit rather than conscious thought, he measured coffee grounds into the blue-speckled pot filled with water and set it on the stove, then headed for his coat and hat which were hanging on pegs near the front door.

He had just slipped into his sheepskin-lined jacket when the door to his bedroom opened. He glanced up, momentarily surprised to see Jennifer standing there.

"Good morning," she said softly.

It had been many years since he'd heard a woman's voice in the morning. And he couldn't recall Christina ever wishing him a good morning. Not once in all the years they were married.

"Mornin'."

"We certainly had a lot of new snow during the night."

"Sure did."

She tugged on the fitted sleeves of her dress. "We're lucky I arrived when I did."

He grunted something which sounded close to agreement, then turned away. "I've got to tend to the livestock." He pushed open the door and stepped out into the sub-zero temperature of dawn.

We're lucky I arrived when I did.

Lucky? He wasn't so sure. Phoebe had taken to Jennifer so quickly, as if they'd known each other all her life. It made him wonder if she'd missed having a woman around the place. She'd only been six when she lost her mother, but he'd thought they'd gotten by well enough. He'd never considered that Phoebe might miss Christina, a woman who had shown her so little affection in her short life.

We're lucky I arrived when I did.

Lucky? No, he didn't think he was lucky to have her there. He'd seen the surprised look on her face when she'd seen Phoebe. She had to be wondering about the child's black hair and brown eyes. She had to be comparing Phoebe's coloring with Christina's. She had to be looking at him and wondering.

We're lucky I arrived when I did.

Lucky? No, it would be better if she'd never come. Once she went back to Chicago and told Dorothea . . .

He jammed his hands into the pockets of his coat as he plodded through the high drifts of snow on his way to the barn.

He knew it was wrong to suspect the worst of her. Jennifer could very well be there just to help Phoebe get well. And wasn't that more important to him than anything else? Would he risk his daughter's health just to keep her to himself? Hell, no, he wouldn't. He would do whatever he had to do, risk whatever he had to risk, if it meant Phoebe would have what she needed.

He thought of Jennifer's tentative smile as she'd greeted him this morning. There was a sweetness there, a goodness that he couldn't argue against. Somehow, even now, it touched his heart, and he began to hope she was all she appeared to be.

"Tell me about yourself, Phoebe." Jennifer turned the sizzling bacon in the frying pan, then glanced over her shoulder.

Phoebe shrugged. "Like what?"

"Like what you like to do when you're not in school or helping your father with the chores."

"Oh, that's easy. In the summer, I liked to ride Panda over to Miller's Pond and go swimming. Panda's my pony. Would you like to see her?

Maybe later Pa'll take you out to the barn and show her to you."

"I'd like that. Tell me more about what you like to do."

"Pa and I used to go skating on the pond in the winter when it froze over."

It wasn't lost on Jennifer, the way Phoebe spoke in the past tense. She wanted to change that. She wanted to be able to tell the little girl that one day she would gallop her pony across her father's fields. She wanted to say that she and her pa could go skating again. But, of course, she couldn't say any such thing. Not until she'd talked to the doctor and had a few more facts.

"I like to read, too. Pa's always liked for me to read aloud to him at night before going to bed. Mr. Miller—he's our closest neighbor—he has a big library full of books, and he lets me take as many as I want as long as I promise to take care of them."

"Sounds like me when I was a girl. I used to hide in the storeroom at my father's store so no one could find me and put me to work. I'd snitch an apple from the bin and climb up on the shelves and read for hours." Jennifer walked over to the table and sat down in a chair across from Phoebe. She reached out, taking hold of the girl's hand. "You know why I've come, don't you?"

"Sure. To take care of me while Pa runs the farm."

"Well . . . yes, that's true. But you don't want people taking care of you the rest of your life as if you were a baby, do you? You'd like to be able to do things for yourself. You'd like to be able to dress yourself and fix your own meals. And if you could, you'd like to go swimming in the pond again and ride your pony, wouldn't you?"

Phoebe nodded.

"Of course you would. But that's going to take lots of hard work. Are you willing to work hard?"

She nodded again.

"You know I can't promise you'll be able to walk again. From what your father said in his letter, the doctor can't be sure if the damage to your legs is permanent." Jennifer leaned forward, her expression serious. "But we're going to do our very best. It's not going to be easy. Sometimes it's going to be very difficult, probably painful."

"I'll work hard, Aunt Jennifer. Really I will."

"Good." She rose from her chair. "We'll get started right after breakfast. *Breakfast!* Oh dear!"

Jennifer rushed back to the stove. The bacon was charred to a crisp. She choked on the thick smoke that rose from the frying pan.

"It's ruined," she cried as she grabbed a towel to wrap around the handle before pulling the pan from the stove top. "It's all ruined."

She felt ridiculously like weeping. She'd wanted to do something to help Mick on her first day here, and she'd ended up burning his breakfast.

Phoebe rolled her chair forward. "Don't worry, Aunt Jennifer. Pa and I are used to burned bacon. It's how we always have it. We like it that way. Honest, we do."

"Really?" The word came out in a squeak.

Despite her efforts, two large tears trickled down her cheeks.

"Phoebe's telling the truth, Jen. We've always been partial to burnt bacon."

She spun toward the door, only now feeling the cool draft of air that had entered the house with him. She quickly dashed away the renegade tears with the back of her hands.

Mick gave her one of his crooked smiles. "You'd be surprised what we've learned to like to eat. Wouldn't she, pet?" he asked, glancing at his daughter.

Phoebe giggled. "Neither one of us is much of a cook," she whispered in a conspiratorial tone to Jennifer. "But Pa says we haven't either one of us starved yet because of it, so we must be doin' all right."

She did feel better. It was, after all, just a few strips of bacon. She wouldn't even remember it by this time tomorrow. At least, not if Mick kept looking at her the way he was now.

Chapter Six

She really did have beautiful eyes. He remembered the way she had watched him as he worked in the back room of the mercantile, her wide eyes following his every move. Come to think of it, Jennifer had almost always been around when he was working, asking him questions, sharing her secret thoughts, sometimes making him laugh. She'd made him feel as if he belonged—not a common feeling for an orphan boy who couldn't remember his own family.

Funny. He'd forgotten that until just now.

After hanging his coat on the peg, Mick crossed the room and sat down.

"Phoebe, will you carry this to the table, please?" Jennifer held out a plate piled high with scrambled eggs.

He started to rise from the table. "Here. Let me . . ."

The look Jennifer shot him stopped him in mid-sentence. "Phoebe can do it," she said with gentle firmness. She set the plate in the girl's lap, making sure that it was level and secure.

Phoebe turned her chair around and wheeled it toward her father. She grinned as she set the plate on the table without spilling a single morsel. "Can I help with anything else, Aunt Jennifer?"

"Not right now. I think we've got everything." Jennifer carried the charred bacon on a plate in one hand and a pitcher of milk in the other as she stepped forward. She set them in the center of the table, then pulled out her chair and sat down across from Mick.

Their gazes met briefly, and he thought again how beautiful her eyes were. And it wasn't just her eyes. She had a pretty face, too. Why hadn't he noticed before?

He'd be better off not to notice, he thought grimly. The last time his head had been turned by a woman, he'd found more grief than pleasure. He didn't need any further complications in his life. He had enough as it was.

Jennifer folded her hands in her lap and bowed her head. After a few moments passed, she glanced up at him with a questioning gaze.

Quickly, he closed his eyes and said, "For this food, Heavenly Father, we are truly thankful. Amen."

When he opened his eyes again, he found her smiling at him. An unfamiliar warmth spread through his chest. There was something very right about this moment, the three of them sitting at the table, the stove belching heat into the tiny house.

His mouth flattened as his gaze dropped to the food. He wasn't about to be fooled by a pair of beguiling eyes and a sweet smile again. Jennifer might not have come to Idaho to try to take Phoebe away from him, but she was still a woman and a Whitmore. He'd been down that road once before, and he'd learned his lessons well.

"I promised Aunt Jennifer you'd take her out and introduce her to Panda," Phoebe said, reaching to fill her plate with eggs.

Mick glanced across the table. Jennifer offered him some sliced bread. "Thanks," he said, taking hold of the plate.

"Will you show her Panda, Pa?"

"Sure, but it'll have to be later. I've got things to do."

"You aren't going into town by any chance?" Jennifer asked.

He raised his eyebrows as he looked at her. "Why?"

"Well, there are a few things I need."

"Why didn't you say something yesterday?" He couldn't disguise the note of irritation in his voice. Her statement seemed to confirm his earlier suspicions. She *was* like Christina in some ways. She hadn't given any thought to the weather or the horses or the time it took to go to town. She was thinking only of herself.

Her reply was soft and gently pleading. "I didn't know I needed anything then."

"It's not like you're in Chicago anymore. You can't just run down to the corner market in a matter of minutes."

"I know that."

Something about her meek reply drew his gaze to her. He was reminded of the time she'd asked him to help her build a bird house to hang in the tree outside her bedroom window. She'd wanted a place for the birds to be safe from the tomcats that roamed the alleys. Mick remembered her huge eyes as she'd looked at him, asking the favor. He hadn't had the heart to say no. They'd spent every evening for two weeks working on that thing, and as he recalled now, he'd enjoyed every minute of it. She'd been a sweet-natured, quiet kid with a good heart. She never could stand to see anything or anyone hurt.

"It really is important, Mick, or I wouldn't ask. If you could hitch up the horses to the sleigh, I'm sure I could manage to get to town on my own. I don't mean to put you out."

Dad blast the woman anyway! Now she was making *him* feel guilty. As if *he* were the one who was being unreasonable.

Mick shoved his chair back from the table. "Well, if it's important, I guess we might be able to go in this afternoon. But only if the weather holds."

"Thank you."

"Sure." He headed for his coat. It wasn't that he was eager to go back out in the cold, but he thought he was a lot better off out there than in here.

"I don't know what's got into him," Phoebe muttered as she stared at the closed door.

"I'm afraid it's my fault." Jennifer got up from the table and started to clear away the breakfast dishes. "I guess I can't blame him."

Phoebe watched her aunt moving back and forth, from table to sink and back again. Eventually, she began to smile, feeling immensely pleased with herself. Pa always did say she saw too much for her own good, but it seemed to her that any fool could have seen what was wrong with him.

Her father had changed since the day of her accident. He was often sad and anxious. He worried about her all the time, and she knew he worried about money a lot, too. But he'd never acted like this before. Grumpy. Irritable for no reason. Almost rude. No, this wasn't like her beloved pa at all.

But now she knew why. He *liked* Aunt Jennifer. He liked her a lot.

A frown replaced her smile. She wondered if Pa was grumpy because he was remembering her mother.

Phoebe didn't remember a whole lot about Christina. She'd been six the last time she'd seen her, and the years had faded most of her memories. Mostly, she remembered her mother's red hair and apple-green eyes. She also remembered the voices raised in anger coming from behind her parents' bedroom door, and she remembered feeling that her ma didn't like her much.

Phoebe always felt a bit guilty for not missing her mother more, but she knew, deep in her heart, that she and her pa were much happier on their own than they'd been when Christina was with them. She supposed that was a sinful thought, but she couldn't help herself. She *liked* it being just her and Pa. She'd always figured that things would go on the same, just the two of them taking care of the farm and themselves. Things probably *would* have stayed the same if she hadn't tripped and fallen out the hayloft door.

But she had to admit she liked having Aunt Jennifer with them. She hadn't been too sure that she would. She'd been afraid Aunt Jennifer would be an angry woman who yelled a lot—just like Phoebe's mother. But she was different, *very* different. Besides her pale yellow hair and her greenish-blue eyes, Aunt Jennifer had a soft, friendly voice and a pretty smile. She didn't scold Phoebe all the time or argue with Pa a lot. She was nice, and Phoebe liked her.

I wish she could stay with us.

That's what was wrong with Pa. He liked Aunt Jennifer, too, but he thought he didn't want her around. Folks were always saying, "Mick, you ought to get married again. A man needs a wife." And Pa was always answering, "I get on just fine the way things are. Phoebe's the only female I want around the place."

Phoebe had always agreed with him. Until now.

Mick's anger was nearly hot enough to keep Jennifer warm as she sat beside him in the sleigh. Several times she considered telling him why she needed to go to town, but she forced herself to remain silent. After all, half the fun of the season was being surprised on Christmas morning.

She knew time was running out. If she didn't order the angel now, it would never arrive in time. And while she waited for it, she could be working on her other gifts. She was going to do her very best to make this a special Christmas for both Mick and Phoebe.

She sent a covert glance in Mick's direction. His coat collar was pulled up close to his ears, his shoulders hunched against the cold, but she could still see his handsome profile. He'd always been handsome, but the past years had added a maturity to his looks that made him even more appealing, even more pleasing to the eye.

She felt a warm tingle in her stomach and thought how nice it would be to draw close to him, to slip her arm through his and snuggle up against his side. She flushed, embarrassed by her thoughts, thankful that her cheeks were already pink from the cold. At least there was no chance he would guess what she'd been thinking.

"I do appreciate your taking me to town again, Mick," she said, hoping to create a diversion from her own disturbing reflections.

"Sure."

It wasn't a very encouraging reply, but it was better than silence. She tried again. "I promise not to ask you to make a special trip again."

"Good."

Perhaps she should talk about something else. Phoebe seemed the best choice of topics. "You know, Mick, you've been coddling Phoebe too much. She's capable of doing a lot of things by herself. She—"

"She came darn close to dyin' when she fell out of that barn." His golden-brown eyebrows drew down in a scowl.

"But she didn't die," Jennifer retorted, her own temper stirring, "and you need to start letting her live again."

"I suppose *you* know what's best for her?"

"I know you need to let her do whatever she can. It won't hurt her to fail a time or two. She doesn't need you to wait on her hand and foot. She's a very bright and ingenious little girl. She might have to do things a little differently than those who have two strong legs, but she'll figure out a way if we just let her."

He turned his head so he could look her straight in the eyes. "I know my daughter better than you, Miss Whitmore. You can't tell me anything I don't already know. I'm going to take care of her as I see fit, and I won't stand for your interference."

"Interference?" She drew away from him, her back as straight as a lightning rod. "Is that what you call it when someone travels halfway across the country to help?"

Mick pulled on the reins, drawing the sleigh to a halt. "Is that why you came, Jen?" His gaze was harsh, suspicious.

Her anger cooled as she stared back at him, unsure how to answer, unsure of what the truth was. She'd thought she'd only come to help out her stepsister's widower, but now that she was here, she wasn't so sure her motives were all that pure. Perhaps, just perhaps, she'd come because she'd wanted to see him again. Perhaps she'd nev-

169

er forgotten her girlish crush. Perhaps she'd been hoping . . .

The urge to lean forward and press her mouth against his was almost overwhelming. Rather than make a fool of herself, she turned away, facing forward, her hands clenched in her lap.

Maddeningly, her voice quivered when she softly replied, "You know very well why I'm here, Mick Gerrard. Phoebe needs a nurse, and I am one. How could I not come and care for my own niece?"

He found the stubborn tilt of her chin charming. He also found her mouth nicely shaped, soft and supple looking. The golden brown lashes that fringed her blue-green eyes were long, curling up toward her brows. Even her shell-like ears were attractive.

Had she always been so obstinate? he wondered. Yes, come to think of it, she had. She'd also been sweet and giving. And whenever she'd fought tears, as he suspected she was doing at this very moment, he'd found it hard to resist giving in to her wishes.

But there was more to Jennifer now than the child he remembered. She was a woman. A damned attractive woman . . .

Mick turned his attention onto the snow-covered road before him. He clicked to the horses as he slapped the reins against the animals' backs. "Giddup there," he called to them.

The sleigh slipped across the white surface with only the faintest of sounds. Mick almost wished he'd put the Christmas bells onto the harness again today, just for a bit of noise. The silence made it too easy for him to think about things . . . to think about Jennifer and her attractively stubborn chin and her supple lips and her cute ears and the long lashes around heart-stealing eyes.

He gritted his teeth, angered by his reflections. He'd thought he'd learned a few things in the past eleven years. He'd thought he'd learned how to curb such desires, to resist such delightful temptations.

He'd be damned if Jennifer Whitmore was going to make him forget what Christina had taught him. The lessons had been too cruel to want to learn them over again.

Chapter Seven

By the end of her second week on the Gerrard farm, Jennifer knew she never wanted to leave. The house was small, but it had an inviting, homey feeling. It was tight against chilly drafts, and although the rooms grew frigid during the night when the fire died down, they warmed quickly in the morning. As far as Jennifer was concerned, it was a perfect house in every way— and so were the people in it.

Mick spent long hours seeing to the daily chores. He made many repairs to the barn and the house, the ring of his hammer often sounding for hours on end. He mended harness and sharpened farm implements. He tended the animals and chopped wood for the stove. Even in the dead of winter, it was clear there was little rest for a farmer.

Phoebe was equally industrious. She was a bright and inquisitive child, and she worked hard on her school work, which her teacher brought by once a week so she wouldn't fall behind the other students in her class. She was a good patient, too. Even when the physical exercises that Jennifer taught her were painful, she didn't complain or try to quit.

It hadn't taken Jennifer long to grow close to her niece. They spent their days together, often laughing over some silly little thing. She taught the girl how to bake her special recipe chocolate cake, and Phoebe showed her how to make her father's favorite apple cobbler. Jennifer made a new dress for Phoebe from fabric she'd brought from Chicago. Phoebe sketched a picture of the barn and horses and gave it to her aunt. Every day was filled with familiar things while always promising something new, and Jennifer loved every moment of it.

Her favorite time of day was evening because that was when Mick joined them. Suppertime discussions were frequently stimulating, never boring. Jennifer and Mick often chose opposing points of view on a great variety of topics, but their verbal sparring was good-natured. Sometimes they would talk about their childhoods in Chicago, sharing old memories of a place and time far removed from the present.

After supper was finished and the dishes washed and put away, the three of them would sit in the parlor. Mick would hold Phoebe in his lap while the girl read aloud. Jennifer would pause in her needlework or whatever task she'd chosen to keep her hands busy, and listen. She would watch the two of them and feel her heart tighten.

It was on one such evening that she acknowledged what she'd tried to deny ever since she'd arrived. She loved him. She'd never stopped loving him. Perhaps her girlish affection had lain dormant in the years they'd been separated, but seeing him had brought it back to life. Only this time, she loved him with a woman's heart.

As she mulled over this revelation, Mick glanced up and their eyes met. She waited breathlessly, wanting to see something in the depths of blue that would give her hope, wanting it so much she ached.

He was the first to look away, his gaze falling to the open book in his daughter's lap. He lifted his arm from behind Phoebe's back and stroked her black hair with his fingers. The gesture was infinitely sweet, an unconscious show of affection. Jennifer wished it was her hair he stroked.

She swallowed the hot tears that burned the back of her throat as she, too, looked away. She knew now that she would never stop loving Mick Gerrard. She knew it would nearly kill her to leave him when the time came.

And come it would. She had already seen encouraging signs that Phoebe would soon walk again. Jennifer wouldn't be needed for long. Perhaps until spring, maybe until the end of summer, but no longer than that.

She swallowed again. Tears were blurring her vision. She wished she could dash them away, but she was afraid that Phoebe would see and ask why she was crying. Jennifer didn't want either of them to know what she was feeling, what she was thinking. It would be too hard to see the pity in Mick's eyes. And she was certain he would pity her—so plain and colorless beside the memory of his long-dead wife, a wife he still loved.

She gathered her mending and rose to her feet, mumbled a quick, "Good night," then scurried from the parlor and into the safety of her bedroom. Once inside, she leaned against the door and allowed the tears to run silently down her cheeks.

"What's wrong with Aunt Jennifer?" Phoebe asked.

Frowning thoughtfully, Mick replied, "I don't know. She seemed all right at supper."

"Maybe you should go ask."

"No." He shook his head. "She's got a right to her privacy."

Phoebe scowled at him. "Maybe she's sick and needs the doctor."

"I doubt it, pet." He ruffled her hair, his gaze meeting hers as he smiled lightly. "She'd tell us if she needed to see Doc Jenkins. She's a nurse, remember?" He lifted the book from where it lay in her lap. "Finish the chapter. I want to know what's going to happen to Tom."

Phoebe was soon engrossed with Tom Sawyer, but Mick couldn't seem to concentrate on the story. His thoughts kept returning to Jennifer, to the unhappy tone of her voice as she'd bid them good night. It wasn't like her. In the short

time she'd been with them, she'd been invariably
cheerful. Even when he made her angry, it wasn't
a mean or spiteful anger. She simply spoke her
mind—quite eloquently, too—and within a short
time, she was her sunny self again.

Sunny—it was a word that described Jennifer
better than any other. Her smile was as warm as
a summer day. Her blue-green eyes made him
think of a clear mountain lake. Her hair was like
the sun itself, yellow and glowing. Her laughter
was infectious, unexpectedly touching something
deep inside him.

He glanced toward the closed bedroom door.
Strange how the parlor seemed to have grown
dim without Jennifer in it. Strange how quickly
she had become a part of this house, this family.
Strange how she made him feel.

His eyes widened. Just what was it she made
him feel? he wondered.

Not certain he wanted to know, he turned his
eyes back on his daughter and forced himself to
listen to her voice as she read aloud.

Jennifer made up her mind in the wee hours
of the night. She decided she would write to her
father and ask him to send money so that Mick
could hire a nurse. As soon as she could find
someone to replace her—someone she could trust
to take care of Phoebe, someone who would love
her as well as see to her physical needs—then she
would go back to Chicago. Back to her position at
the Angel of Mercy Hospital, back to Mrs. Mulligan's Boarding House, back to Saturday dinners

at her father's house, perhaps even back to seeing
Harry on Tuesday and Thursday evenings.

Of course, it really didn't matter what she
was going back to in Chicago. She just knew
she couldn't stay here. The longer she stayed,
the more she would want never to leave. It
had been difficult enough before. Now that she
knew she loved Mick, it made things intolerable.
She couldn't stay, knowing that the memory of
Christina would forever be in his heart.

She rolled onto her side and hugged her pillow
against her chest. For a moment, she allowed
herself to imagine what it might be like to hug
Mick in the same way. Only his body would be
hard and ever so much more intimate.

Mick stared blindly up toward the roof. Try as
he might, sleep continued to evade him. He hadn't
been able to stop thinking of Jennifer all evening,
at least not for more than a few minutes at a time.
It had become impossible after he'd climbed the
ladder to his temporary bedroom in the loft.

Jennifer . . .

He wanted her. He wanted her as he hadn't
wanted a woman in a long, long time. It was a
physical need, yes, but it went beyond that. It was
something deeper, something much more com-
plex than simple lust, much more than just the
natural drive of a man to mate with a woman.

Jennifer . . .

Once before he'd been swept up in passion,
but never had he felt what he was feeling now.
It was ridiculous. She'd only been in Idaho for

two weeks. That wasn't long enough for a man
to . . .

To what? To fall in love? Was that what he
thought he felt for her? Love?

No. It couldn't be. He barely knew her. Okay,
so he'd known her before, but she'd only been a
kid when he'd worked for her father in Chicago.
He'd hardly noticed her back then.

But she wasn't a kid any longer, and he couldn't
seem to banish her from his mind.

Jennifer . . .

Love? Was it possible he was falling in love?
Having never loved a woman, he couldn't be sure.

Chapter Eight

"Mick?"

He dropped the big draft horse's hoof and straightened, surprised by the sudden sound of Jennifer's voice, so unexpected in the silence of the barn.

She was wrapped in her woolen cloak, hugging herself for extra warmth. Even inside the barn, where they were protected from the snow and wind, her breath caused a cloud of steam to form on the air. Her cheeks were pink from the cold.

"May I speak with you a moment?" she asked softly.

"Sure." He leaned his arm against the horse's broad back.

"I think it's time Phoebe had an outing. I'd like to go to the pond where you two go skating. Miller's pond. Will you take us there this afternoon?"

He shook his head. "The doc said she wasn't to go out in the cold."

"That was weeks ago. Mick, she needs to start *doing* things again. You can't keep a child shut up this way."

"I don't know." He shook his head again. "Why would you want to take her to the skating pond?"

Jennifer stepped up to the corral door. "Because she was talking about it again this morning. She misses going skating with you. I think it would be good for her to see you out on the ice again. Maybe it would inspire her to try on her skates, too. She's getting better, Mick. It's going to be slow, and she isn't going to learn to walk again overnight. She may never be able to do all the things she once could. She'll need lots of encouragement along the way, but she will get better."

Jennifer had such an earnest, beseeching look in her eyes, Mick had an insane desire to take her into his arms and kiss her until she was left limp and breathless. If the gate hadn't stood between them, maybe he would have done it.

He cleared his throat, at the same time trying to clear his thoughts. "I guess I haven't thanked you for what you've done for Phoebe. In the short time you've been here, I've seen a change in her. She's been . . . she's been happier since you came. I'm not very good at finding the words to thank you for what you've done. But I do. Thank you, I mean."

"I . . . I'm glad I could help," she whispered in reply.

"Me, too." He stepped forward, one stride carrying him to the gate opposite her.

The color in her cheeks faded slightly. Her eyes widened a fraction.

"To tell you the truth, I wasn't too happy when I got your father's letter, telling me you were comin' to Idaho." He didn't know why he was telling her this; the words just seemed to come out without his wanting them to. "I thought Dorothea had put you up to it. I was afraid she was going to try to use you to take Phoebe back to live with her in Chicago." His voice deepened. "I won't ever let her do that."

"Of course not." Her voice was so soft he almost couldn't hear her. "You're her father. She belongs with you, not in Chicago, no matter what my stepmother thinks. But I shall miss Phoebe terribly when I return home."

Return to Chicago? Why did that have such a melancholy sound?

"When will that be?" he asked.

Jennifer's stomach felt hollow as she looked up into his eyes. He was standing so close to her, only the wooden gate separating them. She could see his breath on the air. She could see the bristles of his beard on his chin.

I don't ever want to leave, she thought, wishing she could say it aloud. *If I thought you could love me as you loved Christina, as you still love her . . .*

"I thought you meant to stay until Phoebe was well." His voice had a sudden sharpness to it. His eyes narrowed, almost suspiciously.

Her throat was so tight she almost couldn't reply. "I . . . I'll stay as long as I'm needed." *Until my father sends the money for you to hire another nurse.*

The tension in his face eased. "You really think this outing would be good for Phoebe?"

"Yes. Yes, I do."

"All right. If the sun stays out, we'll do it."

Impulsively, she reached forward, placing her hand over his forearm. "Thank you."

She turned quickly, hurrying back to the house before she could say or do something she would later regret.

Phoebe's face glowed with excitement as the sleigh whisked across the white terrain. The air was alive with the merry sound of bells, keeping time with the snow-muffled hoof beats of the two horses.

Glancing at his daughter, Mick knew that Jennifer had been right about this. Phoebe had needed to get out. She'd been shut up far too long. She had always loved to be outdoors.

"Look, Pa!" the little girl shouted as she pointed toward a fenced pasture where a mare and a woolly-coated colt cantered. The foal dropped his head, nearly touching his nose to the ground, kicking up his heels. Then he raced away from his mother, running as far as he could before spinning around and hurrying back to her side. "Aren't they pretty, Aunt Jennifer? That's Brian Miller's mare and colt. I got to see the colt the same day he was born."

"Who's Brian Miller?" Jennifer asked with a smile.

"He's my friend. He used to sit behind me in school."

"He doesn't go to school anymore?"

"Of course he does." Phoebe looked puzzled. "He's only a year older than me."

"Then he'll still be sitting behind you when you go back to school."

The girl's face lit up again. "Yes, I suppose he will."

Mick watched the two of them, aware of how often Jennifer reminded Phoebe that she would be returning to the normal world, that she wouldn't forever be shut up in their tiny house, trapped in her small wheelchair. She was constantly challenging Phoebe to push herself a bit harder, a little farther, and it was working.

It had taken him a while, but he'd finally admitted to himself that Jennifer had been right to upbraid him on that day he'd taken her to town. He had been mollycoddling his daughter. He had been doing everything for Phoebe, treating her as if she might break. And in return, Phoebe had grown careful and quiet. Not at all like the laughing, pink-cheeked girl seated beside him now.

Mick shifted his gaze to Jennifer. Her aquamarine eyes were sparkling with the same gaiety as Phoebe's. Her mouth was bowed with a merry smile. When she lifted her eyes to look at him, he felt a warmth spread inside him, a warmth that was at odds with the frosty winter's day.

I'll be darned . . . He turned his gaze back onto the ground ahead of them. *I do love her.*

The thought didn't exactly bring him the pleasure it should. Mick remembered all too well how much Christina had hated living so far from Chicago. She'd thought Idaho was just about the end of the world. She'd never stopped wanting to go back to the city. She'd never stopped hating Mick for bringing her out west, for making her live in their little house on their little farm.

Maybe Jennifer would want to stay . . .

How could he hope for that? She'd already made it clear that she planned to return home as soon as Phoebe didn't need her any longer. She might not be like Christina in any other way, but in that respect, she seemed to be the same. She didn't want to settle on a small farm in Idaho.

But what if she fell in love with him?

Why should she? No woman had ever loved him before. Certainly Christina hadn't.

But Jennifer wasn't *really* like Christina. Maybe she could learn to love him. Maybe—just maybe—it would be worth the risk to find out.

While Mick held Phoebe in his arms, Jennifer lifted the wooden stool out of the back of the sleigh and carried it over to the edge of the frozen pond. Then she returned to the sleigh for the blankets they'd brought with them. She was just turning around when a snowball sailed past her head. Her eyes widened in surprise.

Phoebe giggled as her pa leaned over and packed more snow into a ball. "He won't miss again, Aunt

Jennifer," she called just as Mick hurled the missile in Jennifer's direction.

She ducked in the nick of time. The sudden movement caused her to stumble, and she fell to her knees in the snow.

The little girl's laughter grew louder. "Look out!"

Jennifer looked up just in time to see Mick's hand releasing another snowball. This one caught her shoulder before she had time to take evasive action. Snow splattered onto her face.

Jennifer struggled to her feet, tossing the blankets back into the sleigh while a mock frown creased her forehead. "If it's a fight you want, Mr. Gerrard, you've picked the wrong girl. I didn't spend *all* my time reading books in the storeroom." She bent down and grabbed a handful of snow, shaping it with quick, deft movements.

His gleeful hoot was all the challenge she needed. She waited until he bent forward to grab more of the white stuff, then let the snowball fly. It hit him smack on the top of his head.

Phoebe let loose with a gale of laughter. "Good shot, Aunt Jennifer."

"So it's two against one, is it?" Mick straightened. The smile he wore was playfully ominous.

Jennifer's heart began to race in her chest as he stepped toward her. "Mick . . ." She swirled and tried as best she could to run.

She made a full circle around the wagon and horses, her feet sinking through the crusty surface several times, slowing her escape. She had almost reached Phoebe before he caught up with

185

her. The moment his hands alighted on her shoulders she stopped. Apparently he wasn't ready for her to halt so suddenly, because he didn't do the same. His forward momentum toppled them both into a high drift.

Jennifer sat up, sputtering as she wiped the snow from her face. Opening her eyes, she saw Mick doing the same. He looked so nonplussed she began to giggle. A moment later, Phoebe joined in, and before long, all three of them were laughing hysterically.

"Oh my," Jennifer said when she could speak again. "I haven't done that in years."

"That's too bad." Mick reached forward and brushed a bit of snow from the tip of her nose. "You look very becoming all covered with snow."

Her pulse seemed to hiccup as he rose to his feet, then pulled her up beside him. Their gazes met and held for what seemed a breathless eternity.

Mick was the first to look away. "Guess I'd better get those blankets for you and Phoebe. I don't want you two catching colds so close to Christmas, now do I?"

"No," she whispered. "No, you don't."

"I'll build a fire, and we'll have some hot chocolate before we try out the ice."

"Yes. A fire," she repeated, but she didn't feel the least bit cold. Not the least little bit cold.

"Here. Let me help you with those."

Mick dropped to one knee in the snow and carefully tightened the laces on the skates. His hand on her ankle felt strangely intimate, and her heart quickened at the sight of him leaning so close to her.

She tried to remind herself that he wasn't really interested in her. She tried to remember all the reasons why she'd decided to go back to Chicago. She tried to remember that she had come here to care for her niece, that she was just a nurse. But she failed miserably. She didn't feel like just an aunt or a nurse. She felt like a woman in love, and she wanted him to touch more than her ankle.

She felt her cheeks flame. At just that moment, he looked up. Her heart seemed to stop beating altogether.

"There," he said. "Those seem about right. Why don't you try to stand, see how they feel?"

He held out his hand as he rose from his knee. She placed her fingers within his, and he pulled gently, lifting her from the log on which she'd been sitting.

She wobbled, but his hands on her upper arms steadied her. At least they steadied her body. His touch did something else to her insides.

"I . . . I'm not a very good skater," she said apologetically.

"Too much time spent reading in the storeroom—" his blue eyes seemed to deepen as he looked down at her "—and not enough outside in the snow." He grinned. "Except when you were making snowballs."

His smile—that wonderfully crooked, right-sided smile—was like a bonfire, warming her blood and making her weak in the knees.

187

Robin Lee Hatcher

"Come on," he said. "Let's teach you how to skate like an Idaho farm girl."

Jennifer didn't think she'd ever heard words more wonderful than those.

Heart in her throat, her hand in his, she slid out onto the frozen surface of the pond, trusting him to keep her from falling on the ice, all the while knowing that nothing and no one in the world—not even Mick himself—could keep her from falling ever more deeply in love with him.

Chapter Nine

"I had a wonderful time today, Pa," Phoebe said sleepily as he carried her into her room and laid her on the bed. She yawned, then asked, "Can we go again soon?"

"We'll see, pet." He kissed her forehead, at the same time brushing the stray locks of black hair away from her forehead.

"It was . . . fun . . . to skate . . . again." Her eyes fluttered closed. She yawned a second time. "Lots of . . . fun."

Mick smiled tenderly as he straightened. It had been fun for him to see her skate again, too. Well, she hadn't *actually* skated, but he had helped her put on her skates, and then he and Jennifer had slid her around the pond, holding her upright between them. To be honest, he'd been surprised at the amount of strength and control she'd shown. She wasn't anywhere close to being

189

able to skate—or even stand—by herself, but he understood now why Jennifer was so hopeful of a complete recovery.

Phoebe rolled onto her side, taking the blankets with her. "Pa . . ."

"Yeah?"

"I'm glad Aunt Jennifer came to . . . live with us."

"Me, too, pet." He straightened the blankets, then leaned down to kiss her one more time. "Me, too."

He extinguished the lamp before leaving the room. He paused just outside the bedroom door, his eyes quickly finding Jennifer.

She was sitting close to the wood stove mending one of his shirts, a tiny frown puckering the delicate skin between her eyebrows. A soft green shawl lay over her shoulders. She wore a gown the same color as her eyes, and her hair hung loose around her shoulders. It was the first time he'd seen it that way, and he was tempted to go over to her, to touch the fine tresses and see if they were as soft as they looked.

She glanced up. A smile curved the corners of her mouth. "Is Phoebe asleep?"

It seemed so right for her to be sitting there, asking that question.

He nodded wordlessly.

She laid aside her mending. "I was afraid she was going to fall asleep at the supper table. She was terribly tired. It was a big day for her."

He'd like to see her sitting there every night.

"It was a wonderful day for me, too, Mick."

Her voice was as soft as a gentle summer rain. "Thanks."

He'd like to see her sitting there every night for the rest of his life.

Mick turned abruptly toward the kitchen and went to pour himself a cup of coffee. He noticed his hand was shaking as he picked up the blue-speckled pot. He wasn't surprised. It wasn't every day a man like him thought about marriage.

He splashed coffee onto his hand and grimaced as it scalded his skin.

"Damn!" he swore beneath his breath.

Marriage! He had to be out of his mind. He hadn't found one moment of happiness in his marriage to Christina. If it hadn't been for Phoebe . . .

"Let me look at that."

He turned, surprised to find her standing beside him.

She took hold of his hand, cradling it in her own. "Cold water will help ease the pain." She led him over to the sink. She placed his hand beneath the faucet and began to pump the handle. "Leave it there," she said when he started to pull away.

She was so close he could smell her orange blossom cologne. The fragrance seemed to rise up in a sweet cloud, circling his head, filling his nostrils.

"Jennifer . . ."

Her name was little more than a dry croak in his throat, yet it sent a wave of shivers rippling through her body. She swallowed, almost apprehensively, before turning to look up at him. There was no mistaking the desire she saw burning in his eyes.

Jennifer held her breath as Mick's hands closed around her upper arms. Slowly he drew her closer to him. Ever more slowly, his head lowered toward hers. The touch of his lips against hers was infinitely gentle, yet it started a violent storm in her heart.

In all too short a time, he released her mouth, drawing back just far enough that he could gaze into her eyes. She saw him gathering his resistance, knew that in another moment he would be apologizing for kissing her. But she didn't want his apologies.

Jennifer's hands slid up his chest as she rose on tiptoe. She was guided only by instinct, for never before had she felt this way about a man. Pulling his head down to hers, she put heart and soul into the kiss as her body pressed against his.

She heard the growl deep in his throat, then felt his arms closing tightly around her. Her world began to spin, and she gave herself up to a wellspring of new emotions and sensations.

When his tongue danced across her lips, she opened her mouth, letting out a tiny gasp of surprise and, at the same time, allowing him entrance. Never had she been kissed so intimately. Instinctively she began to pull away from him, but he held her close, and soon she allowed her own tongue to dart forward to touch his.

Her knees grew weak. A strange ache formed in her loins. Her breathing grew labored. Passion—

a feeling so foreign to her—exploded in a flash of heat and bright colors, sweeping away all reason and caution.

She longed for him to caress her. She longed for him to touch all the untouched places of her body. She wanted to feel his bare skin against hers. She knew all the clinical facts, but now she ached to experience lovemaking as a woman. She ached to experience it with this one man whom she loved beyond reason.

She found herself almost gasping for air as his mouth moved away from hers. He trailed kisses down the column of her throat. She let her head fall back, offering him the sensitive flesh.

"Oh, Mick . . . Mick . . ."

Having him hold her, knowing he wanted her, was more wonderful than anything she'd ever known. If only he would say the words she longed to hear, she would never have to go back to Chicago. She could stay right here with Mick and Phoebe.

Jennifer's eyes flew open as her head turned toward the child's bedroom door. As always, Mick had left it ajar. What if Phoebe had heard them? What if . . .

"Mick . . ." she whispered, pressing against his shoulders. "Mick, stop. We . . . we mustn't."

He released her so suddenly she nearly fell to the floor. Stumbling backward, she gripped the edge of the sink to regain her balance. When she looked at his face, she found him without expression. It was if he'd shared none of the wild emotions she'd been feeling—and still felt.

"I'm sorry, Jennifer. You're right. I shouldn't have done that." He spun around, strode toward the door, and left the house, not even pausing to put on his coat.

"Mick," she whispered.

She was answered with silence.

He was shaking all over by the time he reached the barn, but it wasn't because of the cold. He barely felt the frigid temperatures in a body on fire with desire.

No, the shaking was brought on by his realization of how close he'd come to being swept away by the selfsame lust that had torn apart his life once before. He'd acted like a kid of eighteen without enough sense to see trouble when it was right in front of his face.

Perhaps he did love Jennifer. Perhaps there was more to his wanting her than simple lust. But she'd never given him any reason to believe she returned his feelings. She'd made it clear that her intentions were to return to Chicago. Did he want another unwilling wife, resenting him for making her live so far from the life she'd had in Chicago? Besides, unlike her stepsister, Jennifer was most surely a virgin. If he were to take her to his bed, she would feel obligated to marry him—and then she would grow to hate him.

Mick sank onto a bale of hay and cradled his head in his hands. He didn't know what to do. He'd probably already done too much. More than likely, as soon as he'd slammed out of the house, she'd started packing that carpetbag of hers. She'd be demanding that he take her to town for the first train east.

Lord, he was going to miss her when she was gone. He would miss hearing her cheerful greeting in the morning. He would miss looking at her across the table. He would miss seeing the way her pale blond hair fell over her shoulders, and he would miss the sparkle in her aquamarine eyes.

He straightened as his gaze turned toward the closed barn door.

What was he doing, giving up so easily? If he'd given up at the first sign of trouble when it came to farming, he'd be back stocking shelves in a mercantile somewhere. Was he going to let the first woman he'd ever loved just walk out of his life without even trying to keep her with him? He'd be darned if he would.

For some crazy reason, he thought of the angel in the mail order catalog. Phoebe had thought that Jennifer looked like the angel, and he'd begun to think so, too. He'd begun to hope . . .

And why shouldn't he hope? Christmas was a season of love. It was a time of miracles. Maybe, just maybe, this was *his* season of love.

Jennifer was still awake when she heard Mick reenter the house hours later. Hidden in the darkness of her bedroom, the door closed between them, she imagined him crossing the parlor. In her mind, she witnessed him performing all his routine bedtime tasks before he climbed the ladder to the loft.

Feeling sick at heart, she rolled onto her side,

turning her back toward the door. She closed her eyes and tried to will herself to sleep, but it wouldn't come. Instead, the memory of his kisses replayed in her mind, time and time again.

She pressed her hands over her ears, as if that would help to drive out the unwelcome thoughts. She mentally repeated all the things she'd learned in her nursing studies and from her married friends.

A man's physical need for a woman was a strong force. It was God's way of making certain that the race multiplied. It was not necessary for a man to feel love or affection for a woman in order for him to engage in intercourse with her. Just because Mick had kissed her didn't mean he felt anything beyond a natural, basic desire to lie with a woman. *Any* woman. He was, after all, still in love with the wife he'd lost.

Christina . . . Fiery, beautiful, red-haired Christina. What mortal man could ever forget her? And what man would be satisfied with a woman as plain and faded as Jennifer after he'd loved someone like her stepsister?

Besides, it was Jennifer's own fault that things had almost gone beyond mere kissing. When she'd felt Mick trying to regain control of the situation, it had been she who'd thrown herself back into his arms. If she hadn't remembered that Phoebe was there in the house . . .

Her cheeks flamed hot at the memory of her wanton behavior. What must he think of her?

I'm sorry, Jennifer. . . . I shouldn't have done that. . . . The rejection in his voice had been so cold, so complete. *I'm sorry, Jennifer. . . . I shouldn't have done that.*

She would have to leave now. She couldn't wait until her father sent money for another nurse to replace her. She would simply have to leave on the earliest train back to Chicago. She couldn't live in the same house with Mick any longer. Not without bringing more heartache to herself—and perhaps to others—than she already had.

Chapter Ten

Just as Jennifer walked out of her bedroom early the next morning, Mick stepped down from the last rung of the ladder. As he turned around, their eyes met. For a moment, neither of them spoke, neither of them moved.

Jennifer felt her emotions rising quickly to the surface. Afraid he would read her thoughts, she dropped her gaze to the floor.

"Jen . . ." he said softly, stepping toward her.

She raised a hand to stop him. "Please, Mick. Let's not say anything about last night. I . . . I'd rather not talk about it. It was simply an unfortunate incident." She swallowed, trying to remember the words she'd rehearsed so often during a mostly sleepless night. "I . . . I know how you feel about Christina, and I also know that I don't belong here. It would probably be best for me to leave as soon as possible." Her voice fell to a hoarse whisper. "Best for everyone."

"Why?"

Did he have to make it so hard on her? Was he being intentionally cruel? She groped for a reason she could give him. She certainly couldn't tell him it was because she loved him. She had some pride left, and she meant to hold its tattered remains around her as best she could.

"Well, you see, there's a man I've been seeing for some time now. Harry. Harry Reynolds is his name, and . . ." She looked up, and her words died in her throat.

His face was like granite, his eyes as cold as Lake Michigan. "Of course. I understand. If that's what you want, I'll arrange for your passage as soon as possible, but I'd ask you not to go until after Christmas. Phoebe's counting on your being here. I'm sure your Mr. Reynolds can survive without you that long."

She felt woefully close to tears. "I'd like to spend Christmas with . . . with her, too."

"Good." He turned away. "I'd better see to my chores." He crossed to the door, then looked back at her over his shoulder as he put on his coat. "I'd just as soon we don't tell Phoebe that you're leaving. No point in spoiling the holiday for her."

Jennifer couldn't speak around the lump in her throat, so she nodded in reply.

After the door closed behind him, she moved toward the black iron stove. Woodenly she prepared the coffee, then set the skillet on the stove and began to cook breakfast.

What had she expected him to do? Ask her to stay? She knew that even he had to realize the folly that would be. Even though he didn't love her, she was afraid they would end up in bed together if she stayed. And it would probably be her doing, too. Mick was a good and decent father. He wouldn't want his daughter subjected to such goings-on.

In truth, he was more than likely relieved that she had been the first to speak of leaving. That way, he didn't have to tell her she should go.

A sudden sob tore from her throat, and she dissolved into tears.

This was what he got for letting himself believe he was in love. He'd been better off when he'd accepted things as they were, not hoping for something he'd never had. He and Phoebe had done just fine without a woman in their home the past few years. They would do just fine once Jennifer was gone.

There's a man . . . Harry Reynolds . . .

Why had he been surprised? He'd heard similar words from Christina. Only he'd never loved his wife. But Jennifer . . .

There's a man . . .

His first suspicions about her had been right. She *was* like Christina. Faithless. Devious. And he'd allowed himself to think he was in love with her. Well, it was better he'd learned the truth now than later. He hadn't been as lucky with Christina. Their marriage had been a disaster from beginning to end. There had never been a time when either of them had so much as pretended there was love shared between them. Come to think of it, maybe that had been better than loving a woman who didn't return the feeling. Perhaps it was less painful that way.

Perhaps . . .

Phoebe couldn't understand what had gone wrong. Yesterday they had all been laughing and having so much fun, but this morning both her father and Aunt Jennifer were wearing solemn expressions. Neither of them had spoken a single word since sitting down at the breakfast table.

She turned the problem over in her mind as she absently nibbled at the food on her plate.

She knew she wasn't mistaken. Pa liked Aunt Jennifer a lot. He'd been happier since she'd come than she'd seen him in a long time. And she just *knew* that Aunt Jennifer was in love with her pa. So why the quiet, unhappy looks this morning?

Phoebe glanced surreptitiously at her father, then once again toward her aunt, and suddenly she was certain that Aunt Jennifer was planning to leave. That was why they both looked so gloomy. Aunt Jennifer was going away.

An unpleasant memory intruded on her musings. She remembered seeing her mother packing her valise. She remembered her parents' voices raised in anger and the way she'd hidden beneath the covers of her bed, not wanting to hear the ugly things they were saying to each other. She remembered how despondent her pa had been after her mother had gotten into the wagon that had carried her off. She wasn't sure how many days or weeks had passed between that day and the day Pa had told her that her mother wouldn't be returning home, that she'd died in some far-off place of the fever.

Phoebe looked toward her father, knowing she never wanted to see him that unhappy again. She had to do something to keep her aunt from going away. Her pa needed Aunt Jennifer, and Phoebe needed her, too.

It wasn't often that a farmer wished he had more things to do, but that was what Mick was wishing at this exact moment. Anything to be away from Jennifer and the pain he was feeling.

Only there wasn't much left for him to do. He'd already fed the animals and milked the cow. Since Jennifer's arrival, he'd repaired everything he could find that needed fixing, both in the barn and in the house. With a foot of snow on the ground and icy winds blowing in from the northwest, he certainly didn't have to worry about plowing or planting or irrigating his fields.

"Pa?"

He turned his gaze upon his daughter.

"What about a Christmas tree? Shouldn't we have gone to cut one down before now?"

" 'Fraid we're not going to the mountains this year, pet. The ride would be too hard on you. I'm sure even your aunt would agree with me that it would be too strenuous."

"But we can't have Christmas without a tree, Pa. It just wouldn't seem—"

"Don't worry. Mr. Miller's bringing down a wagon full of pines for all the folks who can't get up to

202

cut their own. He said he'd give us first pick. We'll go over to his place tomorrow."

After a moment's consideration, Phoebe seemed satisfied with his answer. Her smile returned as she glanced toward the opposite end of the table. "Will you help me string popcorn for the tree this afternoon, Aunt Jennifer?"

"Of course. I'd like that."

The note of sadness in Jennifer's voice drew Mick's unwilling gaze. The sadness was mirrored in her pretty aquamarine eyes. He wished he could believe that the emotion was real, but he couldn't. When he found himself wanting to reach out and comfort her, he hardened his heart against the urge. After all, *she* was the one who wanted to leave. She was the one who had kissed him with such abandon, only to tell him she belonged to another man.

Phoebe's voice drew his thoughts up short. "You'll go with Pa to help him pick out the right tree, won't you, Aunt Jennifer?" Her voice dropped to a whisper. "I'm still not finished with my Christmas presents." Louder, she added, "I usually get to choose the tree he cuts down, but I'll trust you to pick the best one."

"Well, I . . ." Jennifer glanced up, her gaze meeting Mick's.

"Tell her, Pa. Tell her she has to go with you."

"If she really doesn't want—" he began.

"Oh, please, Pa. She just *has* to go." His daughter's umber eyes pleaded even more eloquently than her words, and he was helpless against them.

He returned his gaze to Jennifer. With a shrug of his shoulders, he said, "It seems your expertise is required. We'll go for the tree tomorrow around noon."

"I'll be ready," Jennifer replied softly.

He didn't know how she did it. *She* was making *him* feel guilty!

Mick rose abruptly from the table and once more retreated to the barn. With as much time as he'd been spending out there lately, he thought, feeling the irritation spreading through him, he probably would do just as well to move his things into one of the stalls.

Dad-blasted female!

The sound of the closing door made Jennifer flinch. She knew he was angry with her for deciding to leave, but what else could she have done? They both knew what would happen if she stayed. She might be an old maid, but she wasn't so innocent that she didn't know his passion had flared as hot as her own. If only . . .

"You're going away, aren't you?" Phoebe asked in a whisper. "You're going back to Chicago."

Jennifer turned toward her niece, uncertain what to do. She'd promised Mick she wouldn't say anything to Phoebe until after Christmas.

"That's why Pa's sad." The child's expression was somber, and she looked far older than her tender years. " 'Cause he doesn't want you to go."

Oh, how she wished that were true. How she wanted to believe the wisdom of a ten-year-old.

"My mother left us, too."

Jennifer resisted a welling up of tears. "It's not the same, Phoebe," she whispered. "Your mother couldn't help leaving."

"Yes, she could have. She didn't have to leave here in that wagon with that man. She wanted to go. She told Pa she hated him and she wasn't ever coming back." She stared at her hands, folded tightly in her lap. "Sometimes I think it's my fault she died 'cause I didn't really want her to come back. I don't think Pa did either."

"Phoebe, I don't understand." Jennifer shook her head, feeling confused.

The girl pushed herself away from the table, turning toward her room. "We thought you were going to stay. We thought you loved us and wouldn't go away," she said quietly as she rolled her chair across the parlor, disappearing into her bedroom.

Jennifer stared after the child, a score of unanswered questions racing around inside her head. Christina had left in a wagon? Mick hadn't wanted her to come back? What was Phoebe saying? Could any of it possibly be true?

Chapter Eleven

A gentle snow was beginning to fall when Mick drove the team and sleigh up to the front of the house the next afternoon. He pulled his coat collar up around his neck, then hopped down from the wagon seat just as the front door opened.

Jennifer lifted her face toward the swirling snow as she stepped outside. A smile of delight curved her pink mouth. The simple expression of joy caused his heart to skip a beat, and he took a moment just to look at her. Her hair was hidden beneath a dark blue hat. White fur trimmed the hat brim, framing her face and making her eyes seem even larger than usual. Her warm, woolen cloak was buttoned tight against the coldness of the day, yet Mick had no trouble discerning the gentle, feminine curves that he'd already assigned to memory.

If only she weren't so darned pretty, he thought

as he held out his hand. "Here. Let me help you into the sleigh."

Her smile disappeared as their eyes met. He felt a stabbing pain shoot through his heart.

"Thank you," she whispered as she placed her fingers in the palm of his hand, her gaze dropping to the ground.

He wanted to recall the anger he'd felt yesterday. He wanted to remember all the bitterness he'd harbored toward the entire Whitmore family, but it just wasn't there. All that was left was a lonely ache where he'd begun to feel love.

And despite everything, he knew that only Jennifer could fill that lonely, empty place inside him.

The team trotted along the country road, the snowfall growing heavier, the temperature dropping noticeably. Jennifer huddled within the warmth of her cloak, wondering if it was the winter weather that made her feel so cold or Mick's tense silence.

You're making a mistake, her heart cried. *Don't leave. Tell him you're not going away. Tell him that Harry means nothing to you. Tell him . . .*

She glanced at Mick, sitting so stiffly beside her, his jaw set, his intense blue eyes staring straight ahead.

It's only wishful thinking, she reminded herself. *Phoebe's wrong about Mick wanting me to stay. It's better to say nothing.*

But what if the child wasn't wrong? What if Mick did care about her enough to want her to remain with them? What if there was a chance, no matter how remote, that he might return her feelings, that he might actually love her, too?

There were so many things she needed to ask, so many things she wanted to know, but she was afraid to speak, afraid to learn the answers. And so they rode on in silence.

Sitting on the edge of her bed, Phoebe massaged her legs, then slowly straightened them, one at a time, just as Aunt Jennifer had taught her to do. It hurt, but she wasn't going to let that stop her. She knew that the best Christmas present she could give her pa was showing him that she was getting better.

She was glad Aunt Jennifer had agreed to go with him this afternoon to pick out the Christmas tree. It gave her a chance to practice without anyone else being in the house. If she fell flat on her face, she didn't want anyone to know what she'd been doing.

Besides, something inside told her that if she could just stand, maybe take a few steps, she would also be able to find a way to keep her aunt in Idaho with them. That would be the best Christmas gift of all, to have Aunt Jennifer with them forever.

Phoebe pressed her lips tightly together as she scooted forward until her feet touched the floor. Her heart was racing, and she felt a little dizzy. She drew a deep breath.

She knew she could do it. Aunt Jennifer had told her she could do it.

Pushing up with her hands, she raised herself off the bed. Her knees wobbled, and for a second she thought she would topple to the floor. But she didn't. Instead, she found herself standing.

A grin burst across her face. She was standing! Now she knew she could find a way to make Aunt Jennifer stay. If she could stand, anything was possible.

Chapter Twelve

The tree filled a corner of the parlor, its fragrant limbs spreading the pine scent throughout the small farmhouse. Jennifer watched as Mick turned the tree first one way, then the other, until Phoebe pronounced it just right.

"Here, Aunt Jennifer." Phoebe held out a box of ornaments. "Help Pa trim the tree." She smiled brightly as Jennifer took the box from her hands.

Despite her earlier gloom, Jennifer found herself returning the child's smile. It was Christmas Eve, after all, and she had much to be thankful for.

Following Phoebe's precise directions, Jennifer arranged the gingham bows and hand-painted pine cones on the tree. Occasionally she would look up and find Mick watching her. Her heart would catch, and she'd find herself hoping he would say something, anything. But he didn't speak.

There was only silence between them—the silence of two people afraid to take a risk and lose. And so they were losing by default instead.

By the time the tree was trimmed, all traces of Jennifer's smile had disappeared. It was impossible to force merriment when she knew she would be leaving Mick and Phoebe in another day or two.

She turned away from the Christmas tree and crossed to the window. Pushing aside the curtain, she stared out at the snowy blanket that covered the earth. The clouds had blown over, revealing a sliver of moon in a star-studded sky. Silvery crystals glittered on tree limbs and from the eaves of the barn and house. The night itself seemed more blue than black. It was a beautiful Christmas Eve.

"It's time you were in bed, young lady," Mick said to Phoebe, drawing Jennifer's gaze from the winter wonderland beyond the glass. "Saint Nick won't come until you're fast asleep. Come on. I'll carry you to your room."

"You don't need to carry me, Pa," the girl responded. She turned her chair, her eyes meeting with Jennifer's. There was clearly a challenge in her gaze. Then she glanced back at her father. "You need to stay here and talk with Aunt Jennifer."

Mick looked across the room, his eyes colliding with Jennifer's once again, and she felt her breath catch in her throat.

"You've always said it doesn't do any good to keep things that are botherin' me all to myself."

Phoebe rolled her chair toward her room. "And you always said it never hurts to try. Seems to me you ought to try, Pa. Seems to me you both should try."

Her gaze still held captive by Mick's own intense stare, Jennifer heard the door to Phoebe's room close. Her chest felt even tighter than before.

"She's pretty smart for bein' only ten." Mick stepped away from the tree. "We do need to talk, Jennifer."

"We do?"

He loomed tall before her. "We do."

The way he was looking at her . . . Her heart began to pump furiously in her chest.

"I've made more than my fair share of mistakes in life, Jen, but if I let you go away without telling you how I feel, that would be the biggest of them all."

His fingers closed around her upper arms.

"The words don't come easy."

He pulled her toward him. She tilted her head back, their eyes still locked.

"Don't go, Jen. Phoebe and I want you to stay. We need you."

His head lowered. His lips claimed hers in a long, passionate kiss that left her shaken to the very core.

It would be so easy to say yes to this man. It would be so easy to stay with him just because he and his daughter needed her. But she wanted more. She wanted his love, and he wasn't offering her that.

She pulled free from his embrace, stepping away from him until her back was pressed against the wall. "I . . . I can't stay, Mick. You see how it is between us. If I stay, we'll . . . we would . . ." She felt the color flare in her cheeks. "I couldn't live like that," she finished in a whisper, knowing even as she spoke that it was a lie. She *could* live like that. She *could* be his mistress and share his bed. It would break her heart, but she could do it.

Mick's eyes widened. The blue seemed to darken from cerulean to indigo. His right hand lifted, and he gently cupped her chin with his fingers as he drew close to her again. "You don't understand, Jennifer. I'm asking you to be my wife."

"Your wife?" The blood drained from her head, and she heard an odd rushing in her ears. Somehow, she found herself back in his embrace.

"I love you, Jennifer." He kissed her forehead, then pressed his cheek against her temple, whispering, "I've never said those words to a woman before. I love you, Jennifer. Stay and be my wife. Stay and be Phoebe's mother. We need you."

It was quite possibly the worst moment of Mick's life. Worse than learning Phoebe wasn't his child. Worse than seeing Christina's hatred and contempt for him.

Jennifer's silence seemed interminable. Confusion swirled in her blue-green eyes.

Maybe he'd been a fool to say anything. Maybe he should have just let her go back to Harry Richards or Reynolds or whatever his name was.

Maybe he'd been wrong to hope. He'd taken a risk, telling her how he felt, and now all he could do was wait for her reply.

"You *love* me?" she whispered, disbelief rounding her eyes. "But I thought . . ." She shook her head slowly, as if denying what she'd heard.

And then he saw what he'd longed to see. She was watching him with a look of love. Try as she might to hide it, it was there.

"But you still love Christina," she said, so softly he could barely hear her.

His daughter had been right. They did need to talk. Jennifer needed to know the truth about his marriage, about Phoebe, about everything. And there were probably things he needed to know about her life. But at this moment, there was only one thing he needed to know.

He cradled her face between his hands. "It's you I love, Jennifer Whitmore. Tell me now. Is there a chance you could love me?"

That odd rushing sound in her ears intensified. *A chance?*

Her voice quivered as she replied, "I've always loved you, Mick. Always."

When he kissed her this time, it was with an overwhelming tenderness. It was a kiss that reached deep inside her, touching her heart as it had never been touched before.

He lifted his head and stared into her eyes. "Tell me you're never leaving."

Perhaps it was because he had touched her heart that she seemed able to see inside his own.

Perhaps that was why she understood how very important her words were. And so she spoke them clearly, the hesitant quiver no longer present in her voice.

"No, Mick, I'm not ever leaving. I'll be with you forever."

Chapter Thirteen

Unnoticed, Phoebe stood on weak, wobbly legs, holding onto the door for support. She watched as the couple moved across the room to stand beside the Christmas tree. Their arms were wrapped around each other. Jennifer's head leaned against Mick's chest.

He chuckled softly. "I think you and I are more surprised about this than Phoebe's going to be."

"Mmmm." Jennifer nodded.

"But it's a nice Christmas present, all the same."

Jennifer lifted her head and looked up at him. "The angel didn't come."

"What?"

"The Christmas angel for the tree. Phoebe had her heart set on it. I ordered it the day you took me to town, but it didn't come. She'll be so disappointed."

Smiling to herself, Phoebe quietly eased back into her wheelchair. Her own surprise could wait until morning. For now she was content to just see how happy her pa and Aunt Jennifer were.

She remembered the night she'd closed her eyes and wished for the Christmas angel. She remembered thinking that the pretty celestial spirit would bring good fortune to her father.

And that was just what had happened, too.

Aunt Jennifer was wrong, Phoebe thought as she closed her bedroom door without a sound. The Christmas angel had arrived, and her pa was holding her in his arms right now.

NORAH HESS
The Homecoming

I dedicate this story to my husband Jack.

Chapter One

New York State, 1776

The wind made an eerie sound echoing around the cabin, reaching down the chimney and scattering ashes on the hearth. Outside, flakes of snow silently fluttered down, covering the shake roof and windowpanes, shutting out the night.

A night that made one glad to be indoors, Kate Harrison thought, scooting her rocker closer to the flames eating into the huge log she had wrestled into the fireplace just before sunset. If anyone was out there tonight, he would surely freeze to death.

The brightly burning fire cast glints of gold on the warm chestnut color of the young woman's hair as she bent her head over a lapful of Christmas ornaments. She sorted through them lovingly and carefully, for some were very old, brought to the new country by her German grandmother, the kind old woman who had raised Kate after her parents had been killed by warring Indians. Her mother had sent her into the woods that morning when the Indians were spotted racing their ponies toward the cabin, half-naked and yelling in a way that made a person's blood curdle. She had crawled into a cave and stayed there, terrified, her small body shaking, until she was found hours later by neighbors.

Kate shook her head as though to banish that day from her mind and continued to examine the treasures that would go on her tree. For a long time she and Grandmother Hesser had been the only family in the area who decorated a tree for Christmas. None of their neighbors had ever seen such a thing, but it was the custom in Germany to go into the forest, select a well-shaped fir, and drag it home. Trimming the tree was a festive occasion in the old country, Grandmother had told her.

Gradually, the children of the other families had become so enthralled with the Hesser Christmas tree that some of the parents had given in to their pleas to have one of their own. Today, most of the cabins in the settlement had a decorated tree at Christmas time.

Kate held up a plumed partridge made from colorful pieces of felt, stitched together with embroidery floss and stuffed with scraps of yarn. How old was it? she wondered, laying it aside. Her grandmother had brought most of the ornaments with her when she arrived here as a young bride.

Kate picked through a bunch of silk baubles of lustrous circles on which bright flowers had been carefully stitched. Each had a hanger of looped ribbon to hang onto the tree's branches.

With a soft smile on her lips, Kate continued to sort through the last of the ornaments, which consisted of needlepoint disks that she had helped Grandmother Hesser to make. She laughed out loud as she picked up her first effort at creating a felt star when she was around eight years old. She had stitched a cross in the center of it; the thread was knotted, the stitches uneven. But Grandmother had praised it, claiming that it would look lovely on top of the tree. Kate had been so proud of herself, she remembered.

With a long sigh Kate leaned her head back against the rocker. She still missed the gentle white-haired woman who had passed away this past spring. It had been March, the weather uncertain, one moment sunny, the next overcast with a chill wind blowing. One day while out looking for early greens, Thelma Hesser had been caught in a heavy shower. Two days later she was in bed with pneumonia. Being frail to begin with, and seventy-five years old, she had been unable to fight off the inflammation in her lungs. She had died in Kate's arms worrying about what would become of her beloved granddaughter.

So far she had fared quite well, Kate thought. All their neighbors had had a warm feeling for the genial and hospitable old woman who had been laid to rest beneath a huge oak tree in the meadow a short distance from their cabin. They showed their liking and respect by checking on her granddaughter at regular intervals, seeing that she was all right, plowing her garden patch, making sure she had enough wood chopped to see her through the bitterly cold days of winter.

She smiled to herself. At first, it was mostly bachelors who had swung the axes, chopping wood into lengths for the fireplace. Grandmother had always discouraged them from coming around, and had always accompanied her granddaughter to the socials that took place in the small community. Once when she asked the old woman why she wasn't allowed to have men callers like the other girls her age, she was told that none of the young men measured up to her grandmother's standards.

Kate had secretly wondered if such a man existed. But then, she hadn't been particularly impressed by any of the young men herself. With the exception of Jase, that was. He was so handsome with his blond hair and blue eyes. But he was eleven years older than she, and she didn't dare hope that he would pay any attention to her.

Then she had outgrown her flat chest and long, coltish legs, and Jase began to see her with different eyes. There was a look of appreciation in them when they roamed over her new curves. When Jase began dropping by in the evenings once a week, she could hardly contain her excitement and happiness, even though Grandmother always made it her business to sit on the porch with them.

That first night after Jase had left, Grandmother cautioned, "Don't set your sights on him, child. He's just using you to make that trashy Olive Worth jealous. He wants to get back at her for stringing him along."

But Grandmother was old, she told herself. She didn't realize that a man could switch his affections if the right woman came along. On the evening of her eighteenth birthday, Jase asked her if she would like to take a walk along the stream that separated their farm from his. She had looked at Grandmother and received a nod of permission.

Jase had only held her hand that first time as they walked along, remaining mostly silent. The second time he had draped an arm around her shoulders, holding her close to his side, their hips brushing against each other. But the third time they went walking, Jase had stopped and pulled her into his arms and kissed her with hot, hungry lips.

Kate still remembered the thrill of the kiss, how her heart had jumped, her pulses raced. He had kissed her several more times, each kiss deeper, more demanding. Then he had put her from him and said in a strained voice, "Enough of that. Let's get back to the cabin before I lose control."

That night, lying in bed, wide awake, she relived the kisses and made her wedding plans. Jase would never have kissed her like that if he didn't mean to marry her.

Those plans of marriage had died when Jase stopped coming by and instead took up again with Olive Worth.

Grandmother had let Kate mourn Jase for a week, then sternly told her that any man who would chase after the likes of that hussy wasn't worth wasting her thoughts on. "Put him out of your mind, girl, and get that dying-calf look off your face."

She had tried not to think of Jase, had tried hard, but every time she happened to run into the couple, she'd sink into a dark gloom and Grandmother would rail at her again, demanding to know where her pride and common sense had gone.

But common sense didn't enter into it when it came to handsome Jase Harrison. She loved him and she was sure she always would. Even when rumors flew around that he and Olive would marry, her feelings for him didn't lessen.

Then, three months after Grandmother passed away, the War for Freedom was on everybody's lips, and all other gossip took a back seat. Some of the young men in the area saddled up and rode to Pennsylvania to join George Washington's forces.

With the previous talk of Jase marrying Olive still fresh in Kate's mind, she hadn't been able to believe her ears when Jase rode up to her cabin that July morning, a scowl on his face, and bluntly asked her to marry him. There had been no leading up to it, no declaration of love, just a short "What do you think about marryin' me?"

"But what about Olive?" she had stammered over her racing heart. "Everyone thinks that—"

"Everyone thinks wrong," he had contradicted sharply. And as she continued to stare at him, he said impatiently, "Well, will you marry me or not?"

Reason, caution, everything had flown from her mind that hot, humid day, leaving only the thought that a dream she'd had since she was fourteen was going to come true. She looked up at his frowning face and said in a small voice, "Yes, I'll marry you, Jase."

Jase had nodded and said, "Get yourself ready then and we'll ride over to Reverend Jones's place and get it done. He's expectin' us." Pride had almost made her revoke her acceptance of him as a husband at that point. Was he so sure that she would marry him that he had made arragements for their wedding before he even asked her to become his wife? Had he known her feelings for him all this time? Had she been so transparent?

She'd opened her mouth to say that she had changed her mind, that she wasn't ready for marriage, and then he smiled at her. Even her bones seemed to melt at the curving of his firm lips and the flashing of his white teeth. "Hurry up now," he said. "We mustn't keep the preacher waiting. I have a feelin' he's not all that set on us marryin'."

She had wanted to ask him why he thought that, but again Jase urged her to hurry up and get ready. She swallowed back the question and walked into the cabin.

Inside her bedroom she had rushed about, changing into her Sunday-best dress of blue sprigged muslin whose bodice followed the curves of her breasts and narrow waist, the full skirt hiding the gentle swell of her hips. She slipped her feet into a pair of soft leather shoes that laced past her slender ankles. That done, she picked up the brush lying on a shelf and pulled it through her thick, shoulder-length curls. After taking a last look at her face in the shiny tin mirror, she joined Jase, who had dismounted and was sitting on the porch.

Jase had stood up and took a full look at the willowy figure of his bride-to-be. With a nod of approval, he took her arm and said brusquely, "Let's go."

No word was spoken between Kate and Jase as they rode along, the stallion's hooves kicking up puffs of dust, the sun beating down on their heads. Kate sat behind Jase, her skirts bunched up to her knees, one hand resting lightly on either side of his waist. She wished that she had the nerve to put her arms around him, but she couldn't help feeling he wouldn't welcome such intimacy. She kept her hands where they were, hoping that he wouldn't urge the stallion into a trot. If he did, she would either have to grab hold of him or fall off the horse.

Although neither spoke, both had much on their minds. Kate was thinking of her wedding night and was filled with anticipation and uneasiness. Grandmother had told her a little of what went on between a wife and her husband in the marriage bed, and she had seen a bull mount their cow several times, but other than the kisses she had shared with Jase, she was ignorant in the ways of pleasing a man. She feared that her new husband would be very disappointed with her. No doubt he had slept with Olive many times, for the older woman had a reputation of giving herself to whatever man was courting her at the time. Olive would know exactly how to please the man that she married.

Kate wondered again why Jase had asked her to be his wife. It wasn't out of love for her, she was pretty sure of that.

And Jase was thinking that he wanted to get this marriage over with so that he could be on his way, to show Olive Worth that she had toyed with him for the last time.

Every time he and Olive quarreled, which was often, he had thought of enlisting in Washington's army to fight against the British. And after what had happened yesterday afternoon, he was going to put that plan of becoming a minuteman into action. Before the day was over he would be on his way to Pennsylvania to join up with General George Washington.

Jase's lips tightened as he thought of the events that had set him on this course. He had ridden early to the Worth farm yesterday to surprise Olive, to make peace with her after a fiery argument they'd had the night before.

The surprise had been his though. As he rode quietly into the Worth's yard, he found Olive in the arms of John Hunter, the biggest womanizer in the county. Their lips had been locked together and Hunter's hand was inside Olive's bodice.

At first Jase was almost blinded by his anger. He wanted to dash up to the porch where they stood, tear them apart, and smash them both in the face. He had been especially angry at Olive, for only last night they had made love several times before quarreling.

As he sat there, he began to wonder if the woman he loved had it in her to be true to any man. Angrily, he turned the stallion around and rode away. That very afternoon he had made arrangements with a friend to take over his farm in his absence.

Jase left off his dark thoughts when the stallion cleared a small rise and the reverend's cabin came into view. The preacher sat on his porch waiting for them, a worn Bible in his hand. He stood up, looking very somber as Jase swung Kate to the ground.

"Kate, my dear," he said, taking her hand, "are you sure you want to marry this young man? Only yesterday he was chasing after Olive Worth. I can't believe he could switch his affections so swiftly."

Kate caught her breath as Jase, his chin stuck out belligerently, grasped her arm and said coldly, "I must have, preacher, since it's Kate I asked to marry me."

The reverend didn't look convinced, but after looking at Kate's willing face, he dropped her hand with a sigh and said, "Come on inside. Annie will be your witness."

Kate set the rocker in motion with a slight shove of her foot as she recalled her wedding day.

Jase's impatience to get it over with had made her so nervous, she was hardly aware of the preacher's words as he made them man and wife.

Was he already regretting his offer of marriage? she wondered, flicking a glance at his stony profile. It told her nothing.

In a daze, she promised to love, honor, and obey Jase Harrison. She then choked back a tear when he had no ring to slip on her finger. But he kissed her when Reverend Jones said, "You may kiss your bride."

Kate shook her head, remembering that kiss. Jase's lips had barely brushed hers. It hadn't been at all like the ones they had shared down by the river.

But she was to have a bigger disappointment, a bitter one, when they returned to her cabin. She had been so happy, so excited. She would pack her clothes, decide what things she would move to Jase's cabin, her new home. His place was much larger than hers, with two more rooms. How nice it would be to have four rooms to move about in.

When Jase reached behind him, taking her arm to assist her to the ground, she stood staring up at him, wondering why he wasn't dismounting also. She felt her face blanch when he spoke.

Avoiding her eyes, he said gruffly, "I'll be leaving you now, Kate. I'm going to Pennsylvania to join the minutemen, to fight in the war. I'll write to you when I can." With a wave of his hand and a "Take care of yourself," he kicked the stallion in the side and loped away.

231

She didn't know how long she stood in the yard, staring after Jase as he rode out of sight. Disbelief kept her rooted to the ground. Why in God's name had he married her? she asked herself over and over. But in the back of her mind, she knew that Olive Worth had something to do with it.

She found that she was right the next afternoon. She was sitting on her porch when Olive came riding up to the cabin, fury in her eyes. "You little bitch," she yelled, her voice shrill, "pretending to be so innocent and all the time you and Jase was sneakin' behind my back, layin' with each other. I guess you think you're real smart, gettin' yourself bigged by him, makin' him marry you. But just remember this, he don't love you and he never will. When he comes back from the war it will be me he'll come to." She brought her riding crop down on the mare's flank and with a protesting grunt the little mount lunged away.

Kate had tried to dismiss Olive's angry words, telling herself that they were spoken out of jealousy. But as time passed, weeks slipping into months, she had realized that the last part of the woman's outburst was probably true. Six months had passed now, and she hadn't received one letter from Jase. She wondered how many he had written to Olive. There was little doubt in her mind that he would go to the woman he loved when he returned.

She would soon find out, she sighed, staring into the flames. Two of the village men who had been with the minutemen had returned home last week and mentioned that Jase would also be coming for a Christmas visit as soon as he could slip away from camp.

She shrank inside. How embarrassing it was going to be when he went to Olive instead of his wife.

In the gloomy silence, the old clock from Germany began to slowly strike. Kate glanced up at its pewter face. It was nine o'clock. She returned the Christmas ornaments to the wicker basket and rose to her feet, reaching up on the mantle for the winding key. The ancient timepiece was running slow.

Kate yawned as she turned the brass key. It was time she went to bed. She would have to get up a little earlier tomorrow morning to shovel the new snow off the path to the barn and privy. When she had wound the clock tight, she laid aside the key and added two small logs of green wood to the fire. They would burn slowly all night, keeping out the cold. She yawned again, then picked up the candle holder to light the way to her bedroom.

The small quarters were cold and damp and she hurriedly changed into a long flannel gown and climbed into bed, sinking down into the warmth of the feather bed.

The snow was still beating against the window as she put Jase firmly from her mind and fell asleep.

Chapter Two

The next morning Kate awakened to the clarion call of her rooster. "Dratted old bird," she muttered, "don't you know it's too cold to get out of bed?"

She remembered then with a shiver all the chores that lay ahead of her. After all the shoveling, which would take the better part of an hour, there was the cow to be milked and her flock to be fed, as well as the mule. There had been two hogs that she had fattened up during the summer, but they had been butchered after the first killing frost in November. Reverend Jones had done the butchering for her, cutting the meat into roasts and chops, then hanging the sow-belly and shanks in the smokehouse where they had cured under a slow-burning bed of maple coals. Instead of paying the preacher for his work, she had shared the meat with him. He was very grateful for it, having six children to feed. He also got a big portion of the cow's milk, and once in a while a small crock of butter. It was the neighbors' way, helping each other out.

The poor preacher felt guilty for having married her to Jase. He had been scandalized to learn that her husband had immediately left her to fend for herself, not caring how she got on.

But he was not alone in feeling sorry for her. Most of the settlers in the area felt sorry for her, and she didn't like it one bit. She knew that they gossiped about her and Jase, wondering why he had married her instead of Olive, and it set her teeth on edge every time a look of pity was directed her way.

What made her shed embarrassed tears in private was learning that the men were laying bets on who Jase would return to and that most of the wagers were in favor of Olive.

It hit Kate suddenly that Jase might have their marriage overturned. They had never been together in the biblical sense. Her hands clenched into fists. She would die of shame if he did that to her.

But he should feel the shame, she thought angrily, staring up at the raftered ceiling . . . unless it was his plan to treat her so shabbily that she would put an end to the sham marriage. She rubbed the spot between her eyes. She was tired of wondering and fretting about what Jase Harrison would or would not do. If he wanted Olive Worth he was welcome to her. She would bear the shame of it somehow.

She sat up, swung her long legs over the side of the bed, fumbling with her feet for her fur-lined slippers. There were only four more ·days until Christmas, and besides all her chores she had to harness the mule and go into the woods and cut down a tree to set up in the corner opposite the fireplace. It would be the first time she'd done it alone, and she dreaded the task almost as much as the thought of decorating the tree. It would bring back so many memories. But she must do it. Grandmother would expect it of her. Tradition must go on.

The cabin was cold, only red glowing coals warming the area around the hearth. Kate picked up the small shovel leaning against the woodbox and raked away the pile of ashes that had gathered through the night, dumping them into the ash-bucket. She then stacked several pieces of well-seasoned wood on the live coals. When they caught and flames leaped up the chimney, she stood up, warming first her front, then turning to toast her backside.

Had it stopped snowing? she wondered. She walked across the floor to the small window and scratched away a patch of frost. It was a clear day, although the winter sun was pale. It was strong enough, however, to strike shimmering lights off the snow hanging thick on cedar boughs and maple and oak trees in the surrounding forest.

It looks like a fairyland, Kate thought as she filled the coffee pot with water from the pail on the table. But very deceiving, she added as she placed the pot on a bed of red coals. If not properly dressed, a person could freeze to death in all that beauty.

While the water heated, she took the coffee mill down from a shelf, put a handful of coffee beans in its round opening, and began turning the handle, grinding the beans into coarse grounds. She sniffed deeply of the aroma of the freshly ground coffee as she pulled a trayful from the grinder.

The water was beginning to simmer when she took the lid off the pot and dumped the grounds in it. Returning the lid, she walked briskly to her room to gather up the clothes she would wear today, then hurried back to the fire. By the time she had changed into her daytime wear, the coffee had finished brewing.

The heat from the fire and the steam from the coffee pot had melted the frost on the windowpanes, and as Kate stood in front of them, drinking her first cup of coffee of the day, she could see more clearly how much new snow had fallen and how much she would have to shovel.

She cringed. There was at least an additional eight inches covering that which had fallen a week ago. It would take nearly all morning to clear the two paths. "I'll need a good hearty breakfast," she mumbled, turning from the window. "It's going to take a lot of energy to shovel through that."

As the bacon sizzled in a long-handled skillet on the fire, Kate heard the lowing of her cow. She knew the animal was uncomfortable with a full udder. She would have to tramp through the snow to milk the poor thing before she did any clearing away.

She removed the crisp bacon from the skillet and broke two eggs into the hot grease. A few minutes later she was sitting at the table eating breakfast and having a second cup of coffee.

Kate covered her mouth with a gloved hand as she stepped outside the cabin, a wooden pail swinging from her other hand. From her knees down she felt the bite of the cold air, for she had tucked up her full skirt and petticoat to keep them from dragging in the snow. Otherwise she was quite warm in her fur-lined jacket and heavy shawl. She stepped off the porch, walking as fast as she could through the snow, for the cow was bawling loudly now.

A few yards from the barn Kate came to an abrupt halt, her heart thudding in her chest. The heavy barn door stood half open and a man's heavy footprints led up to it and disappeared inside. At first she wondered if an Indian had sought shelter in the log building. Then she realized that it wasn't a red man. He wore heavy boots. Whoever was inside there was a white man.

Who? she wondered, chewing on her bottom lip. A stranger or a neighbor? Common sense told her that no neighbor lurked inside. A neighbor would have knocked on the cabin door and asked for a place beside her fire.

She was ready to turn around and beat a hasty retreat to the cabin when a low moan, as from someone in pain, came from inside the barn. She stood undecided, then the moan came again, this time a little louder. She hesitated a moment longer, then went forward and stepped inside the dimly lit structure.

Kate stood just within the doorway, calling out in an uneasy voice, "Where are you, and who are you?" There was no answer, and she stepped further inside, asking again, "Where are you?"

Her eyes were accustomed to the dimness now and she could see everything quite clearly: the stalls housing the cow and mule, the feed bin, the pile of hay next to one of corn. Her eyes were searching the corners when the door banged shut behind her. She spun around to see a large, bearded man, a stranger, stalking toward her.

"Who are you? What do you want?" she squeaked, her eyes searching frantically for a possible way of escaping this man whose very walk told her he meant her some kind of harm. Would he rape her, or maybe kill her? Her blood ran cold. Maybe he planned to do both.

Don't let him see your fear, she ordered herself. *Stand up to him, order him out of the barn.*

Her shoulders squared, but her hands trembling in the folds of her skirt, Kate said firmly, "You're trespassing and I want you out of here immediately."

The stranger gave a short bark of a laugh. "I don't give a whoop in hell what you want. I'm only interested in what I want." His eyes narrowed and glittered. "And I want you. You've been without a man for a long time, and I'm here to take care of that."

"You take one step closer to me and I'll sic my

dog on you," Kate threatened, knowing how foolish she sounded as the words left her mouth.

The man gave his strange laugh again and
sneered, "You don't have a dog, purty little girl.
Now settle down and don't give me any trouble.
If you're nice to me, I won't hurt you. But if you
squeal and carry on, you'll be very sorry."

He lunged at her then, and as she jumped back,
her heel caught in the hem of her skirt and she
toppled over backwards to the dirt floor. The
breath whooshed out of her, and even as she
tried to regain it, the man threw his heavy weight
on top of her, pinning her beneath him. His hands,
rough in his hurry to possess her, tossed her skirt
up over her face, then tore at her underclothing,
his nails biting into her tender flesh. When he
grabbed her legs and tried to pull them apart, she
lifted her clawed fingers and raked them across
his face. He swore an oath and backhanded her
across the mouth, cutting her lip.

"You'll pay for that, you little bitch," he gritted
through his teeth, wiping at the three trails of
blood running down his cheek.

A high scream tore from Kate's lips as the
stranger grabbed her by the knees and jerked
them apart. He was crawling between her legs
when a shadow fell across his beefy shoulders.
Wide-eyed, Kate looked into the furious eyes of
John Hunter, the trapper. Even as relief washed
over her, her attacker was lifted up and hurled
against the mule's stall. He grunted in surprise,
and then in pain as a hard fist smashed against
his mouth and nose.

As Kate sat up and scooted out of the way, Hunter straddled her attacker, hitting him again and again in the face, demanding, "Who sent you here to do this to Kate Harrison?"

The trapper had hit too hard, too often. Before the man could answer, his head lolled to one side in a faint. "You'll answer me when you come to," Hunter muttered, and stood up, walking to kneel down beside Kate.

His eyes grew gentle. "Are you all right?" he asked, smoothing the hair away from her face and pulling down her skirts. "He didn't . . . you know . . ."

"No," Kate answered shakily, licking her cut lip. "You got here just in time. Do you know who he is?"

John Hunter shook his head. "I've never seen him around here before, and you can bet that after I get through with him, you'll never see him again." He took Kate by the arms and lifted her to her feet. "Let's get you to the cabin so you can take care of your lip. It's beginning to swell."

"But I've got the cow to milk and the stock to feed." Kate held back when he would have led her to the door.

"You can do that after you've had a cup of coffee and calmed your nerves a bit." Hunter smiled down at her. "Besides, I could use a cup too, and maybe you could put something on my bruises."

"Oh, I'm sorry," Kate exclaimed, looking at the trapper's split and bleeding knuckles. "We'll soak them in some weak salt water, then I'll smear some balm of Gilead on them." She looked over at

241

the sprawled figure of the man who had attacked her. "What about him? Shouldn't you try to revive him?"

"Naw, let the no-good skunk lay there. I want to question him later on."

Hunter held Kate's elbow, helping her on her shaky legs as they walked to the cabin. "I haven't thanked you," she said as they stepped upon the porch and she pushed open the heavy door. "I think you might have saved my life."

"I don't think he meant to kill you," the trapper said as he followed her into the warmth of the room and closed the door behind them. When Kate laid aside her shawl and fumbled with the buttons on her jacket, he pushed away her shaking fingers and swiftly undid them and then helped her out of the garment, saying, "Go sit by the fire and I'll bring you a cup of coffee."

"But I should be waiting on you," Kate protested.

"Now why should you do that?" Hunter grinned at her. "I'm a bachelor and I know quite well how to do things like serving a lady a cup of coffee."

Kate felt her face grow warm. She had no doubt that there were a lot of things this man could bring to a lady. She watched him as he moved easily about in the kitchen area, adding sugar and cream to her cup, but leaving his black. She thanked him shyly when he joined her at the hearth and put her steaming cup in her hand.

As she sipped at the invigorating coffee, Hunter

sat down in the rocker beside her, the one her grandmother used to sit in, and raised his own cup to his lips. He took a long swallow, then nodded his head in approval. Smiling at Kate, he said, "You make a fine pot of coffee, Mrs. Harrison."

"Thank you, but please call me Kate."

There was silence for a moment as each sipped their drink, then Hunter remarked, "I hear Jase is comin' home for Christmas."

"Yes, I heard that too." Kate stared into her cup.

Hunter slid her a surprised glance. "Don't you know for sure? Haven't you heard from him?"

Kate shook her head. "I expect he's been too busy to write."

John Hunter looked at her downcast face, and pity for the beautiful girl moved through him. He'd heard all the rumors, the gossip that had gone on about Jase Harrison and Kate Hesser's hasty wedding. Olive Worth had spread the nasty word that Kate had trapped Jase by intentionally getting herself in a family way.

He glanced at Kate's flat stomach. Six months had passed since her wedding, and the young wife showed no sign of being in a family way. His gaze rose to her face. The innocence of a virgin was there plain to see. That damn fool Harrison hadn't taken her to bed before he tore off to the war.

Amusement twitched the corners of the trapper's lips. Besides Jase Harrison himself, only he knew why the farmer had married Kate Hesser before he left that July morning. He had done it in a fit of anger to get back at Olive.

That day six months ago when Hunter and Olive stood on her porch, kissing, he had seen Jase approaching the cabin. He hadn't let on, and out of pure orneriness, still watching Jase through his lashes, had slipped a hand inside Olive's bodice. She had moaned and pressed closer to him, and he had debated leading her inside the cabin to see what Harrison would do.

There had always been a rivalry between Hunter and Jase when it came to women. Jase, with his regular features, curly blond hair, and muscular build, was the more handsome, but John Hunter's lean face had a devilish look to it that drew women to him like flame to a moth. And like the silly insect, they'd been badly scorched when he turned his attention to another woman.

Kate Hesser had caught his eye when she was sixteen. And though he wanted her as he had never wanted another woman, he knew it would never happen. First, old lady Hesser would shoot him if he showed his face within a mile of her place, and second, young Kate wasn't the type a man played fast and loose with. She was meant for marriage and children.

As Hunter looked at Kate now, he wished with everything in him that he had braved the grandmother's wrath and had come courting Kate. Two years older now and pretty much jaded, he'd like nothing better than to settle down with the lovely young woman and give her children.

He breathed a sigh and said, "I expect the war has kept Jase pretty busy. Probably doesn't have much time to write." He looked away from her, afraid she would see the lie in his eyes. Harrison hadn't been too busy to write Caleb Malcott, the owner of the fur post. He'd received at least three letters inquiring if Caleb knew how his farm was being taken care. No mention of Kate in it, according to Caleb. And Olive boasted that she had heard from her soldier several times.

He glanced through the window, thinking what fools some men were, then jumped to his feet. "There goes that damn skunk high-tailin' it through the woods. I'm goin' after him."

"Let him go, John." Kate grabbed his arm and pushed him back down on the chair. "I think you've punished him enough. I'm surprised he can see well enough to run. It looked to me like he had both eyes swollen shut."

John sat back down, not at all eager to leave such beautiful company. "Hadn't you better take care of your lip and the bruise on your cheek?" he asked.

"Yes," Kate said as she stood up, "but first I'll take care of your poor knuckles."

A few minutes later, with Hunter's hand soaking in the saline mixture, Kate bathed her cut and bruise, mumbling through the flannel cloth that she had to go milk her poor cow and feed the animals.

"While you do your chores, I'll clear your paths of snow," Hunter said offhandedly.

Kate wanted to refuse his offer. What if a

neighbor came along and saw the infamous womanizer shoveling snow for her? Gossip would run
wild. But she didn't have the heart to hurt his
feelings. After all, he had saved her from being
raped, possibly killed.

She smiled at the trapper and said, "Thank you,
John. That's very kind of you."

Chapter Three

Hunter had shoveled the path to the privy and half of the path to the barn when Reverend Jones rode up. The reverend reined in his horse beside John and frowned down on him. "What are you doing here, John, shoveling snow for Kate Harrison?" he demanded.

"Well, it's like this, preacher," Hunter began, leaning on the shovel handle. "It occurred to me that I am the only male around here who hasn't pitched in to help Kate." His eyes twinkled devilishly. "I figured it was time I gave her a hand."

"Now look, Hunter," Jones said, dismounting, "you know very well that the bachelors no longer come to help Kate now that she's married. The married men in the community help her now. Mostly me."

"I didn't know that," Hunter lied, the teasing

look still in his eyes. "I'll just finish this job and be on my way."

"You'd best leave now before someone comes along and spreads the tale that you're hanging around Jase Harrison's wife. I'll finish the shoveling."

"Thing is, preacher, I like to finish what I start." Hunter stubbornly held on to the shovel. "There's no harm in bein' friendly to a neighbor."

"No, there's not if the circumstances were different. If Kate was an old woman, or even a plain young married one you wanted to help, nobody would think much about it. But Kate is beautiful, and you know how people like to gossip."

"If there's any gossipin' to be done, I think it should be about that husband of Kate's for goin' off and leavin' her to take care of herself the best way she can."

"There is talk about Jase Harrison, and I'm sure you're aware of it. But until Kate gets a bellyful and sets her marriage aside, she's off bounds to you or any other man." He gave Hunter a sympathetic look. "In the meantime why don't you just step back and wait, see what happens. We don't want any gossip started about Kate."

"It's too late for that, preacher." Hunter looked past the mule stamping his hooves against the cold. "Here comes Olive Worth, the biggest gossip around."

"And Kate's worst enemy," Jones added on a sour note. "God only knows what kind of tales she'll spread."

Hunter's jaw tautened and his eyes narrowed.

The preacher spoke the truth. Olive hated Kate Harrison. Hated her for her youth, her beauty, her good name. She hated her all the more because Kate had married the man that she, Olive Worth had planned to marry someday.

He sighed inwardly. It was up to him now to pacify the jealous woman, to pretend an affection that was opposite from the truth. It would be easy to fool her. He had known for a long time that it was he, John Hunter, that Olive now hoped to marry. She had done everything but come right out and ask him.

There was a sullen pout on Olive's face when she rode up to the two men and climbed from the saddle. Ignoring the preacher, she looked at Hunter and sneered, "So, John, you take care of Mrs. Harrison's needs while Jase is off fightin' for his country."

"Are you talkin' about Kate's need to have the snow shoveled away from her paths?" Hunter asked, a dangerous note in his voice.

Not put off by his tone, Olive snapped, "You know very well what needs I'm talkin' about, John Hunter. Jase has been gone for six months, and she's bound to be twitchy by now."

Hunter was hard put not to lay hands on Olive, to tell her that, unlike herself, some women were able to control such feelings. He knew that was the worst possible thing he could say, so instead he draped an arm across her shoulders and said in low tones, "The preacher is gonna take over here. It's too bad you don't have any shovelin' I could do for you."

The dark scowl left Olive's face. Mollified by Hunter's soft innuendo, she leaned into Hunter and with a coy look murmured, "Maybe I'll see you at your cabin later?"

"You do that." The trapper gently squeezed her shoulder, wishing that he could dig in his fingers and leave a big bruise on her plump flesh. The last thing he wanted to do was spend time with the simpering bitch tonight. What he wanted now was for her and the preacher to ride away, to leave him alone with Kate, even though he knew they would never be any more than neighbors who would nod pleasantly at each other when they chanced to meet on Crown Crossing's winding dirt street.

Nevertheless, he had looked forward to spending a short time with the woman who was forbidden to him, to feast his eyes on her fresh beauty, to listen to her soft voice when she talked to him. His eyes darkened. This one pressing her hip against his was putting a stop to that. If he did not ride away, she would do everything in her power to come between Jase Harrison and his wife when and if he came home for the holidays. Kate was going to need someone to run interference for her. Someone like himself who knew how Olive's conniving mind worked, who could second-guess every sly bit of trouble she was about to attempt. It would mean keeping a close eye on Olive, but the gentle Kate deserved a chance to keep her husband.

Of course there was the possibility that Jase would go straight to Olive and completely ignore his wife. The trapper's lips firmed in a tight, determined line. If that should happen, he would give the handsome farmer a beating he would never forget. Kate didn't deserve such treatment.

Hunter stiffened suddenly. Kate had just stepped through the barn door, a pail of milk in her hand. "Let's go to my cabin now," he said to Olive, trying to keep the apprehension from his voice.

But Olive had seen Kate and she spun around, her eyes narrowing on Kate's pretty face. "You're a little late gettin' your milkin' done ain't you, Kate?" she sneered when Kate walked up to them. Her eyes found Kate's cut lip, and she shot a suspicious look at Hunter. "I didn't know you could be such a rough lover, John."

The preacher, who had been silent all this time, now made an angry protesting sound at the same time as Hunter made an impatient gesture. "I had nothing to do with Kate's cut lip," he said tightly. "She was attacked by a stranger this morning, and I came along just after he had struck her."

"Dear Lord, Kate, are you all right?" the reverend exclaimed. "Did he . . ."

"No, he didn't," Hunter answered brusquely for Kate. "And I think that he'll think twice before tryin' rape on another woman. I beat the livin' hell out of him." He raised his bruised and cut knuckles for Olive and Jones to see.

"I see they've been nicely taken care of," Olive said, her lips lifting in a sneer when she saw the salve that Kate had spread over the large knuckles. "I wonder if that's the only way she thanked you for rescuing her."

"Miss Worth, you have no right to speak of Kate that way," the preacher said sharply. "She's a good Christian woman who would never put horns on her husband. I think you owe her an apology."

"Hah!" Olive snorted. "She owes me one. Didn't she sneak around and marry the man who was supposed to marry me?"

"I didn't have to sneak to marry Jase," Kate flared out, her hazel eyes blazing fire, tired of the older woman's insults. "Jase came to me and asked me to marry him without any encouragement from me. Nobody forced him to. He came of his own will."

Angry red spots mottled the coarse skin of Olive's cheeks. "The only reason Jase did that was because we argued and he wanted to spite me," she cried furiously. "But he's over his anger now and he's sorry he ever married you. He tells me that in his letters, and that when he comes home for Christmas he's comin' straight to me."

Both men were furious, but Reverend Jones spoke first. "I tell you this, Olive Worth," he said, his voice trembling with emotion. "If Jase Harrison goes to you, the pair of you will be ostracized in this community. There won't be a decent man or woman who will speak to either one of you."

"Hah!" Olive sniffed. "Who cares. I'll have Jase, and he'll be so glad to have me he won't care if anyone speaks to him or not."

Hunter glanced at Kate. Her face had gone so white he was afraid she was going to faint. Again it took all his will power not to slap Olive in the

The Homecoming

mouth. His hands were not overly gentle when he grabbed her around the waist and practically threw her in the saddle. He mounted his stallion and gave Kate an apologetic look. She smiled weakly at him, and he thumped his heels into the horse's sides and galloped away. Olive was hard put to keep up with him.

When the two had disappeared out of sight, Reverend Jones looked at Kate and said, "There goes a resentful, unforgiving woman, Kate. She'll hurt you in any way she can."

Kate nodded. "I know. She never has liked me, although for the life of me I don't know why. I've never done or said anything against her."

"It's no mystery to me," the preacher snorted. "She's blind jealous of you."

"I don't know why," Kate said, her voice trembling. "She's the one Jase loves. It's her he'll be going to whenever he returns."

"Don't be too sure of that, Kate," Jones said as he picked up the shovel Hunter had discarded. "If he's got half a brain he'll come to you."

Kate watched the kindly man thrust the shovel into the snow, her eyes full of doubt.

Chapter Four

Kate was still seething the next morning as she went about her chores. God only knew what kind of rumors Olive was spreading about her and Hunter, she thought as she mechanically milked the cow, the jets of milk striking the bottom of the wooden pail, creating a bubbly foam. She would spin out quite a tale of finding the trapper at the Hesser cabin.

Kate sighed. She could only hope that her friends and neighbors would give no credence to the woman's vicious lies, but would realize that they came from a female who felt that she had been scorned.

She pressed her head against the warmth of the cow as though seeking comfort as she wondered what Jase would think when he heard of Olive's charge of his wife's wrongdoing. Would he be angry? Would he even care? One minute she wished that he would come home for a visit, the next minute she wished he wouldn't. Wouldn't she be happier not knowing what was in Jase's mind and heart?

Until recently she had been content to live in a dream world. If the unwanted thought that her marriage was a sham came to her occasionally, she pushed it away, telling herself that Jase loved her, that he had only been waiting for her to grow up before making her his wife.

But yesterday her dreaming had ceased, replaced by reality. She had Jase's name, but his heart belonged to Olive. Not once had he written to his wife, but he had corresponded with Olive all this time.

Swallowing the lump in her throat, Kate drew the last of the milk from the cow's deflated udder and stood up, vaguely noticing that each day the cow gave less milk. Soon she would dry up altogether and would have to be taken to the neighbor's bull for a visit. Come spring she would drop a calf and there would be milk again.

Kate wished that the new calf would be a little bull. It was embarrassing to lead her cow to her neighbor for mating purposes.

It was hard being a woman alone, Kate sighed again.

As she passed the hen house, the fussing of hens and the gobbling of turkeys made shrill sounds on the cold, silent air. She tried not to mind the noise. They were hungry, she knew, and it was her fault. She had overslept this morning, because she hadn't fallen asleep until well past midnight.

She would not let herself think about why sleep had evaded her. She would think of other things.

As her feet crunched along on the frozen snow, Kate recalled the way she had come to own turkeys. One day while out gathering greens in the meadow back of the barn where she let her cow and mule graze in the warm weather, she had found a nest of wild turkey eggs. She was about to walk on when an odd idea came to her. She carefully picked up six of the eggs and put them in her apron pocket. When she arrived back at the cabin, she slipped them under one of her hens that had been insisting on nesting. Her neighbors had laughed and joked about it, asking her if she intended to start a turkey farm, and wouldn't it shock the poor old hen if by some miracle the eggs hatched.

They had stopped laughing when ten days later every egg had hatched. As for the mother hen, she had taken the best of care of the young turkeys even though they soon outstripped her in size. Kate hoped the old biddy wouldn't be too upset when one disappeared. It was going to reappear on her table Christmas day, stuffed and roasted to a golden brown.

Maybe I will start a turkey farm, Kate thought as she strained the milk into a brown glazed bowl. She could make a few dollars selling them to her neighbors. Raised on milk and cracked corn, they would be more tender than their relatives in the wild. The money in the little box in her chest of drawers was disappearing fast. If Jase decided to continue to fight, she would be hard put to provide for herself.

As Kate prepared to go out into the cold again to feed her mixed flock, she realized with a tightening in her chest that she was slowly coming to terms with the idea of living out her life as a spinster. Jase would marry Olive, and as the years went by Kate Hesser would turn into one of those strange old women who kept to themselves, scaring children, and the neighbors would refer to her as that crazy old Kate Hesser. Olive would teach her children to taunt her, to peg rocks at her and her cabin.

"What in the world is wrong with you, woman?" Kate snapped out loud to herself as she went out the door. If Grandmother Hesser were here and could read her mind, she'd give her granddaughter a rap on the head, then remind her that Thelma Hesser had survived with dignity without a man and that she expected Kate to do the same, and she had better straighten out and behave like a Hesser.

Half an hour later, her mood raised somewhat, Kate had fed her turkeys and hens and one rooster and was harnessing the mule to ride up the hill a short distance away to chop down her Christmas tree. She knew the one she wanted. She had spotted it this past summer on her way back from visiting Reverend Jones and his family. It was a cedar tree, its branches dark green with short needles. Grandmother had always chosen cedar, claiming that it gave off more fragrance than its cousin, the pine.

Kate had thought of her grandmother often the past two weeks. The old lady had made the holidays a cheery, special time. She would go about her Christmas baking softly singing songs she had learned in Germany. The little girl following her around had begged to be taught the happy-sounding tunes, but Thelma Hesser had always refused, answering that Kate was an American and that she owed it to her country to speak English.

But Kate remembered the tunes if not the words, and she hummed them to herself as she climbed onto the mule's bare back and headed up the hill,

It was numbing cold as Kate rode along, a winter fog drifting down from the hills. She was thankful she'd had the foresight to put on her jacket with the rabbit-fur lining. It had belonged to her grandmother, a gift from an old squaw whose life she had saved when the Indian woman had been bitten by a copperhead three summers ago. It was a beautiful garment with bead designs worked down the front. As she gained the top of a hill, a bitter wind blew up and she dug her chin into the collar to nestle in the fur's soft warmth.

In a short time Kate pulled the mule beside the tree she had chosen and slid to the ground, transferring the axe from her lap to her hand. The snow came almost to her boot tops as she swung the axe into the trunk of the trees.

The sharp blade had bitten halfway through the thick bole when Kate paused to rest, and saw the figure of a man coming through the trees.

John Hunter walked fast in the bitter cold as he made the rounds of his traps. He hunched deeper into his heavy jacket, his mind on two women, Olive Worth and Kate Harrison. Yesterday when he and Olive arrived at his cabin he couldn't bring himself to bring her inside to lie with her on his bed. Much to her displeasure, he had given the excuse that he'd just remembered he had to ride to the post to talk to Caleb Walcott about his furs. He wanted to ask the post owner what prices pelts were bringing this season. Olive had pouted, then became sullen when he wouldn't change his mind about taking her to bed. She had brightened a little when he said that they would get together later in the week.

John wondered now what reason he could give the determined woman for not keeping his word when she came calling. For she would be back, he had no doubt about that. And he would have to be careful not to rile her too much. She was a vindictive female and she hated Kate Harrison. Jase had shamed her when he married Kate, a younger, more beautiful woman.

He wished he knew just what Jase Harrison felt about his wife. Kate was sweet and shy, whereas Olive had a disagreeable disposition and had slept with her share of men, if gossip was to be believed. At any rate, she hadn't been a virgin the first time he took her to bed. He pitied the man who would be foolish enough to marry her. Jase Harrison didn't know how lucky he was to have escaped the woman's clutches.

The people of Crown Crossing were still wondering what had happened between Jase and Olive. Many opinions were expressed: that Jase had only been killing time with Olive while he waited for Kate to grow up, that he had waited a decent time to elapse after Thelma's passing, that he felt sorry for Kate, being alone and all, that he and old Thelma had been quite friendly and he felt duty bound to marry her granddaughter and take care of her. Some voiced the belief that Jase had caught Olive with another man and that he had married Kate out of spite.

Hunter's lips twisted in a wry smile. Those who believed the latter were right. Jase Harrison had looked furious enough to kill that morning when he found Olive in his arms.

"If the damn fool only knew it, finding Olive in my arms six months ago was the luckiest day of his life," Hunter muttered, climbing to the top of a hill. "If he's smart he'll . . ." The trapper broke off his thoughts as he came to an abrupt halt.

Below him in a snow-covered meadow was a feminine figure chopping away at a cedar tree while an old mule stood patiently a couple of yards away. His keen eyesight soon told him that it was the young woman who had been taking up too much of his thoughts since yesterday. It annoyed him how deeply she affected him emotionally. Not since he was a young man of twenty had a woman touched his heart.

And that one had played him false.

It took the trapper a minute to figure out why Kate Harrison would be out in the cold chopping down a tree. Without her awareness of it yesterday he had checked her wood supply and found several cords of small logs stacked between the trees back of the cabin. He remembered then Thelma Hesser's habit of bringing a tree into her cabin at Christmas time and hanging bright little geegaws all over it.

When Kate paused to rest a minute, Hunter adjusted the pack strapped to his back and walked down the hill, moving toward Kate. She shouldn't be out here alone, he thought, the snow kicking up around him. That low-life who attacked her yesterday could still be lurking around somewhere.

"Good morning, Kate," he called when he was a few yards away. "I haven't seen you all winter and now I come across you two days in a row." He smiled as he walked up to her.

Kate returned him a friendly smile. She liked the trapper, although he didn't have the best reputation in the world. He drank too much, brawled too often, and chased women like a rutting buck, but he was always a gentleman around her.

"I see you've had a good catch so far," she said, looking at the furs on Hunter's back as he took the axe from her and with one swing of the blade brought the tree down.

"Yeah, pretty good," he answered, leading the mule to the cedar and bending over to fasten the single tree to its trunk. "And you'd be a good catch if that man who attacked you yesterday should come upon you out here alone," he added as he straightened up. "Why didn't you have that oldest kid of Jones's come along with you?"

"I didn't think about it actually," Kate said, her face paling as she remembered her encounter with that awful man in her barn. "But I can't stay shut up in the cabin all the time, John. I have chores to do, and I have to go to the village once in a while. Anyhow, I think that stranger got your message yesterday. I'm sure he'll be afraid to come within sight of my cabin again."

"Let's hope so," Hunter said, slapping the mule on the rump, stirring him into motion. As they followed along behind the plodding animal, the tree dragging through the snow, he asked, "Do you know how to shoot that Kentucky rifle your grandmother used to carry around?"

"Oh, yes," Kate answered proudly. "I'm a crack shot. Good as any man, Grandmother used to say."

"Good. From now on don't leave the cabin without it, even if you're only makin' a trip to the privy. You never know who might be sneakin' around."

Kate walked alongside the trapper, her feet crunching through the snow as she thought sadly that her husband hadn't cared enough to warn her of the dangers a lone woman might face. She felt sure that if it was Olive he was married to he wouldn't have gone off and left *her* alone.

No more was said between Kate and Hunter until they reached the cabin. "How will you get this tree to stand up?" Hunter asked as he bent over and unfastened the tree from the mule.

Kate picked up two boards about three inches wide and sixteen inches long that had been nailed crosswise together. "I nail this to the end of the tree trunk."

Hunter nodded. "Where's your hammer and nails?"

Kate picked up the hammer from beside the tree stand and teased as she handed it to him, "Is your eyesight bad or don't you know what a hammer looks like?"

"My eyesight is perfect, and I know the difference between tools, Miss Smarty." Hunter grinned at Kate. "I also know what a nail looks like, but I don't see one layin' around."

"That's because it's in my pocket." Kate grinned back.

She handed over the long nail, and after Hunter had given his thumb a couple of good whacks the tree was attached to its stand. It leaned a little to the left, but Kate didn't mention it, the trapper looked so proud of his accomplishment. She did ask if he would shake the snow off the branches.

After Hunter had shaken the tree so vigorously that Kate feared all the needles would fall off, she opened the door and he carried it inside. "Where do you want it?" he asked. Kate directed him to set it in the corner where the Christmas tree had stood for as long as she could remember.

Kate stood back and gazed at the tree. It was a beautiful specimen, she thought, even though it stood a little crooked. After John left she would turn it around until that fault was hidden. It would take a while for it to dry out so she could decorate it.

"What about a cup of coffee and some sugar cookies before you leave?" She smiled at Hunter as she removed her shawl and unbuttoned her jacket.

"Sounds right good." Hunter smiled back. "I'll just lay my catch outside the door." *I shouldn't stay here,* Hunter told himself as he unstrapped the fur pack and let it slide to the porch floor. *I'm only tormenting myself. And what if a neighbor should happen along? Maybe Preacher Jones. He'd have a fit, finding me here a second time in as many days. And God forbid that Olive should come nosing around. Tongues would really wag once that one finished telling her lies.*

For several moments Hunter was tempted to ride to Pennsylvania and kick Jase Harrison's rump all the way back to Crown Crossing. The damn fool didn't deserve Kate, but he had married her and he should treat her like a wife, not like someone of no importance. If he, John Hunter, were married to her, he would treat her like a queen. She wouldn't be living alone, fending for herself.

When Hunter came back into the cabin, Kate had poured their coffee and placed a plate of cookies on the table. As he took the chair she indicated he looked around the neat room that served both as kitchen and the main living area.

Besides the kitchen table and four chairs there were two rockers in front of the fireplace, comfortably padded in red and yellow calico. A basket of yarn sat beside one of the rockers, two knitting needles sticking out of it. On the small table between the rockers was a pewter candle holder, a book lying beside it.

Against one wall was a hutch with pretty plates and dainty figurines gracing its shelves. A spinning wheel and a loom stood in one corner, the loom holding an unfinished piece of material. He could picture Kate sitting at it, working the foot pedal, creating cloth for some purpose she had in mind.

Hunter shifted his gaze back to the fireplace. A tinderbox, along with a clock, sat on the mantle, a long-handled skillet and iron spider rested on the hearth. He looked next at the bare cedar tree, wondering what it would look like once Kate finished putting her bits and pieces on it.

He'd never know, he thought gloomily. Kate wouldn't be issuing him any invitations to come look at it. For the first time in his life he was sorry about the life he had lived. It had cut him off from decent people who lived nice ordinary lives. Because of his reckless way of life he would always be on the outside looking in. There would never be hearth and home for him.

Kate sat down across from Hunter, and he put aside his depressing thoughts as she pushed the cookies within his reach and said, "Help yourself, John."

Hunter bit into a flaky cookie, which seemed to melt in his mouth. The cookie certainly didn't taste like the rock-hard ones that Olive had served him once. He'd finally had to soften one in his coffee.

"I haven't eaten anything so good since my mom used to bake," he said, reaching for another sweet.

"Are your parents still living?" Kate asked, pouring milk into her coffee.

"No, they're both dead. My pa passed away eight years ago and my ma followed him a year later. My brother lives on the family farm."

"It's hard, losing your parents," Kate said gently. After a pause, she asked, "where is the family farm?"

"It's a distance from here. Lower Kentucky."

"You're quite a ways from home." Kate smiled at him. "Isn't the trapping any good in your home state?"

"There's none better anywhere," Hunter answered, then added with a crooked grin, "It was a woman who sent me high-tailin' out of those hills."

"Oh? Do you mind telling me about it?"

Hunter shrugged. "There's not much to tell. She decided she didn't want to be a trapper's wife and married a farmer instead. The man was eighteen years older than she and had a passel of younguns, but he owned the largest farm in the county."

"She sounds like a very mercenary woman. You're probably better off without her."

"I expect you're right, but I don't blame her too much. Her folks were as poor as church mice, and I expect she thought I'd never give her much in the way of material things."

"But trappers make good money, don't they?"

"Yes, we do, but she couldn't see that, considerin' that we don't do anything in the summer months. In her opinion we're all a bunch of lazy louts who'll never amount to anything."

Kate stood up to stir the pot of beans cooking slowly over the fire. As she walked across the room she said, "I still think you're better off without her, but I also think that you should find yourself a nice woman and marry her, settle down. You'll live longer with a wife to take care of you."

Hunter didn't answer until Kate sat back down. Then, forgetting common sense, he fixed a soft look on her and, his meaning crystal clear, said, "There's only one woman around here I'd like to settle down with, and she's already taken . . . for the time bein'."

Kate was too stunned to speak for several seconds. She could only stare at Hunter as her mind took in his double meaning. He had declared his feelings for her, and let her know that he believed that Jase wouldn't be coming back to her. That in the near future Kate would be free to marry another man.

She was saved from having to answer when Reverend Jones called her name outside. Her face flushed with confusion, she jumped to her feet and rushed to open the door. Hunter sat on, silently cursing at the preacher and at himself.

He had probably scared Kate away for all time. Why couldn't he have kept his dumb mouth shut and waited to see what happened when Harrison came home? If Jase went to Olive, a man could wait a decent time and then begin to court Kate, like the preacher had said.

Reverend Jones looked thunderstruck as he stepped inside after stamping the snow off his boots and saw Hunter at the table calmly drinking coffee and eating cookies.

"What in the blue blazes are you doing here, John Hunter?" he demanded, his eyes snapping angrily. "Are you trying to ruin Kate's reputation? Two days in a row now I've caught the two of you together. Olive Worth is spreading her lies all over the countryside. If one of your neighbors had happened to drop by and seen you here, all those lies would be believed."

"Look, preacher," Hunter bit out angrily, "I came upon Kate choppin' down her Christmas tree and gave her a hand with the job. After we got it back here, I nailed a stand on it and brought it inside the cabin. Kate, as she would do for any other neighbor, gave me a cup of coffee and some cookies. What's wrong with that?"

"You know dratted well what's wrong with that, John Hunter. You should have refused and gone on your way."

Hunter had no answer for that, knowing that the preacher was right. He shouldn't have come inside the cabin, let alone sat down and had refreshments with her. But Kate was an innocent when it came to what was proper and what was not. He had done her a favor, and she had thought it the right thing to do to offer him coffee and cookies in return.

He stood up and pushed his chair back in place. "Thank you for the refreshments, Kate. I'm sorry if I cause you to be talked about."

Kate started to protest, to say that they had done nothing wrong, but Hunter was already opening the door and stepping outside. When she would have followed him, the preacher grabbed her wrist, staying her.

"Let him go, Kate," he said soberly. "It's best this way. Hunter has had his eye on you for a long time. If you call him back, it will only encourage him to come around again."

Kate sat down with a sigh. "He's a very nice man, you know. He's never once said or done anything disrespectful."

Reverend Jones nodded. "I expect he didn't. Even hell-raisers recognize a good woman when they see one. Nevertheless, he knows that you're married and that he shouldn't set foot in your door when you're alone. I just hope that Jase doesn't get word of him being here. He'd go after Hunter and there would be a fierce fight."

Kate made no response, but her face showed what she was thinking. Jase wouldn't care if John moved in with her. It was almost a sure thing that he would go to Olive when he returned.

"Wait until Jase comes home, Kate," the preacher said gently. "You'll know where you stand then," he added as he unbuttoned his jacket and hung it over the back of a chair. "What about giving me a cup of coffee and some of those cookies? I've come to talk about the Christmas party tomorrow night, to remind you to show up."

Kate gave him a startled look. She had forgotten about the social that took place during Christmas week at the post. It had started when only five families lived in the community. Now there were nineteen, excluding ten bachelors who trapped for a living. Crown Crossing was a growing little village.

Jones quickly drank the coffee Kate poured him, explaining that he had to call on old lady Shrivers, who was feeling poorly. "Me and Annie and the younguns will be here around six o'clock to pick you up," he said, shrugging into his rather worn jacket. "Make sure you bundle up good."

"I will, and thank you for taking me with you and Annie." Kate followed him to the door and watched him climb onto his mule. When he lifted a hand in farewell, she quickly closed the door, shivering as she hurried to the fire. It was growing colder by the hour it seemed. She hoped that tomorrow would bring a warming trend.

I'll have to get busy with my baking, Kate thought, excitement building inside her as she warmed her front and then her backside. She and Grandmother had attended the parties each season, bringing cakes and cookies. She had enjoyed the gatherings to a degree, but her grandmother had kept her by her side all the time. Kate hadn't liked sitting with the older people, and longed to be with the young girls who chattered and laughed together and danced with the young men. Grandmother had allowed her to dance with the older married men, but the younger, single ones had stopped approaching her to ask for a dance. They had learned a long time ago that they would be refused.

Of course she wouldn't be dancing with any of the bachelors this time either. Not that she wanted to, nor did she want the gossip that would spread if she took a turn with any of them on the floor. She was married now, and her husband was off fighting in the war. She felt sure that Olive had started plenty of gossip about her and John Hunter.

Later that night, lying in bed, as she listened to the frost pop in the frozen trees, Kate's thoughts drifted to John Hunter again. What would she have said to him if the reverend hadn't interrupted?

Chapter Five

Kate discovered the next morning that the weather wasn't going to warm up as she had hoped it would. Just the opposite was true. Snow had fallen again last night, and as she trudged through the new snow to the barn to milk the cow and feed the mule and fowl, it was bitterly cold.

What would it be like tonight? she wondered later as she kneaded a large round mass of bread dough. How would she and the Jones children fare, sitting in the wagon bed, bouncing over frozen ruts, breath escaping their lips in clouds of white vapor?

Of course the preacher would have put down a thick layer of hay for them to bury themselves in, she thought as she fashioned three loaves of bread, placed them in tall pans, and shoved them into the brick oven built on one side of the fireplace. And if people dressed warmly enough, their teeth shouldn't chatter out of their heads.

"And what should I wear tonight?" she asked herself. She had two warm dresses to choose from. Both were woolen, the yarn made by her own hand at the spinning wheel, then woven into cloth at the loom.

One dress was blue, the color made from indigo roots, with white bone buttons down the front of the bodice and a white lace collar she had crocheted. The other was deep purple, the color derived from boiling pokeberry juice. It had the same adornments as the blue one except for white lace cuffs on the long sleeves. She decided to wear the purple one. The color suited her fair skin and dark brown hair, and it had a fuller skirt, which would feel nice and warm around her thighs and legs.

Would Hunter be at the party? she wondered as she gathered ingredients for a pumpkin cake. She felt a quiver of anticipation as she cracked four eggs into a bowl and then began to whip them into a frothy liquid with a long-tined fork. Everyone would be watching them, thanks to Olive Worth.

Kate knew she was well liked by her neighbors, but she also knew how much they enjoyed gossip. After all, what other entertainment did they have during the long winter months?

The cake batter was finished, and after she poured it into two cake tins she set them aside to wait their turn in the oven. Her grandmother had been known for the moist, delicious pumpkin cake and had taught Kate how to make it. It would go fast at the party.

She opened the oven door and checked the bread. The loaves had risen to double their size and were beginning to take on a light tan color. Another ten or fifteen minutes and they would be ready to put on the table to cool.

While she waited, Kate decided she had time to start some molasses candy. She quickly combined a cup of molasses and a cup of water and set them on a bed of hot coals to boil until the mixture came to a hard-ball stage. After it cooled enough to handle, she would grease her hands with butter and pull it until its color changed from brown to light yellow. Then she would roll it into long ropes and cut them into small pieces. She smiled to herself as she pictured the children fighting for the last piece.

Kate spent the entire day in the kitchen area baking things she would take to the party, then making two pies from apples she brought up from the cellar, plus one made from sweet potatoes. These last she set aside for her own Christmas dinner. She couldn't believe it when she looked out the window and saw that the sun was setting. A glance at the clock on the mantel showed the hour hand on four. The Joneses would be coming by in another couple of hours, and she had the cow to milk, the stock to feed, and eggs to gather.

She rushed about, clearing the table and putting away the items she had used in making her pastries. She then took a basket off the wall, and after lining it with a sun-bleached fustian towel carefully placed the cake, one loaf of bread, and the molasses candies inside it. After covering it all with another towel she set the wicker container down beside the door, ready to be picked up when the preacher and his family arrived.

Before bundling up for her trip to the barn, Kate put two large kettles of water on the fire to heat. Her bath would have to be a fast one, she told herself, glancing at the clock again.

At ten minutes to six Kate was dressed in her purple dress and was gazing into the tin mirror as she brushed her hair. She had washed it two days ago and the curls were tame, lying loosely on her shoulders, a perfect frame for her flawless, healthy skin and large hazel green eyes. Her cheeks were pink, flushed from the cold and being around the fire all day as she baked her goodies. Her eyes sparkled with the anticipation of seeing her neighbors after so long a time, of hearing people laughing and talking. It had been a lonely time since winter set in. She had mostly seen only Reverend Jones when he came to check up on her. And John Hunter twice, she tacked on.

The rattle of wagon wheels bumping along sent Kate hurrying for her fur-lined jacket and heavy shawl. She walked outside just as the creaking vehicle rolled to a stop in front of the porch. Greetings were called to her from behind scarves pulled across mouths and chins as the reverend reached down and took the basket from her. As she climbed into the back of the wagon she gave a tickled laugh. Annie and her five children looked like bundled-up mummies. All she could see of them were bright shiny eyes.

The moon was still a sickle shape as Kate burrowed in beside Mrs. Jones, but with the millions of stars reflecting off the white snow on the ground it was almost like daylight. As she and Annie chatted, catching up on each other, the children broke into muffled Christmas songs. Kate hadn't felt so light of heart in a long time. Jase hadn't entered her mind once. All too soon the village loomed ahead.

Judging by the number of wagons and mounts tied up among the trees behind the post, every family in the area had ridden in to attend the festivities. The preacher steered his mules as close as he could to the post's long porch and held them steady as Kate and his family scrambled to the ground, which had been cleared of snow for the ladies.

"I'll see you in a minute," he said and drove away to find a tree to tie his mules to.

The community room attached to the post was brightly lit by dozens of candles carefully placed not to be accidentally knocked over. As Kate and the Jones brood opened the door and stepped inside, cries of welcome greeted them. The older women clustered around Annie as her children rushed off to join their peers in play. Kate's young friends gathered round her, drawing her over to the corner they had been occupying. Kate wasn't aware of it, but the eyes of all the single men in the room followed her, watched her remove her shawl and jacket. She looked like a rose in the middle of a daisy patch. Everyone was envious of Jase Harrison and hoped that he would go to Olive Worth when he returned. Each was determined to court Kate then, to make her *his* wife.

Kate sat down on a bench with her friends and looked around. She wasn't surprised to see Olive standing with a group of men, tittering at some crude joke one of them had probably told. Kate knew that none of the men were careful of their language around the man-crazy Olive. According to gossip, most of them had lifted her skirts at one time or the other.

Kate released a sigh of disappointment when she saw no evidence of Hunter, nor of any of the other trappers. It was early yet though, and they could still come, but she somehow doubted it. This little get-together was too tame for them. There were no spirits to drink, no women who'd allow them any familiarities. They would prefer the company of the tavern whores, whose shrill voices she could hear through the thin walls. She couldn't help wondering if Olive wouldn't rather be in the next room also.

Feet started tapping as a fiddle and banjo began tuning up. When a tune was finally struck up, partners were grabbed and the wooden floor bounced and popped as the couples hopped and jumped all around the floor. The single men looked longingly at Kate, but none crossed the floor to ask her to dance. She was married and out of bounds to them. They silently gritted their teeth when a married man old enough to be her father swung her out among the other couples.

Outside in the shadows another man watched Kate being swept around the room. John Hunter wished he dared to walk in there and ask the beauty for a dance. Kate was too kind to refuse him, he knew, even though her reputation would be in shreds if she did. When Olive danced past the window he swore under his breath. He had promised the bitch that he would attend the party and dance with her. If he didn't keep his word, the spiteful woman would take her spleen out on Kate, whispering lies about her, bragging that Jase Harrison was coming home to her and not Kate. It would start the shameful betting all over again.

He hadn't laid any bets because he truly had no idea what Harrison would do. If the man had any brains, he would go to his beautiful wife, but Hunter had come to the conclusion that brains were not the farmer's strong suit.

Hunter stepped farther back into the shadows when the high-spirited musicians stopped for a rest after the rollicking tunes they had been playing. Some young man might decide to take his girlfriend for a walk, and they would see him peering through the window like a lovesick calf.

The male dancers, red-faced and sweating from their exertions, hurried to the cider keg to quench their thirst and cool down. The young women resumed their seats on the bench, waiting for their partners to bring them a cup of the refreshing liquid.

Kate looked down at her clasped fingers lying in her lap. If she wanted any refreshments she would have to get it herself. All her partners had been married men and had their wives to attend to.

A pair of boots appeared before her, and a young voice with a crack in it spoke. "I've brought you some cider, Miss Kate."

Kate looked up into the shy eyes of Sammy Jones, the preacher's thirteen-year-old son. "Why, thank you, Sammy, how very thoughtful of you." She smiled as she took the cup from him. "Maybe you'll dance with me later on."

Sammy blushed a bright red. "I'd like that, Miss Kate," he said. "I hope I don't step on your toes. I ain't never danced too much."

"Don't worry about that. I'll probably step on yours." They both laughed, and young Sammy strutted away. He was going to dance with the prettiest girl there.

Each of Kate's friends had their drink now, and Kate was sipping on hers when Olive sauntered over and squeezed herself in between Kate and the girl next to her. The arrogant look on Olive's face said that it made no difference to her that she wasn't welcome.

"Well, *Mrs. Harrison*," she sneered, "have you got it out of your head that your husband will be spending Christmas with you?" As Kate's breath caught in her throat and her companions gasped, Olive continued her attack. "I received a letter from Jase this mornin'. He wrote that he can't wait to get home and spend Christmas with *me*."

Red spots of anger appeared on Kate's face. How could she answer this awful woman? How could she deny Olive's words when she didn't know if they were true or not? Jase might very well have written to her. She opened her mouth to retort that she couldn't care less who her husband spent the holiday with, then snapped her mouth shut.

John Hunter had walked up to them, his face hard and cold, his eyes furious as he glared down at Olive.

"I can see from everyone's face that you're still tellin' your same old tired lies," he ground out at Olive, whose face had paled considerably. "I thought that we'd agreed you'd stop that."

"But, John, I was only visitin' with my young neighbors," Olive whined and looked at the young women to confirm her words. When no one spoke up but merely looked at her with scorn-filled eyes, Hunter grasped her wrist and jerked her to her feet.

"I want a private word with you," he growled and started walking toward the corner where everyone had stored their coats and jackets, Olive practically running to keep up with his long, angry strides.

When they reached the relatively private spot, Hunter swung Olive around to face him. Watching her with narrowed eyes he voiced a suspicion he'd had for some time. "If you speak one more lie to or about Kate Harrison, I'll let it be known that you sent that stranger to her place to attack her."

Olive's face became paper white. "I did not," she gasped in a low voice, sliding a look around the room to see if anyone had heard Hunter.

But the trapper saw the guilt on her face and gave a disbelieving grunt. "You're lyin' and we both know it."

A slyness came into Olive's pale brown eyes. "If it is true, how are you gonna prove it, John Hunter?" she challenged him.

"Very easily. I've got the man tied up in my woodshed," Hunter lied. "I'm keepin' him there until Harrison shows up. If he goes to you all on his own, without any lies from you, I'll let the stranger be on his way. But if you get hold of Jase and fill him with a bunch of lies before he can talk to his wife, I'll bring the man to the next village meetin'. When he finishes talkin', the decent people in this community will take sticks to you and drive you out of Crown Crossing."

As curious eyes watched, Hunter gave Olive a push toward the men still gathered around the cider keg. "Get over there with the men and stay there," he ordered. "Don't let me see you around Kate Harrison again." As she gave him a sullen look, he added, "I'll be outside watchin' you through the window."

When Olive had joined the men, Hunter left the big, drafty room, a grim look of satisfaction on his face. He had played a hunch and it had paid off. Olive had been behind Kate's attack. He went around the building and entered the door to the tavern part of the post. He didn't think that Olive would need watching. He felt that he had scared her enough that she would behave herself.

Also, he thought with relish, she couldn't blackmail him into sleeping with her anymore. He now had a heavier stick than she did.

And though the tavern whores came rushing up to their favorite, inviting Hunter into the back room with them, he politely turned them down and ordered a glass and a bottle of whiskey instead. He found a table in a dark corner and spent the rest of the evening staring gloomily into the whiskey, wondering why in the hell he didn't strike out for new territory. The one woman he could truly love . . . did love . . . would never be his.

When he finally stood up and staggered toward the door, he had reached a decision. He was going to Kentucky; he would spend Christmas with his brother and sister-in-law and nieces and nephews. When he reached his cabin and sprawled across his bed, he wondered how many youngsters his brother had sired just as he fell into a drunken sleep.

Kate's young friends didn't know what to say to her after Olive's outburst, so they chatted about unimportant things, but let it be known through smiles and friendly touches that they sympathized with her. Kate kept a smile pasted on her lips, although she hurt so much inside she wanted to cry. She danced to every tune that was played, many with a puffed-up Sammy, but there was a leaden weight in her chest. She wanted to sob aloud her relief when finally the party began to break up and Revered Jones signaled her it was time to leave. She said goodbye to her friends, and as she pulled on her jacket and arranged the shawl over her head and shoulders, she was told over and over to make sure that Jase brought her visiting on Christmas day.

Unshed tears shimmered in her eyes as she climbed into the wagon. It was her neighbors' way of telling her that they believed that Jase would come to her when he returned. She only wished she had the same confidence.

Annie Jones didn't bring up Olive's name as they bounced along, but she held Kate's hand all the way home. When they reached her cabin, Kate said good night and hurried inside. She threw herself across the bed, her violent sobs shaking the mattress with their force.

Chapter Six

Darkness deepened and a pale moon rose, shining weakly on the horse and rider. John Hunter had been caught in the dark before he'd been able to find adequate shelter. He had overslept this morning, due to his drunken spree, but he'd been so eager to leave Crown Crossing that he had set out for Kentucky anyway. His head ached and his hands trembled. And every hour or so he had to dismount and heave his insides out, swearing that he would never touch that rot-gut whiskey again.

And on top of his misery, he hadn't been able to find anyone who would be willing to to run his line until he returned from Kentucky.

But the stallion was moving at a fast clip and John felt sure he'd come to a settlement before long. Then the moon slid behind a cloud and stayed there as the wind died down. In the total darkness of the forest John gave the stallion his head. The animal could guide himself among the trees much better than John could guide him.

An hour later, however, when the moon moved from behind the cloud and John could see a little, he found that he was lost. The stallion had been wandering around in circles. Tired and discouraged, his head still hurting, John turned the mount around and headed him in the direction he thought was right. Half an hour later the stallion stepped in a hole and lamed himself. He could hardly walk.

John dismounted and examined the sprained and swelling joint. Midnight would be unable to carry his weight. From here on he would have to walk. But walk where? he asked himself. Perhaps he should hole up under some tree and wait for daylight. Maybe then he could find a familiar marker of some kind—a glade, a grove of trees he might recognize. At least when the sun rose he'd know in which direction to walk.

But common sense told him that he could very well freeze to death if he stopped walking in the bitter cold. He must keep moving, even if he walked in circles.

As John wearily stumbled over rocks, tree roots and rotting branches, he didn't notice when it began to snow. It wasn't until his eyebrows and lashes were covered with ice that he became aware of the changing weather.

He lifted his head to stare through the white curtain of snow. It fell straight down, huge flakes rapidly covering the old snow. "Damn," he grated out between cracked lips. He was caught in a blizzard.

John walked slowly, conserving his strength. He would need every ounce of it for his battle against nature. He was fighting for his life. For some reason he was chanting Kate's name when he saw the dim light ahead. He stopped and peered through the darkness. For a moment he was afraid his brain was playing tricks on him, that the light was just an illusion. He rubbed the snow from his lashes and saw the light more clearly. Hope gave him new strength, and he pressed on.

The yellow glow continued to beckon him, finally leading him to the bulk of a cabin. "Thank you, God," he said as he tripped on a small porch and fell against a door that stood ajar.

When Kate awakened she burrowed deeper into the feather bed until only her eyes and cold nose were visible. The winter chill had crept into the cabin, finding all the corners and frosting over the windowpanes.

From her bed she could see into the main room and the fireplace. Red glowing coals assured her that she had remembered to add wood to the fire before retiring last night.

A bleakness came into her eyes as she stared unseeing into the other room. She was surprised that she remembered anything, she had been so numb with hurt and humiliation. How could Jase cause her so much shame with her friends and neighbors? she asked herself. She could still see the glittering triumph in Olive's eyes as she bragged about the letter she had received from him yesterday, telling how he longed to see her. Hadn't he realized that the malicious woman would brag about it?

Kate wondered what Hunter had said to Olive when he dragged her away for their private talk. His firm lips and snapping eyes had said that he was furious with her. Was he, too, in love with Olive Worth? Had he been jealous of the men she had been talking to?

Whatever the trapper had said to Olive, it had dampened her high spirits somewhat. For one thing, she hadn't returned to the group of young women to continue her talk of Jase, going on and on about how much he missed her. Only occasionally did her loud laugh ring out as she danced with some man. And she had left the party early, clinging to the arm of the last man she had danced with. Brows had been lifted as the pair went through the door and into the night. The man was married, his wife at home expecting their third child any day.

The cow lowed from the barn, and Kate put Olive Worth from her mind as she gathered the courage to get out of the warm bed and make a dash for the fireplace. She threw back the thick feather comforter, shivering as she swung her legs over the side of the bed, her feet searching for her fur-lined slippers on the floor. Finding them, she grabbed up the heavy woolen robe lying across the foot of the bed and shrugged into it as she hurried into the main room.

It took but a few minutes for Kate to have a roaring fire going, bright sparks flying up the chimney. Tying the robe's belt more tightly around her small waist, she went to the window and, scratching away a patch of frost, peered outside.

"Oh dear," she whispered. "I've slept through a blizzard." More shoveling to do, she thought, dreading the chore. She couldn't remember ever having to clear away as much snow as she had this winter. The path to the barn and privy was piled waist high on either side.

Kate turned away from the window and crossed to the table, where she had to break up a skim of ice in the wooden water pail in order to fill the coffee pot. It took but a short time to add coffee grounds and place the pot on a bed of red coals to brew. That done, she went back into her room and gathered up the clothes she would wear for the day, then hurried back to the fire to change into them. A short time later a blast of cold air hit her in the face as she opened the cabin door and made a dash for the barn.

Inside the small log structure it was warm and dry, warmed from the body heat of the cow and mule. She forked some hay into the mule's feed trough, then did the same for the cow. It was while she sat on the three-legged stool coaxing the milk from the cow that the thought hit her that maybe there was a letter for her at the post. Maybe Jase had written to her also.

Kate was immediately sorry the idea of a letter from her husband had entered her mind. If indeed there was a letter from him, it would be to tell her he had made a mistake in marrying her and that he wanted his freedom.

Still, as she trudged through the snow to the cabin fifteen minutes later, the half-pail of milk steaming in the cold air, she couldn't banish the hope that a letter from Jase did wait for her, one that would finally let her know what to expect from him.

The aroma of freshly brewed coffee filled the cabin when Kate opened the door and stamped the snow off her feet on the rug put there for that purpose. When she had discarded her outer garments, she poured a mug of the strong dark liquid and sipped it as she strained the milk through the cloth kept for that purpose. She had a second cup sitting in front of the fire, her feet stretched out to its heat, debating whether or not she should make the cold trip into the post to see if a letter waited for her.

She sternly told herself to put such foolish notions out of her head as she went about making up her bed, then cleaned the ashes out of the fireplace. There would be no message from her husband at the post.

But as she decorated the tree with the bright ornaments she had brought out and examined with fond memories, her mind wouldn't give up the idea of riding to the post. For some reason, she felt sure there would be news of Jase there today. Finally, she admitted to herself that she was only killing time until Caleb Walcott opened the post for business. She knew that when the clock struck seven she would climb onto the old mule and make the two-mile ride to Crown Crossing.

An hour later Kate was calling herself all manners of a fool as a cold wind brought tears to her eyes. She'd had no idea it was so cold when she started out. Her feet felt like chunks of ice dangling in the air as the mule trudged on, breaking trail in the deep snow. Her only saddle was a folded blanket, providing no stirrups to slip her feet into.

She pulled the shawl up over her mouth, wanting to cry at her stupidity. She was making a useless trip to the post, freezing herself in the process. There would be no mail from Jase.

At last the little village lay in the distance, nestled in a small valley. Smoke rose from chimneys, drifting up to be lost among the pines and cedars surrounding the community.

Kate's heart dropped when she rode up to the post. Two other mules were tied to the hitching post fronting the long building, and the gray one belonged to the Worth family. Was Olive inside? She swung from the mule's back, bracing herself for any scathing remarks Olive would send her way.

The first person Kate saw when she pushed open the door was Olive. To her surprise, however, her old enemy hurriedly looked away when Kate stepped inside. This was so unusual, Kate's steps faltered a moment. Olive usually never lost a second to start in on her.

The other early shopper was Reverend Jones. He and Caleb called out cheery greetings to her.

"What brings you out so early in the day, Kate?" Caleb asked. "It's cold enough out there to freeze the horns off the devil."

"I've run out of coffee and sugar," Kate lied as she undid her shawl but left it to rest on her shoulders. "I have some last-minute baking to do," she added to her falsehood.

"What about the turkey you plan on roasting for Christmas?" the preacher asked, a teasing in his tone. "Have you chopped his head off yet?"

Kate looked at him and grinned. "You know I don't have the nerve to do that. Do you think your Sammy would come over this afternoon and do it for me?"

"I think Sammy would do most anything for you," the reverend laughed. "He's quite smitten. He'll be there, you can depend on it."

All the while the three had talked, Olive hadn't entered into the conversation. Kate slid her a glance from the corners of her eyes and wondered at the sullen look on her face. The older woman was very displeased about something. Kate wished again that she knew what the trapper had said to Olive. She felt that whatever had been said had involved her in some way. Why else was Olive leaving her alone?

She shrugged mentally. She didn't care what John had said to Olive as long as it kept the woman's sharp tongue off her.

Caleb was measuring out her sugar and coffee when the door opened and three neighbor women came in, exclaiming that they were near frozen and wondering if the cold snap would ever end. They greeted Kate, telling her how well she looked these days and asking if it was because her handsome husband would be home any day. Kate blushed, not knowing what to say. She stood with her back to the entrance, so she had no idea why all three suddenly stopped laughing and stared past her at a new arrival.

Kate turned and froze at the sight of Jase Harrison standing in the doorway. At last he was home! She whispered his name and started toward him. She was nearly knocked over as Olive rushed past her and threw herself into Jase's arms. Everyone, including Caleb and the preacher, gasped when Harrison held Olive close to him and kissed her hungrily.

"Hold on there just a damn minute, Jase," Caleb growled, finding his tongue, "Your wife is here. Don't you think that kiss should have been for her?"

Still keeping Olive in his arms, Jase turned cold eyes on Kate. "Do you mean the woman who has been carryin' on with John Hunter? She's no longer my wife. I'll not have that womanizer's leftovers."

He turned to Reverend Jones. "Set the marriage aside as quickly as possible."

"But, Jase," Kate cried out brokenly, "it's not true what you accuse me of. John Hunter is a friend. I've only talked to him twice in all the time you've been gone. Someone has been telling you lies."

"That's not the way I've heard it," Harrison said coldly and turned his back to her. "Come on,

Olive," he took her arm. "I'm anxious to get to my farm and see if it's been well taken care of."

When the door closed behind them, the silence was so complete it hurt the ears. Before anyone could speak, Kate dashed to the door, snatched it open, and climbed onto the mule. As she turned its head toward home, she saw Jase and Olive riding down the winding, snow-packed street, talking and laughing, holding hands. She gave the mule its head. She couldn't see through the scalding tears that ran down her cheeks. What a homecoming it had turned out to be.

Chapter Seven

John awakened to the sound of stamping hooves and a violent shivering of his body. He opened his eyes to find Midnight standing beside him in a strange room. He lay facing a window that was grimy with dirt and had two broken panes. A rag that had been stuffed into one of the panes fluttered in and out as a cold wind blew on it.

"Where in the hell am I?" he muttered out loud, then became acutely aware of stiff and sore muscles. He felt with his hands beside him and discovered that he was lying on bare ground so frozen, the cold seemed to have seeped into his bones.

He turned his head and saw the fireplace that had burned so brightly last night, guiding his footsteps here. Now there was only a black gaping hole with no sign of a fire having recently burned inside it.

The Homecoming

That's strange, he thought, and got to his feet with a painful grunt. After he had stretched, easing his sore muscles somewhat, he crossed the floor to hunker down beside the hearth. He scooped up a handful of ashes and let them drift through his fingers. They were as cold as the air that swept down the chimney. He felt the blackened ends of burned wood in the grate and frowned in troubled confusion. A fire hadn't burned in this grate for days.

John stayed where he was, staring thoughtfully at the cold remains of a fire. There was something very odd here. He'd swear a fire had burned in this fireplace last night. He could see it as plainly as he could see these dead ashes now. Its light had beckoned him, had led him here. Had some divine providence guided his footsteps to this old cabin to keep him from freezing to death, or wasn't he meant to leave Kate right now? She might be in desperate need of him.

He had never been a religious man but he strongly believed in a Supreme Being. Something told him now to forget about his visit to Kentucky and get back to Crown Crossing.

The stallion nudged John on the shoulder and he stood up. "I know you're hungry, old fellow," he said, rubbing a hand down his shiny black neck, "but there's not much I can do about it. I'm so hungry I could eat a horse." He grinned wryly. "But not you, of course," he apologized as though Midnight had understood his words.

He crossed the floor and looked out the door that had stood open all night. The sun was well up and the snow had stopped falling. He could see his and Midnight's tracks coming from the west. They had been traveling back toward Crown Crossing, but that was all right. That was where he intended to go anyway. He recognized some landmarks and grinned. He wasn't all that far from his own cabin. Maybe another five miles. Shouldering his rifle, he started out, the stallion limping along behind him.

As usual Kate was up as the first rays of the sun peeped over the eastern horizon. And though she felt empty inside, she began her usual routine, building the fire, putting on a pot of coffee to brew, heating a kettle of water to wash up in.

The sky was overcast as she walked to the barn to milk the cow and feed the stock. "It's going to snow again before the day is over," she muttered darkly, vowing it could pile up past the windows before she would pick up a shovel again.

As she picked up the stool and placed the milk pail under the cow's udder, yesterday's event was strong in her mind. She cringed, remembering her embarrassment and shame when Jase denounced her in front of everyone at the post. She could still see Olive's smug face, her pale eyes taunting her.

It serves me right, she thought. *Deep down all along I knew, but I refused to admit that it was Olive Jase loved, that he had only used dumb Kate Hesser to make his real woman jealous.* All the signs had been there. The hasty marriage without even a ring to put on her finger. And then

to ride off to the war less than an hour after the
ceremony, and not write to her once.

As all this ran through Kate's mind, her anger
grew. She told herself that she was the one who
should have had the marriage set aside. She wondered if the reverend had filled out the papers
yet. Could she ride over to his cabin and tell him
that she wanted the marriage dissolved? It would
salvage her pride a little if she could be the one
who initiated the action.

Kate gave a firm nod of her head. As soon as
she finished her chores she would ride over to
Reverend Jones, to try to beat Jase Harrison to
the punch. Let the word go out that she wasn't a
complete idiot.

A few minutes later as she changed into a fresh
dress and brushed her hair, she yawned several times. She hadn't slept well last night, and
strangely her disturbing dreams had been of John
Hunter, not Jase. John had been in some kind of
danger, calling out to her. Then John and Olive
had stood in front of her, their arms entwined,
their lips twisted in a mocking smile as Olive
gloatingly announced that John loved *her* and
that soon they would marry.

She had awakened once, crying out, "No! No!"
As she puzzled over the strange dream, it had
taken her close to an hour to fall back asleep,
only to dream again that John was in trouble, in
a dangerous situation.

When she woke up this morning, however, she
felt that John was all right, that whatever danger
he might have been in was over now.

Kate made herself some breakfast, then bundled herself up for the trip to the Jones cabin.

According to the position of the sun, John figured it was around eight o'clock when he rode into Crown Crossing. As Midnight clomped up to the post, John was surprised at the number of wagons pulled up alongside the post. Had something happened while he was gone? As he stepped up on the porch he could hear the excited voices of women inside, all talking at once. He stopped young Sammy Jones as the teen-ager was about to enter the post.

"What's all the chatter about in there?" he asked. "Sounds like a flock of hens cackling."

Sammy looked at him in surprise. "You must be the only person within twenty miles who doesn't know that Jase Harrison rode in yesterday mornin'. The store was full of people, includin' Kate, when Olive Worth flew across the room to him and he hugged and kissed her. Caleb got onto him about that, and Jase turned to Kate and said real cold like that he knew all about her foolin' around with you, and that he was havin' their marriage set aside. Told my pa to get right on drawin' up the papers."

Blinding anger at Jase Harrison and deep pity for Kate rushed through John. He didn't know which of them to seek out first. "Thanks, kid," he said and mounted Midnight again.

"I'm sorry, old fellow," he said as he lifted the reins, "but I've got to ask you to go another little distance." He was going to the Harrison farm first, to see if he could talk some sense into Jase.

John wasn't surprised to see Olive's mare saddled and waiting at the Harrison hitching post when he rode up and swung to the ground. His lips curled in a sneer. He had no doubt that she had spent the night here and was getting ready to go home.

He saw a curtain move at the window and Olive's round face peek out at him as he stepped up to the door and rapped on it. He heard a chair scrape across the floor, then the door was flung open. With a belligerent look on his face, Jase demanded, "What in the hell do you want, Hunter?"

"I want a few words with you, to set you straight about me and Kate. You've been fed a pack of lies by that whorin' bitch standing behind you. Kate is an honorable woman who wouldn't dream of being unfaithful to her husband."

"Don't give me that hogwash, John Hunter." Jase's fist clenched. "I've heard about your winnin' ways with women. You had Kate on her back before I even reached the war. You're tired of her now and you want me to take her off your hands."

"You rotten bastard," John gritted between his teeth as his knotted fist lashed out and landed squarely on Jase's mouth and chin. As Jase fell against the wall, then slid down to sit on the porch floor, John stood over him, panting, "Get

up, you low-belly copperhead, and take the beatin'
you deserve."

Stunned, Jase shook his head as though to clear
it, then stood up. "You'll never see the day you
can—" His words were cut off as the punishing fist
hit him again, this time between the eyes. Blood
streamed from his nose as he lunged at John,
taking them both off the porch to roll around in
the snow, their fists striking out at each other.

Olive stood on the edge of the porch watching
the panting, grunting pair.

John finally managed to straddle the tiring
Harrison and his fist struck the handsome face
until Jase muttered weakly, "Enough. Enough."

John heaved himself to his feet and stood looking down at the beaten man. "You fool," he said
quietly. "You've cashed in gold for a piece of
worthless red clay." He swung onto Midnight
and headed toward the Hesser cabin.

Around noon, Kate was hanging garlands of
cedar across the mantle. Maybe her life had been
turned upside down, but she would carry on, keeping the Christmas spirit the best she could.

She had arrived back home a couple hours ago.
Her trip to visit the preacher had been successful.
"No," he had said when she asked him if he had
drawn up the papers Jase had requested. "I was
hoping the fool would come to his senses and
realize that Olive had written him lies."

Kate shook her head. "I don't want a man who
is so dumb he can't see what is plain to everyone else. To my shame, I was like him for a

while, but thank God my eyes are finally open. I'm petitioning to have the marriage set aside."

"Good for you, Kate." Jones beamed at her. "I'll start on it as soon as you leave. And when it's squared away, you can start looking over the fine bunch of men who used to be eager to court you."

"I don't know, Reverend," Kate said, her eyes shadowed. "I don't know if I can trust a man again."

"You're wrong there, Kate," Jones said as he walked with her to the door. "You mustn't judge all men by Jase Harrison. He doesn't know the difference between love and lust. There's a good man out there for you, you'll see."

I don't want to see, Kate thought now as she finished hanging the cedar. She didn't know what it was like to have a man in her life, and she was in no hurry to find out. The way she felt now, she would probably remain an old maid the rest of her life.

She wished that the holidays were over, that winter would come to an end, so she could get on with her life. She could be outside once spring arrived, occupied with planting her garden, tending her flower beds, putting away food for the next winter. She would have no time to pity herself.

Kate settled down to work on the shawl she had started just before her grandmother had passed away. But after dropping several stitches she impatiently placed the half-finished garment back in the basket with the other yarn and stood up. She would pop some popcorn, string it, and add it to the tree.

She was taking the bag of corn off the shelf when she glanced out the window and saw a horse and rider approaching the cabin. Her heart gave a strange flip-flop. John Hunter. She didn't know that a shining light had jumped into her eyes as she hurried to open the door.

As John looked down at her, giving her the gentle smile reserved just for her, she said, "Come in and warm up, John."

"Should I? Aren't you afraid the neighbors will talk?"

Kate shrugged. "As you know, they are going to talk anyway."

John grinned and swung to the ground and tied the stallion to the porch railing. "You sound pretty brave today," he said, seeing the hurt deep in her eyes. "Any reason for that?" he asked, following her inside the cabin and closing the door behind him,

"I guess so," Kate answered as he took off his jacket and hung it on the back of a chair. "I went to the preacher's house this morning and told him to prepare the papers that would make me single again."

"And how do you fell about that?" John watched her face closely.

"I feel fine," she said, then cupped her hands to her face, the tears she had held back all morning rushing down her cheeks.

"Oh, honey, I'm sorry." John went to her and pulled her into his arms. "He's not worth one of your tears." He stroked her head as her tears soaked his shirt.

"I know that." Kate's words came muffled. "I guess I'm crying because I've been such a fool."

"Let them all out then, once and for all," John soothed, stroking her back now. "Cleanse your mind of the past six months."

As Kate's sobs lessened, she became aware of how nice it was to be held against John's warm body. She could feel the steady beat of his heart against her breast, and it was a good feeling, a safe feeling. Something she hadn't felt in a long time.

She realized suddenly that she was feeling a sensation she'd never felt before. Not even with Jase when he had kissed her so passionately that evening of her eighteenth birthday. It was a tingling that started in her breasts and traveled all the way to her lower body. She pulled back and stared up at John with bewildered eyes.

"What is it, honey?" John asked, wiping away her tears with his thumb.

"I don't know," she answered, stepping out of his arms. "I just felt funny for a minute there. Sit down and I'll pour some coffee."

John sat down, wondering, hoping that Kate in her innocence had felt her first stirring of desire. If that was the case, Jase Harrison had never affected her that way. There was a stirring in his own loins as Kate poured their coffee, then sliced into a pumpkin cake. Was it possible he might have a chance with this lovely girl? He was afraid to hope.

John and Kate talked and laughed and drank coffee until the bellow of the cow brought them both to look out the window. The sun was going down, dusk ready to settle in.

"My goodness," Kate exclaimed, "where has the afternoon gone? I've got to milk that poor cow."

"Can I stop by tomorrow night after I finish runnin' my traps?" John asked as they stood up. "See how you're gettin' on and all."

Kate didn't answer for a moment, then, looking up at him with twinkling eyes, she asked, "Are you saying that you want to come courting, John Hunter?"

John blushed for the first time since he was a teen-ager. He smiled his special smile. "I reckon you could say that, Kate. How do you feel about it?"

"I don't know. I have to think about it. But come, we'll see how we suit."

"I know you're gonna be leary of men for a while, Kate," John said, "and I can't fault you for that. But I swear by all that's holy, I'll never treat you the way Jase Harrison has done."

"But you courted Olive too, one whole winter. She was crazy about you, everyone said."

"Aw, honey." John stroked a finger down her cheek. "I never courted that one. I only slept with her like half the men in Crown Crossing."

As he shrugged into his jacket, John said, "I can see on your pretty face that you still have some doubts, but give me a chance. I'll put them all to rest."

"We'll see," Kate answered, and walked with

him to the door. She could see in his eyes that he wanted to kiss her but she gave him no encouragement. She would not be rushed this time. Look where haste had gotten her with Jase.

Later, as she milked the cow and then tossed hay to her and the mule, she replayed John's words in her mind. He had sounded sincere, and she found that she wanted to believe him.

Chapter Eight

The mantle clock had struck two the next day when the wind picked up and it began to snow again. As the flakes struck lightly against the windows, Kate gritted her teeth. She paced the floor. The snow made her restless. So much had fallen this winter, it would be July before it all melted.

As she passed the window she glanced outside. Young Sammy Jones was coming up the trail, the top of his head and shoulders covered with snow. He carried a rifle in one hand and a hatchet in the other. He was here to kill the turkey, and she had forgotten about his coming today. She opened the door and smiled at him. "Would you like to come inside and warm up before you take care of the turkey, Sammy? You must be near frozen."

Sammy shook his head. "I ain't cold, Kate. Which tom do you want killed?"

"Whichever one you can catch. They're all the same size. I'll set a pail of hot water on the porch for you to douse him in."

Sammy nodded and turned toward the barn. Then Kate called after him, "Pick out one to take home with you. It will be my Christmas gift to your family."

The boy turned around, a wide smile on his face. "Mom will like that," he said.

Kate closed the door and went to check the pail of water pushed up close to the coals. It was full and steaming, and after she filled her scrub bucket with water she set the pail outside the door for Sammy.

Half an hour later the boy was handing her a dressed turkey. "He's a fine-lookin' bird," he said.

"Will you come in and have some cookies and milk before you start back home?" she invited.

Sammy glanced back at the trail he'd have to follow back home. Already his tracks were beginning to fill up with snow. He looked back at Kate and answered, "I'd better not. Pa said not to linger, that this squall might turn into a blizzard and I might get lost." He grinned. "Besides, I want to get back home before the wolves start prowlin' around." He held up the turkey he had killed for his family. "They'd smell the turkey blood and be all over me to get it."

"I never thought of that," Kate said, concerned. "You must get home right away. I'll just wrap you up some cookies and you can eat them as you walk along."

Sammy, ever hungry in his growing state, thanked Kate warmly when a few moments later she handed him a cloth bag of ginger snaps. With a wave of his hand he struck off through the forest to make the mile-and-a-half trip home.

As Kate turned back into the kitchen, closing the door against the cold air that swirled into the cabin, she thought of John out in this weather and hoped there wouldn't be a blizzard. He too could become lost in the white curtain of snow.

She smiled to herself as she laid the turkey on the table. She had never before worried about a man. Come to think of it, she hadn't once worried about Jase when he was fighting in the war.

What had her feelings for Jase really been? she wondered as she took a large roasting pan from a peg on the wall. Had it been just a young girl's infatuation for a handsome older man?

A thoughtful frown creased her forehead. Could it be just infatuation with John, too? He was very attractive and even older than Jase. She hoped not, for she was beginning to have a very warm feeling for John. A feeling altogether different from what she had felt for Jase. Of course she still had to find out what, if anything, John still felt for Olive. She hoped that he got home all right and would be able to come visit her tonight. She needed to get to know him.

When Kate had placed the turkey in the roasting pan, she carried it to the cellar, where it would keep half-frozen until she was ready to stuff and roast it for Christmas dinner.

She asked herself why she should bother making a big dinner on the twenty-fifth of December. There would be no one but herself to eat it. She might just as well eat a bowl of beans and a piece of cornbread.

"Habit I guess," she muttered, climbing the open steps back up into the kitchen area. Ever since she could remember, Grandmother had followed the custom of a big dinner on Christmas. Maybe John would eat the special dinner with her.

"One must hold to tradition," she told herself.

A glance at the clock showed Kate it was time to trudge to the barn, to begin the routine she did day in and day out. In addition, this afternoon she would have to make sure the woodbox was filled and stack some logs on the porch. The blowing snow didn't look as if it was going to stop soon, and she had heard of people going out to their woodpile in a blizzard and getting turned around and lost in the thick whiteness. More than one man or woman had frozen to death within feet of their cabin.

The wind had turned into a gale when Kate returned from the barn. She braced herself against the wind, fighting her way toward the candle she had left lit in the window. When she at last reached the safety of the cabin, she prayed that John was all right in this storm, that he had finished checking his traps and was safe and snug in his little one-room cabin.

But as she strained the milk and covered it with a cloth, she couldn't shake the feeling that he was in danger. It was almost like the dream she'd had.

* * *

A strong wind blew in from the north, bringing snow with it, and John swore in disgust. "It looks like me and you are in for another blizzard, Midnight," he said through chattering teeth.

The stallion snorted as though he understood, and John wrapped his hands around his body and dropped his chin into his collar.

Because of the storm, total darkness descended early, and John gave up the thought of finishing the round of his traps. The air felt frozen in his lungs, and Midnight was growing weary of plowing through snowdrifts. He finally pulled the stallion to a halt and swung to the ground. The snow was past his knee-high moccasins as he took hold of the reins and pulled Midnight after him, leading the way by pure instinct.

His legs became like lead, his feet had no feeling, but he told himself that he must press on if he was ever to see Kate again. He couldn't see a foot in front of him, and he thought of the light that had guided him to the abandoned cabin and wished that it would appear again.

As he plodded on, praying he wasn't walking in circles, he suddenly heard a dog barking. He paused and turned his head to listen. He heard nothing for a moment, then it came again. A wide smile of thanksgiving split his nearly frozen face. He knew that long-drawn-out yowl. He had heard it for years. It was Reverend Jones's old spotted coon dog letting his discomfort be known. The preacher's cabin was a mile and a half from Kate's place. He only needed to veer to his left a bit and he'd be knocking on her door in less than an hour.

John tried to quicken his pace as he trudged along, but it was an effort to put one foot in front of the other. When he finally saw the wavering candle flames, his eyes were tired and red-rimmed from looking for it, and he was clinging to the stallion to keep from falling on his face.

The candle grew brighter, and then without warning John was almost tripping over Kate's porch. He pounded on the door with the side of his fist, calling, "Let me in, Kate, I'm almost frozen to death."

As an early dusk settled in, Kate lit a candle and put it in the window to serve as a beacon. The wind whistling around the cabin and the strong fear that John was out there somewhere in the blizzard had her nerves on edge. She made numerous trips to the window, peering through the solid whiteness, praying she would see the broad shoulders of John Hunter coming up the trail. Nothing but cedar and pine branches waving wildly in the wind met her view.

Finally she sat down and picked up her knitting. Sometimes the click of the needles was soothing to her. She had just finished making a cable stitch when she heard a step out on the porch. She stood up, the knitting falling to the floor. When a voice called, "Let me in, Kate, I'm almost frozen to death," she whispered, "Thank God, it's John."

She flung open the door and stared at what resembled a large snowman. Her voice trembling with a mixture of happiness and concern, she grabbed his arm and pulled him inside. As she helped him out of his jacket, murmuring soft, soothing words, John thought he had never seen anything as beautiful as those leaping flames in the fireplace. As he was gently pushed into the rocking chair, he had the strange urge to step inside the flames to melt the ice in his bones.

Kate knelt down and removed his soaked moccasins and pulled the wet socks off his feet. Then she jumped to her feet and poured a mug of hot coffee, added a good amount of whiskey and sugar to it, and brought it to him. When John took it from her with a thankful smile and trembling fingers, she knelt back down and began to massage his ice-cold feet, willing the blood to warm and reach his toes, praying that they weren't frozen.

John emptied the mug in two long swallows and placed it on the floor. A few seconds later he gripped the arms of the rocker, his face contorted with pain. His blood had warmed and was now circulating through his body. Each pump of his heart brought an added ache. But his toes were turning pink, and Kate thanked God that they hadn't remained white. He wouldn't lose them to frostbite.

Knowing that he must be hungry, Kate went to get a bowl from the cupboard and filled it with some of the strength-giving stew she had made for supper. She placed it on a tray with a spoon and a thick slice of bread. John's eyes thanked her as she set it in his lap, but before he started to eat, he said, "I hate to ask this of you, Kate, but would you mind taking Midnight to the barn and giving him something to eat? He's as beat as I am."

"Oh, the poor thing," Kate exclaimed and took down a loop of rope from the wall and reached for her heavy shawl. "There's plenty of stew in the pot if you want more," she said as she opened the door and stepped out into the freezing weather. She tied one end of the rope to the doorknob, then let it string out behind her as she picked up the stallion's reins and battled her way toward the barn. She could scarcely see the black shape of the building before she bumped into it and felt her way to the door. After she had tied what was left of the rope to a peg on the wall put there for that purpose, she pushed open the door and led the stallion inside. She fumbled her way to the stall next to the cow and led Midnight inside it. Then she unsaddled him, removed his bridle, and carried an armful of hay to the stall and tossed it at his feet.

She went back outside and, grabbing hold of the rope, followed it back to the cabin. Inside the warm room again, she took off the shawl and walked over to John. A smile touched her lips as she looked down on him. He was sound asleep.

He looks so different in sleep, she thought, her eyes ranging over his features, the straight nose, the firm jaw and chin. The deep lines that etched his lips, which had kissed her so gently yet so passionately, were relaxed, and his lids covered the dark eyes that looked so hard unless they were turned on her.

Suddenly she knew with certainty that she loved John Hunter with a deep and abiding love. She didn't know if she could bear it if he didn't love her back.

She stroked the black hair off his forehead and gently shook him awake. He looked up at her with sleep-filled eyes, then lifted his hands to cup her face. "My beautiful Kate," he whispered.

She smiled down at him and said, "You must get out of those wet clothes and get into bed."

John cocked an eye at her and, eyes twinkling, teased, "Get into whose bed, Kate?"

She blushed and pulled her head away. "My grandmother's, of course."

"Oh," he said, disappointment in his voice.

Kate laughed and straightened up. "It's the door left of the fireplace. Do you need anything before you retire?"

"Kate, Kate, you are an innocent," John said huskily as he rose to his feet. "I need *you*, but I'll settle for a kiss." He pulled her into his arms and kissed her with so much fever it left her reeling when he released her and went into Thelma Hesser's bedroom.

Her blood racing, her heart singing, Kate stoked the fire, then sought her own bed. As she fell asleep she told herself that John did love her. She had felt it in every fiber of his being.

The sun had just crept over the eastern horizon when Kate awakened, its early softness bathing her face and tousled hair. Curled on her

314

side, she opened her eye and blinked. John was leaning in the doorway, watching her, love in his dark eyes. She gazed back at him, hers reflecting her happiness. He swiftly crossed the room and knelt down beside the bed. Taking her small hand in his, he asked huskily, "Will you marry me, Kate?"

"Oh, John, do you mean it?" she cried, her eyes shimmering with tears.

John gathered her into his arms, whispering huskily, "I never meant anything so much in my life. I love you, Kate. I have loved you for a very long time. I just never dreamed I could have you."

"You can have me, John," Kate whispered, pulling his head down to feel his lips on hers.

John broke off the kiss and released Kate. "I'd better get out of here before I crawl into bed with you," he said, his voice shaking, "I'll stir up the fire and have a cup of coffee before I take off to run my traps."

"Oh, but you must have something to eat before you go." Kate sat up and swung her feet to the floor. She shoved her feet into her slippers and pulled on her robe. John kept his hands in his pockets as he followed her into the kitchen. Otherwise they would have reached out and grabbed her, and he was afraid he might lead her back to bed.

Kate was just placing a platter of ham and eggs on the table when Reverend Jones called to her from outside. "Oh, dear." Kate looked at John with widened eyes. "You know what he will think."

"Well, honey, we can't stop him from thinking," John said and rose from the table and opened the door at the preacher's knock.

"You're just in time for breakfast, preacher." He grinned at the frowning man. "Me and Kate were just about to dig in. Come in and share it with us."

"Since when did you become the head of this household, John Hunter?" Jones growled, looking past him at Kate still in her gown and robe.

"Since last night," John said, laughter jumping in his eyes as he helped the man of the cloth off with his heavy coat. "Kate has promised to marry me."

"You have?" The stunned man looked questioningly at Kate.

"Yes, I have," Kate answered proudly. "I feel very honored that John has asked me."

"Well, you don't have to get huffy about it," Jones said with a grin. "I think you two suit very well, even though it will be like marrying the devil to an angel."

After they all laughed at Jones's remark, Kate said, "John is no devil and I'm no angel. We're going to do just fine together."

When the two men had left, Kate went outside to do her chores and was surprised that the snow had stopped. She was so caught up with thinking about her coming marriage with John, she hadn't even looked out the window. With the outside chores done, she made up the two beds, smoothing her hand over the pillow where John's head had rested, then started mixing the bread, sage, and eggs that she would stuff the turkey with. Tomorrow was Christmas, and she wouldn't be eating alone after all. The man she loved would be sharing Christmas dinner with her. She didn't know if she could contain her happiness.

She had roast beef and baked potatoes waiting for John when he arrived at the cabin just as night was settling in. He stamped the snow off his feet and came in without knocking, the way a man of his household should. "It sure smells good in here." He smiled and pulled Kate into his arms. He kissed her so thoroughly she had to cling to him a moment after he released her.

"I'm sleeping in your bed tonight, you know." He looked deeply into her eyes, his meaning clear.

Her eyes twinkled up at him, then pouting her lips she said, "But, John, I don't want to sleep in Grandmother's bed. Her mattress is too hard."

"Well," John said, giving her a playful slap on the rear, "you'll just have to share your bed with me."

Kate sighed heavily. "I guess so. I expect I can bear it."

"Oh, you think you can bear it, do you?" John made a swipe at her again but she eluded his hand.

Neither ate much, other things being on their minds, like the big, soft bed in Kate's room.

It was shamefully early when they went there to see if Kate could bear sharing the bed with John.

* * *

The next morning Kate opened her eyes and gazed at the man sleeping beside her, the man who had made love to her so tenderly for half the night. He opened his eyes and smiled at her and said, "Merry Christmas, my love."

"Merry Christmas to you too," Kate said, smiling shyly. "How are you this morning?"

John was silent a moment, then said solemnly, "I've never felt better. I feel that at last I've come home."

CONNIE MASON
The Greatest Gift of All

*To all the incurable romantics who still believe in
the special magic of Christmas.*

Chapter One

Montana, 1855

The cabin sat snugly in the bosom of a snow-cloaked mountain, camouflaged by tall pine trees whose thick branches bowed gracefully beneath a fluffy white blanket. Huge drifts of fresh snow piled against the cabin and the howling wind whistled eerily through the treetops. Six feet away from the hearth, where the children sat reading before the fire, Jenny Montgomery shivered as she stared out the window into the swirling storm, thinking that the haunting beauty of the Montana landscape caught in the throes of a winter blizzard was deceptive and lethal.

Turning from the window, Jenny brushed a wisp of rich chestnut hair away from her thin face and secured it firmly to the prim bun at the back of her head. Her hair was severely skinned back, her small face appeared pinched and drawn, and her jewel-like green eyes were dull and lusterless. During this joyous holiday season Jenny should have been happily anticipating the sharing of festivities with her small family, but nothing could be further from the truth.

Jenny Montgomery had never felt more alone or been so consumed with bitterness.

"Mama, Luke won't pay attention," eight-year-old Annie complained. Small and serious, her expressive face was screwed up into a frown. "I'm trying to read him a story, but all he wants to do is play with that little wooden horse Papa made him."

Jenny knew without being told that blonde, blue-eyed Annie was far too solemn for her meager years, but tragedy affected children in different ways. Five-year-old Luke worked out his frustrations by being naughty and deliberately disobedient, while serious-minded Annie became quiet and somber.

"I've heard that story before," Luke said, sticking his tongue out at his sister. "I want to play outside."

Jenny directed her gaze out the window. Nothing had changed in the past few minutes except that it had grown darker. Large, fluffy flakes of snow were still being pounded to earth by the shrieking wind, and the trees surrounding the house were bent nearly double. Venturing into the storm was tantamount to suicide.

"It's much too cold, darling," Jenny said, trying to maintain a reasonable tone. It was difficult after being trapped in the small house for days on end with two fretful children.

Suddenly an arrested look came over Annie's face as she directed her gaze out the window. "It's not too cold for St. Nicholas, is it, Mama? His sleigh can travel over snow, and he never freezes because he knows exactly the right kind of clothing to wear," she explained to Luke who had snapped to attention the moment St. Nicholas's name was mentioned.

"How many times must I tell you," Jenny snapped irritably, unable to bear the children's hopeful expressions. "There is no St. Nicholas, and if there were he most definitely would not be coming here."

Luke's chin trembled as his serious gray eyes regarded his sister, waiting for her to contradict Jenny. Annie patted Luke's head, sending Jenny a baleful glance. "Of course there's a St. Nicholas, Luke. Mama says mean things sometimes because she misses Papa. You'll see, St. Nicholas will come Christmas Eve, just like he did when Papa was alive."

Oh, God, Jenny thought despairingly. She was only twenty-seven years old and already so damn bitter and cynical her children thought her an ogre. And Christmas was the worst time of all. It had been a year ago Christmas Eve that Evan Gillespie had arrived on her doorstep with the devastating news that her husband, Lucas, had drowned in the Republican River on a trail drive to Abilene.

Lucas had learned about the drive when he

went into town one day over eighteen months ago and heard that Evan Gillespie was hiring men to drive his cattle to the railhead in Abilene. Usually content with trapping animals for their hides during the winter months and riding herd for a nearby rancher during the summer, Lucas had become excited about the prospect of driving an entire herd of cattle from Montana to Kansas. For days he talked of nothing but the generous pay Evan was offering intrepid cowboys willing to brave the hardships of a long, arduous trail drive.

Though he made a good living at trapping, Lucas had wanted one more chance to explore his wild side before age caught up with him. They had been married so young that the responsibilities of parenthood, which had come hard on the heels of marriage, had taken their toll on Lucas. In the end no amount of pleading from Jenny had swayed Lucas's decision to join the trail drive. He had departed in April, leaving her and the children all the money they had in the world, promising to return by Christmas.

Lucas never kept his promise. Evan Gillespie had informed her that Lucas had been buried beside the river after they found his body. Evan had paid Jenny the amount Lucas would have earned had he completed the drive, which she thought was quite generous of him, and she and the children had learned to live without a man in the house. She hadn't cried, not once. How could she mourn a man who had left his family for such selfish reasons? Every day Jenny grew more embittered, more cynical, more withdrawn, until she no longer recognized herself as the happy, carefree woman who had married Lucas Montgomery.

The approach of Christmas brought a painful reminder of that terrible day when Evan Gillespie had arrived at her door.

"Is it true, Mama, will St. Nicholas be here on Christmas Eve like Annie says?" Luke asked hopefully. He wanted to believe. He *needed* to believe.

"There's no money for such foolishness," Jenny said harshly. Why must she be the one to dash the children's hopes and dreams? she asked herself bitterly. What must she do to make them believe there was no magic in Christmas?

"You're wrong, Mama," Annie said with such quiet conviction it left Jenny shaken. "You'll see, Mama, Christmas is a magic time. St. Nicholas will come and you won't have to marry Mr. Gillespie."

"What do you know about Evan?" Jenny asked sharply. Her perceptive daughter never ceased to amaze her.

"I know he wants you to be a mama to his five children. Luke and I don't want to share you, Mama. Why are you even thinking of marrying Mr. Gillespie?"

Jenny sank down beside Annie, cradling her small face in her hands. "You're old enough to understand what I'm going to tell you, Annie, so is your brother. The truth is, I don't know how long we can go on like this. Our money is nearly gone, and I'm not half as good a trapper as your papa was. Mr. Gillespie has asked me to marry him. We'll have a home, and you'll have lots of brothers and sisters to play with."

"Do you love him?" Annie asked with the innocence of an eight-year-old.

"We're not talking about love, darling, we're talking about survival. I'll be a good mother to his children, and he has pledged to be good to us. I've promised to give him my answer after Christmas."

"I don't like Mr. Gillespie," Luke announced in a petulant voice. "He called me a runt. I can't help it if I'm small, Mama. One day I'll be as big as Papa was."

"Of course you will, darling," Jenny said, hugging him tightly. She knew she didn't demonstrate her love often enough these days and gave him an extra squeeze. "Mr. Gillespie was merely comparing you to his sons, who are all big for their ages. We owe him a great deal. If he hadn't sent one of his men over to chop wood for us, I don't know what we would have done."

Suddenly a particularly ferocious gust of wind rattled the windows, and Luke leaped to his feet, his face radiant. "It's St. Nicholas, Mama!"

"Christmas is a whole week away," Jenny reminded him gently.

Luke's face fell as he reluctantly turned away from the window and sank back down to the floor beside his sister. Patting Luke's hand consolingly, Annie picked up the book and continued reading. Half listening, Luke played with the wooden horse, now and again turning to stare out the window.

An air of expectancy hung in the air; even Jenny felt it. It permeated the isolated cabin like a haunting melody and made the children edgy. Jenny turned her thoughts from the children to Evan Gillespie, the man who had offered her a way out of her dilemma. The possibility that she'd be little more than a drudge once she married Evan had occurred to her. Evan was basically a good man, but there was nothing soft or sentimental about him. He had never given her the slightest impression that he cared for her romantically or wanted her for any reason other than to be a mother for his children.

The only reason she had even considered Evan's rather sterile proposal was for the children's sake. Lord knew what would happen to them if she didn't marry again. Few opportunities existed on the Western frontier for a penniless widow with two children to raise. After Christmas was over she'd give Evan his answer. If she was fortunate, he wouldn't be too demanding a husband. If she was *very* fortunate, in time they'd learn to regard one another with fondness.

Darkness fell over the land; the only light for miles around shone like a beacon through the cabin windows. Driving snow pelted the windows and blew in beneath the door, leaving a little pile just inside the jamb. Close to the hearth the room was warm and toasty, but six feet away Jenny's expelled breath hung in the air like a ghostly mist. She shivered and moved closer to the fire. Pulling a chair up to the hearth, she perched gingerly on the edge, glancing uneasily toward the barred door.

Hairs stood up on the back of her neck, and an unexplained disquiet settled over her. Suddenly Annie stopped reading, and Luke grew watchful, the wooden horse forgotten for a moment. The pounding on the door was anticlimactic. Both children looked at Jenny, who seemed frozen to the spot.

"Someone's at the door, Mama," Annie said as the pounding grew louder. "Do you suppose it's Mr. Gillespie?"

Jenny's face cleared instantly. "Of course, but why Evan would venture out on a night like this is beyond me. Perhaps one of the children is sick," she added as she rose quickly and hurried to the door. It took several minutes to lift the bar, and when she did, the door flew open from the force of the howling wind. Jenny stepped back in alarm as a huge, snow-encrusted figure staggered over the threshold.

The man was shrouded in white, from the top of his fur hat to the tips of his booted feet, on which were strapped snowshoes. His beard and eyebrows were frosted with snow and ice, and his face was red from exposure to the elements. He carried a large pack over one shoulder, stuffed to overflowing. To Annie and Luke, seeing this man here at this time of the year, appearing like magic, was no coincidence.

Annie's face assumed an "I told you so" expression, but it was Luke who whooped with joy and shouted, "It's St. Nicholas! He's come!"

The man's face crinkled in a smile, cracking the frosty crust around his eyes and mouth. With great care he heaved the pack from his shoulder and set it beside the door. Then he took two giant steps into the room and made a slow spiral to the floor, collapsing before the hearth with a thud.

"What's wrong with St. Nicholas, Mama?" Luke wailed as he dropped to his haunches before the fallen man.

An icy draft whipped under Jenny's dress, chilling her legs and reminding her that the door was still gaping open. It took all of her strength to shove the door shut against the persistent wind. Only when the door was shut and barred did she attempt to answer Luke's question.

"Don't be ridiculous, Luke, there is no St. Nicholas!" Her patience was wearing thin. "I don't know who this man is, but there is nothing magic or special about him."

"You're wrong, Mama," Annie said. "The Christ Child was born on Christmas Day; it *is* a magical time." Her steady gaze rested solemnly on the unconscious stranger. "St. Nicholas came to us because we needed him."

Just then the man stirred, groaned, and opened his eyes. The heat of the fire had begun to melt the snow and frost covering his beard and eyebrows, and Jenny saw that his hair was as black as midnight and his eyes a deep, penetrating blue. He looked up at her and grinned, revealing a deep dimple in his left cheek. Mesmerized, Jenny smiled back, the first genuine smile she'd given in months.

The stranger, rising to his elbows, searched Jenny's face with an intensity that made her breathless and slightly giddy. His gaze diverted briefly to the children, who were squatting beside him with an air of anticipation, then returned to Jenny.

"Hello, Jenny." His voice was deep, raspy, and slightly breathless, as if the act of breathing was painful.

Jenny recoiled in horror. How could this man know her name when she'd never set eyes on him before? "Who are you? What do you want? How do you know my name?"

"Is it Christmas yet?" He was wheezing now, every breath an agony.

Taken aback, Jenny wagged her head in a negative motion.

"Thank God, I lost track of time these past weeks."

"Who are you?" Jenny repeated on a rising note of panic.

"You're beautiful."

"You're delirious," Jenny said ruefully. She wasn't beautiful, far from it. At one time she might have been considered pretty, but life on the Western frontier was difficult for a woman. She knew she was painfully thin, her face gaunt and aged beyond her years. Since Lucas's death she had done little to enhance her appearance. "I'm going to ask you one more time, stranger. Who are you?"

"My name is Nick. Nick St.—"

That's all Luke needed to hear. Leaping to his feet, he began jumping up and down, his eyes dancing merrily. "I told you! It *is* St. Nicholas! It *is* St. Nicholas!"

"Hush up, Luke," Jenny warned as she glared at the stranger in rapt confusion. Let Mr.—Mr.—Nick continue. Go on, mister, what did you say your name was?"

"Nick. Nick St. Clare."

"I don't care what he says," Luke announced stubbornly, "I *know* he's St. Nicholas."

Annie merely smiled. Though her youthful expression held all the wisdom of the universe, she remained uncharacteristically silent.

Chapter Two

Nick St. Clare gazed bemusedly at Luke. It was the first time in his life he'd ever been mistaken for St. Nicholas. But he could understand the lad's mistake. He supposed he was so encrusted with ice and snow his best friend wouldn't recognize him. Besides, it was rather flattering to be mistaken for St. Nicholas.

Jenny stared in consternation at Nick St. Clare. His beard and eyebrows were beginning to thaw, and she was concerned over his flushed face. He was wheezing deeply, his chest heaving as he fought to fill his lungs with painful puffs of air. When he began to cough, she realized that he was a very sick man.

"Take Mr. St. Clare's snowshoes off, children," Jenny said crisply as she took charge in her usual no-nonsense manner. Questions could come later. The man was probably wet to the skin, chilled to the bone, and on the verge of pneumonia.

"I can manage," Nick said as he sat up to assist the children.

"Let me help you with your jacket," Jenny said, noticing that a puddle was beginning to gather beneath him. Before he could protest, she had the sheepskin jacket stripped from his broad shoulders and hung by the hearth to dry. When she turned back to him, she was startled to find him staring at her with an intensity that left her confused and shaken. Who was this man and what did he want with her?

"Can you stand, Mr. St. Clare? We've just finished supper, but there is plenty left over."

Nick struggled to gain his feet. Jenny stood aside, becoming alarmed when he finally uncoiled his lean length and began swaying from side to side. When he started to fall, she rushed forward to steady him.

"What's wrong with St. Nicholas, Mama?" Luke asked.

Gnashing her teeth in frustration, Jenny bent Luke a quelling look. "*Mr. St. Clare,*" she stressed, "is ill. Help me get him to your bedroom. He can use Annie's bed, and Annie can bunk in with me."

Nick tried to protest, but a sudden bout of coughing rendered him so weak he meekly allowed Jenny and the children to assist him to the bedroom. The room was barely large enough for two single bunks, and when Nick stretched full length on Annie's bed his feet hung over the end. Both children began to giggle, but a stern look from Jenny brought their mirth to a halt.

Jenny bent to light the lamp. "Make Mr. St. Clare a cup of tea, Annie," she instructed. "And Luke, see if you can get his boots off. I don't want him dirtying up the bed."

"I don't want to be a bother," Nick gasped between paroxysms of coughing. "I hadn't expected to be caught out in a blizzard, and the hike from town through drifting snow took longer than I expected."

"You walked from town?" Jenny asked, astounded. "In this kind of weather? It's over ten miles; you must be mad."

"I had no choice. I didn't think my horse would make it through the snow drifts. I left him at the livery and hiked out here on snowshoes."

While they talked, Luke had managed to pull off Nick's boots and one by one they hit the floor with a thud.

"Go help Annie with the tea," Jenny said when he looked at her expectantly. She wanted to question Nick St. Clare without the children in attendance. The man didn't look or act menacing, but one never knew in this day and age. He appeared to have come with a definite purpose in mind, and she needed to know that purpose before he regained his full strength. She was alone, without a man to protect her, and she had to think of the children.

Jenny studied him through watchful eyes. He had pulled off his fur cap, revealing a full head of shiny black hair badly in need of cutting. It curled in thick unruly strands just above his collar. His deep blue eyes were watching her, the intensity of his gaze sending a shock shuddering through her. For the first time since Lucas's death Jenny became aware of another man's physical attributes.

Nick St. Clare was a handsome devil with the rugged good looks of an outdoorsman accustomed to vigorous daily exercise. Even beneath his heavy clothing she could see that his muscles were well developed, his body trim, his shoulders enormous. Every well-honed inch of him exuded power and strength. Unaccountably her eyes were drawn to his hands. They were huge, rough, and callused—and oddly erotic. Startled to find her thoughts taking her on a journey she hadn't traveled in a long time, she forced her mind onto more practical matters.

Just then Annie came into the room carrying a mug of tea, which she offered to Nick with a tremulous smile. Luke stood beside his sister, staring at Nick in awe.

"Mama said you wouldn't come this Christmas," he said in a small voice. "But Annie and I knew you wouldn't forget us. We just didn't expect you so early. Christmas isn't until next week. Are you lost?"

Disconcerted, Nick took a swallow of tea. It burned all the way down and his raw throat constricted painfully. "St. Nicholas never forgets anyone," he responded hoarsely, neither admitting nor denying he was the mythical St. Nicholas. "Christmas is a magical time."

Jenny glared at Nick furiously. How dare he encourage their belief in a silly legend! "Mr. St. Clare is too sick to talk right now, children," she said evenly. "There is still time before bed to work on your lessons. I'll be there to help you as soon as I see that Mr. St. Clare is made comfortable."

Reluctantly the children left the room. Annie lingered in the doorway a moment, turning her serious little face toward Nick. "I don't care if you're not really St. Nicholas. Children like Luke need to believe in something."

"Oh, God," Jenny groaned, burying her face in her hands. When had her small daughter become so wise? Or so solemn?

Nick frowned. "What have you done to Annie to make her so serious?" he asked with a hint of censure.

Jenny's restraint flew out the window. "Who in blazes are you? What do you want? You have no business coming here like this and disrupting my family."

By now Nick's voice was so hoarse his words were reduced to a low whisper. "I'm fulfilling a promise."

"A promise to whom?" Jenny asked suspiciously.

"To your late husband."

Jenny rocked back on her heels, stunned. "You knew Lucas? Funny, he never mentioned you."

"We met on the trail drive," Nick rasped. "We struck up a friendship immediately. He must have had a premonition of death, because shortly before he drowned he made me promise to make sure that you and the children were all right if something happened to him. I always keep my promises."

Jenny snorted derisively. "You've taken your own sweet time, Mr. St. Clare. It's been over a year since Lucas's death."

Nick's flushed face grew even redder. "I know, and it couldn't be helped. It took longer than expected to work my way back to Montana. I broke my leg on the trail and was laid up for months. And then I did some trapping in the mountains on my way here. But I always meant to keep that promise to Lucas. He loved you and the children very much, you know. He told me so much about you that I felt—well, let's just say I knew you in my heart and in my mind long before I met you. Lucas told me you were beautiful."

Jenny gave a cynical hoot. "Then you must have been disappointed when you finally saw me. And if Lucas really loved us he wouldn't have left us to fend for ourselves while he went off chasing a rainbow."

Nick went into a fit of coughing, reminding Jenny that he was a very sick man. Bustling into action, she left the room and returned a few minutes later with an old woolen robe that had once belonged to Lucas. "Get out of those wet clothes, Mr. St. Clare," she ordered crisply. "And get under the covers as soon as you're undressed. Put on Lucas's old robe, it's patched but warm. I'll heat something for you to eat. We'll discuss your reason for being here later. Right now I think a good night's sleep is in order. But be forewarned, there's a loaded shotgun beside my bed and I know how to use it."

Nick managed a weak smile. "I mean you no harm, Jenny. I'm merely fulfilling a promise to Lucas. I'll move on as soon as I'm able."

Jenny searched Nick's face, failing to find anything threatening in his words or expression. Though his eyes were bright with fever, she was satisfied that he spoke the truth. Turning abruptly, she left the room.

Nick stared after Jenny, his expression thoughtful. All that glorious chestnut hair Lucas had described so accurately had been skinned back from her face into a tight bun, pulling the skin so taut that her cheekbones stood out in stark relief. Though her skin was flawless, it was so pale and translucent he could see tiny blue veins beneath the surface. Purple smudges marred the delicate flesh beneath her incredible green eyes, making her appear vulnerable and so fragile he could break her in two with one hand. She was thin, but still shapely enough to make her desirable in every way. And despite her denial, she *was* beautiful, although the rusty black dress she wore didn't do her justice.

Lucas Montgomery had spoken about his family so often Nick felt that he knew them intimately. Jenny became the model on which he had built his dreams for the future. Annie and Luke were the children he hoped to have one day. Nick suspected that Lucas had regretted leaving Jenny and the children for his one last ride on the wild side. Personally, Nick couldn't conceive of leaving a loving family, had he been fortunate enough to possess one. But at thirty-three years of age Nick had begun to think that he wasn't meant to enjoy a wife and family. He was a drifter, a saddle tramp who earned his living riding herd and busting broncos.

When he first met Lucas he had envied the man his wife and family. Lucas's death had placed Nick in an awkward position. Lord knew he'd intended to keep his promise to Lucas, but he couldn't help wishing it was his own family he was going home to. This last year had been a nightmare. First Lucas's death, then his own accident, which laid him up for months. Then he was robbed of his money while he was laid up and had to spend precious time earning enough to get him back to Montana.

While Jenny was preparing something for him to eat, Nick slipped out of his wet clothes and donned the wool robe she had given him. He had just settled back into bed when the children slipped unnoticed into his room. They stood in the doorway staring at him, until he happened to look up and see them. He motioned them closer. When they stood beside the bed, Nick reached out and caressed Annie's smooth cheek. "Except for the color of your hair and eyes you look just like your mother." His voice sounded like sandpaper rasping across wood.

Luke nudged Annie aside. "Why is your beard black instead of white?"

Nick looked startled, then his lips parted in a smile.

"Luke," Annie chided with a hint of exasperation, "you ask too many questions. St. Nicholas can make his hair and beard any color he wants."

Luke assumed a thoughtful expression, then seemed to accept his sister's explanation. "Is your bag filled with presents for us?"

"Luke!" Annie said, aghast. "Don't be greedy. There are other children besides us expecting gifts."

"I'm sorry," Luke said, distressed. "I didn't—"

"Children, what are you doing in here?" Jenny had returned with Nick's dinner, appalled to find the children in serious conversation at his bedside. "Please don't bother Mr. St. Clare with your nonsensical talk about St. Nicholas. Christmas is the time of the Christ Child's birth, nothing more."

"They're not bothering me, Jenny," Nick rasped. He didn't feel comfortable addressing her more formally as Mrs. Montgomery for he felt as if he had known her all of his life.

"Nevertheless, they are becoming quite annoying with all their talk about St. Nicholas and gifts. They're old enough to realize there is no St. Nicholas and Christmas has no magic to it."

Nick was stunned. When had Jenny become so cynical and hard? Didn't she realize that when children stopped believing they ceased to be children? When he was a child, Christmas was just another day filled with drudgery and despair. He was only eight when his parents were killed in an Indian raid, and he had gone to live with an uncle who used him like a slave until he was old enough to run away. He recalled listening to other children discuss Christmas and the gifts St. Nicholas would bring them, and he had vowed that when he married and had children of his own he would keep alive the dream as long as he could. He couldn't believe that Jenny was openly discouraging her children from treating Christmas as a special time.

"Get ready for bed, children," she added tersely. "If Mr. St. Clare is better tomorrow, you may visit with him."

Dutifully the children filed out of the room. Jenny pulled a small table up to the bed and set the tray on it. "It's just venison stew but it's nourishing."

"It smells wonderful. I know you're a good cook, Lucas told me."

"What else did he tell you?" Jenny asked, growing annoyed. She would never be able to look Nick in the eye if Lucas had told a complete stranger about the more intimate side of their relationship, which had always been warm and passionate.

Nick knew when to retreat. "Only that you were a wonderful wife and mother."

The tenseness left Jenny's body. "If I was so wonderful, why did he leave?"

"Partly for the money and partly for the adventure, I reckon." She handed him the spoon and he lifted a spoonful of stew to his mouth, almost too exhausted to chew. He took two more bites, then gave up. "I'm sorry, I'm not as hungry as I thought." He fell back against the pillow and closed his eyes. A lock of ebony hair fell over one eye, and Jenny had an uncontrollable urge to smooth it away from his forehead. Her hand had actually begun to move toward his face when he opened his eyes. She drew it back instantly.

"I have some medicine I always rub on the children's chest when they have colds. I'll go fetch it." She turned abruptly, before Nick could see the softness that had turned her eyes a luminous green.

When she returned, Nick was sleeping. She almost turned around and left, but he was wheezing so badly she decided he needed the medicine she had brought him. Perching on the edge of the bed, she carefully opened the upper part of the robe and smeared a glob of wintergreen ointment across the broad expanse of his chest. The moment her hand touched his burning flesh, his eyes flew open. He grasped her wrist, stilling her hand. If she touched him again he didn't think he could stand it.

"Thank you, but I can do that myself."

Jenny nodded, drawing her hand away. The strength of his grip surprised her, and she felt the vibrations all the way to her shoulder.

Chapter Three

By early the next morning the snowfall had diminished, but deceptive layers of ominous gray clouds still hung over the mountains, shrouding the jagged crests and threatening to spill more snow. Nick awoke slowly, startled to find himself snug in bed beneath a feather tick. He hadn't known such comfort in more months than he cared to remember, even if his feet did extend over the end of the bed. Outside the covers the air was bitter cold, and Nick realized that the fire in the hearth had gone out during the night.

He tried to rise, thinking that the least he could do to repay Jenny for the care she'd given him since he'd arrived so unexpectedly in the middle of a blizzard was to build a fire. Still ravaged by fever and chills, punctuated by intermittent bouts of coughing, he found the effort to get out of bed more taxing than he'd imagined. A frustrated groan slipped past his lips. He wasn't the kind to indulge himself and he hated the helpless feeling that came with illness. He tried again to push himself from the bed.

"What do you think you're doing?"

Turning his head sharply, Nick was startled to see Jenny rising fully clothed from the mountain of covers on the bunk adjacent to the one he was occupying. Had she slept there all night? he wondered.

"I was going to kindle the fire," Nick rasped. The sandpaper hoarseness of his voice had improved little during the night.

"Lie still, Mr. St. Clare. You'll keel over if you attempt to get up now, and you're much too heavy for me to lift."

"I'm sorry," Nick apologized. "It's not like me to be ill. I feel so helpless."

"I'm sure you'll be up and around in a day or two, Mr. St. Clare," Jenny assured him. She stood beside him now, bending over to settle the tick more closely around his shoulders.

"I'd like it if you called me Nick," he said. He found himself staring at the back of her neck where the prim bun had become dislodged during the night, releasing strands of chestnut hair. They tumbled around her narrow shoulders in lustrous disarray, captivating Nick. He inhaled sharply, wondering why in the devil she hid all that glorious hair in a tight bun when it added nothing to her natural beauty. It was as if she were deliberately trying to deny the soft womanly part of her. Had

Lucas's death done that to her? he wondered curiously.

Nick felt acutely the hurt and rejection that Jenny must have felt when her husband joined the long trail drive to Kansas. Being left alone in so isolated a spot with two active children to support had to have been a bitter pill to swallow, he reasoned. Learning that Lucas would never be coming back must have destroyed her hopes for the future.

With a start Jenny realized that Nick was staring at her hair, and her hand flew up to rearrange the unruly mass that had become dislodged from its confines. "I should kindle the fire before the children get up," she said, flustered by his rapt regard. "Stay in bed, Mr.—Nick. I'll bring your breakfast. There's a—a chamber pot under the bed," she added, blushing.

Nick watched her leave, forgetting to ask why she had slept in the bunk beside him last night. He heard her moving around in the other room and wished he felt well enough to take some of the burden from her instead of adding to it. When she returned with his breakfast, Nick had taken care of his needs and was sitting up in bed. Annie and Luke trotted in behind her.

"See, I told you St. Nicholas was still here!" Luke crowed delightedly. "Will you show us what's in your pack now, St. Nicholas?"

"How are you this morning, St. Nicholas?" Annie asked gravely. "You'll have to excuse my brother, he's very young."

Nick made a serious effort not to laugh at the prim little miss. "Much better, thank you. Your mother is a wonderful nurse. Let's keep the contents of my pack a secret until Christmas," he added cryptically.

Jenny frowned, deliberately turning the conversation in a different direction. "I hope you can eat something." She set the tray on his lap. "There's porridge and tea and biscuits. Our sugar is gone, but there's plenty of honey."

"Thank you." Nick saw that she had changed her wrinkled black dress for another of the same color. Black definitely wasn't her color. With the alabaster paleness of her skin, she needed something more vibrant and colorful to bring out the incredible green of her eyes. She had also combed her hair, drawing the shining curtain into orderly primness at the nape of her neck.

"Can we stay and talk to St. Nicholas?" Luke asked as Nick began to eat.

"How many times must I tell you, his name is Mr. St. Clare," Jenny said crossly. "Let him eat in peace." She started to herd them from the room.

"Let them stay," Nick argued. "I've never had much truck with children and I enjoy them."

Jenny looked skeptical but caved in under the children's pleading looks. "Very well, but don't tire Mr. St. Clare. And don't talk his ears off."

"Mama doesn't mean to be cross with us," Annie said defensively. A forlorn sadness settled over her small features. "She can't help it. I don't think she really wants to marry Mr. Gillespie."

"Who?" Nick asked sharply. "I assume you're referring to Evan Gillespie, the rancher whose cattle your father and I drove to Kansas. I understand he's a wealthy man. What makes you think your mother is thinking about marrying him?"

"She told us," Luke offered. "Mr. Gillespie needs a mother for his children, and Mama says he'll take care of us. He's a widow."

"A widower," Annie corrected.

"What do you children think about having Evan Gillespie for a stepfather?"

"I don't like him," Luke said sullenly. "If you're St. Nicholas, why can't you find us a papa who will love us? If you'd do that, I promise not to be disappointed if you forgot to bring the sled I asked for. And I'm sure Annie would rather have a new papa than a baby doll with glass eyes and real hair."

Luke's words nearly tore Nick's heart apart. He remembered himself as an unwanted, overworked lad whose childhood had had no bright moments. "Maybe your mother loves Mr. Gillespie," Nick suggested.

"I don't think so," Annie returned. "She said love had nothing to do with her marrying Mr. Gillespie. She's to give him her answer after Christmas. But don't tell Mama I told you, she'd be mad."

"Trust me, Annie, I'll keep your secret."

Just then Jenny returned with a basin of water, soap, towel and razor. "Run along, children. I suspect Mr. St. Clare would like to clean up. If you bundle up you can go outside and carry in some firewood from the shed. We're nearly out,

347

and another storm appears to be brewing over the mountains."

Once the children were out of the room, Jenny rounded on Nick. "What kind of secrets were you sharing with my children?"

"Nothing important, just kid stuff," he hedged, unwilling to violate the children's trust.

"They're quite fanciful," Jenny continued, "as you well know. All this nonsense about St. Nicholas has gone too far. I believe another talk with them is in order. They just don't seem to understand that there will be no Christmas this year. I had hoped there'd be enough money to buy yarn and knit them warm hats and mittens, but even that proved impossible."

The stubborn angle of her jaw was clenched so tight that a muscle twitched convulsively beneath the fine skin of her pale cheek.

"It's difficult to disabuse children of their hopes and dreams," Nick said quietly.

"What about my hopes and dreams?" Jenny cried, forgetting that she was spilling her heart out to a man she barely knew.

"Perhaps St. Nicholas will bring you your heart's desire," Nick suggested.

"Bah!" Jenny said with a look of censor. "You're as bad as the children. I've learned the hard way to expect nothing out of life. Fantasies are a luxury common folk can't afford. I suggest you gain your strength as quickly as possible, Mr. St. Clare, for the sooner you leave, the sooner the children will curb their imagination and settle down." Spinning abruptly on her heel, she left the room.

Nick stared after her, acutely aware of what his promise to Lucas Montgomery was going to cost him. How could he leave Jenny and her children when they seemed to need him so desperately? He hoped it wasn't too late to save Jenny from a disastrous marriage and her children from a bleak existence with an uncaring stepfather.

A nap later that afternoon helped Nick regain some of his lost strength. By evening his body had shaken off the fever, and he left the bed to sit before the fire with the children. Never having had a real home—at least not one he could remember—Nick savored the closeness of the family. Annie read to him from a book of Christmas tales while Luke rested against his knee. Jenny had pulled a chair close to the fire so she could attend to her mending in the flickering light.

When Jenny happened to glance over at Nick she found him regarding her with undisguised interest. Tiny flames from the fire reflected in the luminous blue depths of his eyes, and a thrill of hot excitement rushed through her. She looked away quickly, before her eyes betrayed the utter confusion his unexpected presence in her home had wrought in her.

The next day Nick arose early and kindled the fire. Glancing out the window, he saw the faint glimmer of sun just rising over the mountains. He looked for coffee in the cupboard but found only a small amount of tea.

"What are you looking for?"

"Coffee. I prefer it to tea."

"I used the last of the coffee a month ago."

"It hasn't been easy for you, has it?"

"We've managed. Things will get better soon."

Her words hinted at her decision to marry Evan Gillespie, and Nick felt compelled to ask, "Are you referring to your marriage to Evan Gillespie?"

An astonished expression slowly disintegrated into one of fury. "What have the children told you? What gives you the right to interfere in my life? I'm doing what's best for my children."

"Can't you see what you're doing to the children? You're condemning them to live with a man who will never love them as he does his own children. You might be content to live without love, but the children deserve better."

"What makes you such an expert on love, Mr. St. Clare?" Jenny bit out, chagrined that he saw through her so easily. "Have you never heard of companionship? Does respect and warm regard mean nothing to you? I married for love once, and look what it got me."

"Two wonderful children," Nick said wryly. "I seriously doubt that companionship and regard will warm your bed at night."

Jenny puffed up indignantly. How dare Nick St. Clare criticize her? "If you were a gentleman you wouldn't discuss matters of such a personal nature. Besides, it's my life, and if I prefer a comfortable life for my children to frivolous fantasies of love, it's my business."

"I'm no gentleman, Jenny," Nick drawled in a voice that sent a shiver down her spine. The intensity of his gaze probed her deeply, delving past the beauty she tried so desperately to camouflage into her very soul. Had he known how empty her heart was, he wouldn't bother to interfere where he wasn't wanted, Jenny reflected as she returned his steady regard.

"Mama, St. Nicholas, only three more days till Christmas!" Luke shrieked as he danced into the room.

"For heaven's sake, Luke, if you don't stop calling Mr. St. Clare St. Nicholas I'm going to smack you!"

Stricken, Luke halted in his tracks. His little chin quivered and his eyes grew luminous with unshed tears. Turning on his heel, he ran back into the bedroom. Annie appeared a few minutes later, looking even more solemn than usual. She gave Nick a passing glance, then fixed her mother with a baleful look.

"Don't look at me like that, Annie," Jenny scolded sternly. "If you must blame anyone, blame your father for leaving us the way he did."

"Papa is dead," Annie said in a tremulous voice. "But we're alive. What can it hurt if Luke believes that Mr. St. Clare is St. Nicholas? Why are you being so mean, Mama?" Her shoulders slumped dejectedly, Annie turned and followed her brother into the bedroom.

"Oh, God," Jenny sobbed, burying her face in her hands. "What have I done? I love my children. I wouldn't hurt them for the world."

The sight of Jenny, her slim shoulders bent under the terrible burden she had borne these past months, tugged at Nick's heartstrings. With a need born of the deepest longing, he drew her

Connie Mason

into his arms, soothing her as he would one of her children. "Go ahead and cry, Jenny. I suspect it's just what you need. You've carried the burden of your husband's death inside you too long. Let it come out now and cleanse you of your grief. You're no longer alone. I'm here to help you."

Suddenly Jenny pulled away, her face contorted in furious denial. "I don't need you to console me, Nick St. Clare! I don't even know you. You show up out of nowhere and expect me to believe you were a friend of my husband, but how do I know you're telling the truth?"

"Why would I lie?"

"How do I know? There are many reasons for a man to lie. Turning up on my doorstep at Christmas doesn't make you St. Nicholas. A child like Luke might believe in miracles, but I'm too practical to believe you were sent here for a purpose."

"I've never pretended to be other than what I am. But I *have* come with a purpose in mind, Jenny Montgomery. I wanted you to know that someone besides your husband cared for you. And according to the children, I arrived in the nick of time. You can't marry Evan Gillespie. You'd be wasted on a man like him. I know him. He's a thoroughly passionless man, while you, Jenny, are a beautiful woman of fire and passion."

Jenny gave a derisive hoot. "Look closely, Nick. Do I look like a beautiful woman? Do I look like a woman with the kind of passion you just described? If you were honest with yourself you'd see me for what I am. A mean-spirited, downright plain woman devoid of passion and utterly lacking in fire. Now if you'll excuse me, I'm going to see if I can make peace with the children."

You're wrong, Jenny Montgomery, Nick thought as he watched Jenny walk away. *You're vibrant and beautiful, and somewhere in that slim body of yours is a spark of passion just waiting to be ignited. Some day,* he solemnly pledged, *some day I'm going to release you from your passionless existence.*

And you are most definitely not going to marry Evan Gillespie!

Chapter Four

When a weak sun filtered through the clouds later that afternoon, Nick suggested that the children dress warmly and help him carry firewood inside. Squeals of delight filled the small cabin as the children rushed to find their warmest wraps.

"Was that wise?" Jenny asked testily. "You're still not fully recovered from your illness."

"I'm not going to let a sniffle keep me in bed. I'm accustomed to being outside in all kinds of weather."

"It was more than a little sniffle and you know it, Nick St. Clare," Jenny declared. "You're still wheezing."

One corner of Nick's full lips curved upward in a lazy grin. "I didn't think you cared, sweet Jenny."

Flustered, Jenny's heart began pounding and her skin felt too tight for her body. She said the first thing that came to her mind. "I suppose I'm accustomed to ordering the children around and coddling them when they're ill."

"I don't mind at all," Nick said. "Coddle me all you want."

"We're ready, St. Nicholas!" Luke said, appearing before Nick encased in so many layers of clothing he was barely recognizable. Annie joined him, similarly bundled against the bitter cold.

"I'll be with you in a moment," Nick said, reaching for his sheepskin jacket. Turning to Jenny, he asked, "Do you have a shovel? I'll probably have to clear a path to the shed."

"It's sitting beside the door," Jenny answered as she watched him pull his fur cap down over his ears and don a thick pair of gloves. "Would you like an extra pair of stockings? I still have most all of Lucas's things." He nodded his head, and she hurried off to get them.

An icy wind blew in through the open door as Nick and the children trooped out into the cold. Jenny watched from the window as they carried wood from the shed and piled it beside the back door where it could be easily reached. When the task was done, the children began romping in the snow, making snowballs and throwing them at each other. Jenny was astounded when Nick joined them in their play. When they tired of the game, Nick taught them how to make snow angels in the snow, and while they made row upon row of angels he began rolling snow to build a snowman. At that point Jenny turned away, deciding to use the last of the canned milk and cocoa to make hot chocolate.

Jenny set a pot of fresh snow to melt over the hearth, gathered the milk and cocoa, and sat down to wait for the pot to boil. As so often happened these past few days since Nick's arrival, her thoughts strayed to the rugged cowboy who had blown into her life with the storm, leaving an impression on her and the children that would be difficult to forget after he was gone. And he *would* leave, Jenny thought with an acute sense of loss. She felt certain Nick St. Clare had had a specific purpose in coming to Montana. She just didn't know yet what that purpose was.

Sometimes Nick looked at her as if he wanted to devour her, and at other times his searching glances seemed to puzzle him as much as they did her. What did he want from her? More importantly, what did she want from him? Had he really turned up on her doorstep merely to fulfill a promise he had made to Lucas? Her musings came to an abrupt halt when Nick and the children burst through the back door, laughter on their lips, their noses red from the cold, their clothing crusted with ice and snow. Nick's beard was no longer black, and to Jenny's dismay he actually *did* look like St. Nicholas.

"What's that I smell, Mama?" Luke asked, sniffing the chocolate in the air.

Giving her head a vigorous shake, Jenny fought to dispel the picture of the way Nick had looked the first time she had seen him, his clothing and hair frosted with white and carrying a pack over his shoulder. Though she was curious, she had no idea what was inside the pack, which still sat undisturbed beside the door.

"I've fixed you all some hot cocoa. Hang your wraps beside the door to dry and come sit by the fire. You must be frozen."

"St. Nicholas taught us how to make snow angels," Annie said with more animation than she'd displayed in over a year.

Jenny frowned, still uncomfortable hearing the children refer to Nick, a virtual stranger, as St. Nicholas. It sounded to Jenny as if they were conferring some magical power on the man. She couldn't help but wonder what would happen when Nick moved on. Men like Nick St. Clare seldom stayed around long. Why did he have to drop into their lives now and give them all false hope? Or was it just the Christmas season that was making her *feel* again? She had existed so long in the numb void of hopeless despair that it had become a way of life.

"And we built a snowman," Luke added excitedly. "Nick says tomorrow we'll cut a Christmas tree. But you have to come with us."

A Christmas tree! Jenny had no intention of erecting a Christmas tree, and the children knew it. She gave Nick an austere look. "There will be no Christmas tree," she said slowly and firmly. "Until you came, the children knew there would be no Christmas this year. You disrupted our lives the moment you walked through the door. Drink your cocoa, children. It will be the last for a long time to come. Until after the wedding and we move into Mr. Gillespie's house."

Disheartened, the children sipped their cocoa in silence while Jenny moved away to check on the dough she had set to rising. For years she'd baked bread in a small oven Lucas had built over the hearth, and she recalled that he had promised to buy her a real cook stove when he returned from the trail drive. Nick followed her, his face set in angry lines.

"Why do you do that to them?" he asked. His voice was low and tense, as if he were trying to understand her and failing.

"Why does anyone do what they do?" Jenny bit out crossly. "You should have consulted me before you told the children they could cut a Christmas tree."

"Do you have something against Christmas trees?"

"No!" Jenny hissed angrily. "Just against Christmas. And men who show up on my doorstep pretending to be St. Nicholas."

"I'll be moving on in a few days."

Jenny searched his face, but his expression remained purposely bland. "You don't have to tell me that. It's obvious you're not the kind to stick around for long."

"All that could change, Jenny. It's up to you. I've never felt so content in my life as I have these past few days with you and the children. You've opened up a whole new way of life to me, one I've only dreamed about. A man could make a good living here, hunting and trapping and selling prime pelts. The land would even support a small herd of cattle should a man be so inclined."

"Please, don't, don't say things you don't mean. I'm going to marry Evan Gillespie. I've as good as given my promise. You don't even know me. I'm cold and hard and bitter. You heard the way I rounded on the children a few minutes ago, refusing to allow a Christmas tree in the house. Even my own husband didn't find many redeeming qualities in me, or he wouldn't have left me to chase a bunch of cows across the prairie."

"I never would have left you, Jenny. And I don't believe for a minute that you're as heartless as you pretend. Or as hard. If the children weren't here, I'd kiss you right now and prove there's a softness in you. You can deny it all you want, but I know it's there, hidden beneath that shapeless black dress."

His eyes lingered on her lips; she felt them tingle and burn beneath the explosive heat of his gaze. "Don't look at me like that."

"I'm going to keep looking at you like this until you relent and allow the children to have a tree."

"There are no decorations."

"Do you have popcorn?" She nodded. "There seems to be an abundance of holly growing in the woods, with beautiful red berries. And pine cones. We'll improvise."

"Do you always get your way?" Jenny said in a low voice.

Nick flashed another of those devastating smiles. "Almost always. Do you want to tell them or should I?"

Jenny chose to tell them herself.

*   *   *

The next day dawned cold and clear. A perfect day to chop down a Christmas tree. The children gobbled their breakfast in record time, then waited impatiently for Nick. To their consternation, Nick plopped himself in a chair and refused to move unless Jenny came with them. After much cajoling and wheedling, Jenny grudgingly consented. Nick's wide brow furrowed into a frown when she tugged on an old threadbare jacket that had once belonged to Lucas.

"Have you no coat of your own?"

"This will do just fine," Jenny said, clamping her lips tightly shut. Didn't he realize that growing children needed new clothing from time to time? Her own well-being came after that of her children. There was simply no money to waste on herself.

Nick must have realized her predicament, for he dropped the subject. But when he noticed that she had no proper footgear for the snow, he solved the problem in his own way. When the four of them trooped out into the cold air, he retrieved the ax from the shed and handed it to Luke. Then he swung Jenny off her feet and carried her into the nearby woods.

Finding herself riding in Nick's strong arms, Jenny squealed in protest. "Nick St. Clare, put me down! I'm perfectly capable of walking."

"Not in those shoes," Nick growled, scarcely aware of her slight weight. The children, delighted by Nick's shenanigans, danced playfully around them.

"St. Nicholas is carrying Mama!" Luke shrieked in pure joy.

His enthusiasm was catching, for Annie joined him, chanting, "St. Nicholas is carrying Mama! St. Nicholas is carrying Mama."

Despite Jenny's protests, Nick carried her easily to a stand of thick pine trees a few hundred feet into the woods, where he sat her down on the snow-dusted limb of a fallen tree.

"Well, Jenny, look around and tell me which tree it will be," Nick said, motioning toward the literally hundreds of trees on the side of the hill. "Just keep in mind that we have to drag the tree back to the house and it has to fit inside the cabin."

Jenny's lovely features assumed a thoughtful expression as she pretended to examine each and every tree. How wonderful it was to join in the children's games, she reflected happily. She hadn't felt this carefree in longer than she cared to remember.

"That one," she declared, pointing to a rather lofty pine whose huge trunk was thickly branched.

Nick gave it a rather doubtful, measuring look. He was almost certain it wouldn't fit inside the cabin. But if it was the one Jenny wanted, then Jenny would have it. He took the ax from Luke and brought his arms back to deliver the first blow.

"Wait! It's all wrong. That's not the tree I want after all." Nick heaved a sigh of relief. He had no idea how they would get it back to the cabin once it was felled. "Over there, see that little tree at the foot of the hill?" Though it wasn't the tree Nick would have chosen, he moved to comply. Once again he heaved the ax over his shoulder.

"Are you sure?" he asked. Jenny nodded happily. Nick picked the place on the trunk where he planned on landing the first blow, but once again Jenny stopped him. Groaning in frustration, Nick asked, "What's wrong now?"

"I've changed my mind," Jenny said pertly. "I think the children should choose."

Whooping with joy, the children scampered off, flitting in and out of the trees until they were out of sight. Nick rested the ax against a tree trunk and sat beside Jenny on the fallen limb. "This is apt to take a long time. Are you cold?"

"A little," Jenny admitted. Large fluffy flakes of snow began filtering down from the mountains. "I can't imagine a more beautiful place to live," she said, lifting her face to the snow. At that moment, Nick decided he couldn't imagine a more beautiful woman.

"Perhaps this will help keep you warm," he said, sliding an arm around her shoulders and pulling her against him. She stiffened, then relaxed, as if realizing that protesting would serve little purpose. Nick usually managed to have his way. "Better?"

Jenny didn't trust herself to answer. Being so close to Nick was a sobering experience. She not only felt warm, but safe and protected. She wanted to lay her head on his shoulder and let him take care of her forever.

"You're much too thin."

"What?"

"Your bones are so frail I could easily crush them beneath my hands. You should eat more." His eyes lingered on her face with an undeniable hunger. "You have a radiant beauty few women possess. Your bones are so fragile and your skin so transparent I'm afraid to touch you without causing you injury. Your lips—" A tormented groan slipped past his lips. "My God, I want to kiss you!"

Jenny sucked in a great gulp of air, realizing that she *wanted* to be kissed by Nick, yet fearing what his kiss would do to her. The choice was taken from her when Nick bent his head and kissed her gently, his lips barely brushing hers. The feeling was exquisite. Her head rested against his chest; she could hear the strong beat of his heart as he kissed her. It matched the pulsing rhythm of her own. She drew back to look at him, her eyes wary, and their gazes met in a rare moment of mutual understanding.

Nick bent to her, claiming her lips again. He moved slowly, carefully, aware of the fragile thread binding them and unwilling to break it. The kiss was soft and tender, and Jenny trembled with the suggestion of restrained passion behind that gentle kiss. She sensed that Nick would be a fierce lover, holding back nothing of himself, demanding everything in return.

The world as she knew it ceased to exist as Nick's mouth plundered hers with gentle insistence. She wanted to melt into him, to feel him invade and surround her, to feel herself become a part of someone as vital and alive as Nick St. Clare. His arms tightened, and a small moan slipped past her lips. When the hot moistness of his tongue prodded her lips apart, Jenny tried to refuse him entrance, but he was so eager to taste her sweet nectar he wouldn't tolerate her refusal. Then his tongue was exploring the soft sweetness of her mouth, and Jenny felt a tugging ache begin somewhere inside her.

"Look, Annie, St. Nicholas is kissing Mama!"

Hearing Luke's startled cry, Nick broke off the kiss instantly. But there was no guilt visible in the blue depths of his eyes or in the lopsided grin he gave the children as they ran up to join them.

Annie made no comment, merely staring at them with round eyes. But there was no censure in her guileless gaze. Quite the contrary. If anything, Annie's expression was one of supreme smugness.

Of the four of them, Jenny appeared the most flustered. Her face was flushed, her eyes sparkled, and her cheeks were reddened, and not just from cold. At a loss for words, she looked to Nick for help.

A deep chuckle rumbled from Nick's chest but he gallantly complied. "Did you find a tree, Luke?"

Luke was far too inquisitive to drop the subject. "Why were you kissing Mama, St. Nicholas?"

Jenny groaned.

Annie giggled.

Nick's eyes twinkled mischievously as he answered Luke's question. "I kissed your mama because she looked like she needed kissing."

Jenny's groan grew louder.

Annie's giggle erupted into a belly laugh.

Luke's candid gaze searched Jenny's face for several tense minutes before he announced rather grandly, "She *does* look like she needed kissing." Having come to that momentous conclusion, he quickly lost interest in the subject. Grasping Nick's hand, he said, "Hurry, St. Nicholas, Annie and I have found the perfect tree."

Chapter Five

The tree the children had chosen was indeed perfect. It was nearly six feet tall, with thickly needled branches spreading out in perfect symmetry. Nick placed it in the shed to allow the thick coating of ice and snow to melt before setting it up and decorating it the next day—Christmas Eve. The children were so excited at the prospect that for once they offered no protest when bedtime arrived. Suddenly uncomfortable being alone with Nick, Jenny, pleading exhaustion, excused herself and would have escaped into her bedroom if Nick hadn't placed a restraining hand on her arm.

"Don't go yet, Jenny, it's still early."

"I—I'm tired. There's so much to do tomorrow. Since there are no gifts for the children, the least I can do is scrape together a decent meal."

"I never figured you for a coward, Jenny Montgomery."

A spark of defiance flared to life in the green

depths of Jenny's eyes. "I'm not a coward and you know it!"

"Prove it," Nick argued. "Stay here and talk to me."

"We've nothing to talk about."

"I think we have. Let's begin with Evan Gillespie. Do you love him? I've not seen him at your door once since I've arrived. You'd think a man about to be married would care how his fiancée was faring during the worst storm of the year. And what about Christmas gifts? Your children will soon be his children if you carry through with this marriage. Why hasn't he acknowledged them with gifts? Or at least sent treats to make the holiday more enjoyable?"

"You don't understand," Jenny said, clinging to the remnants of her pride. "Evan has his own children to provide for during the holidays. Since we're not yet married, there is no need for him to pamper mine with gifts. All that will come later, after we're one family."

"I asked you if you loved Evan Gillespie. You haven't answered."

"Evan is a good man," Jenny temporized.

"That's not what I asked."

"Why should you care? Once you leave here there will be no reason for you to be concerned about us."

"You're wrong, Jenny Montgomery. I'll never forget you or Annie or Luke." He dropped down on the rug before the fire, taking her hand and pulling her down beside him. "And I won't leave unless you tell me to."

367

Jenny looked stunned. "You can't stay here. It isn't right. You're a drifter. Drifters don't settle anywhere for long. Besides, what will people say?"

"Haven't you figured it out yet? Did our kiss this afternoon mean nothing to you? I adopted you and the children as my family long before I met you. Long before Lucas's death. Yes, dammit, I envied Lucas, but I never wished his death. At first I felt guilty that he was dead and I was alive. Why should God spare my worthless life in that raging river when Lucas had so much to live for?

"When I finally arrived on your doorstep after so many delays, I knew the moment I saw you and the children that God works in mysterious ways. He delayed my arrival until Christmastime for a purpose. If you can't figure it out for yourself, I'm not going to explain."

"I was doing just fine until you arrived," Jenny insisted, tilting her chin at a stubborn angle.

"The children would disagree. Bitterness, hostility, and resentment don't suit you. And marrying a man you don't love will only produce more bitterness and resentment."

"You don't understand a damn thing, Nick St. Clare! If I don't marry Evan, the children and I won't last another six months. I'll do anything to keep them safe and protected. What would you have me do?"

"You could marry me," Nick said earnestly.

Stunned, Jenny laughed harshly. "How long would you stay before moving on? A week?

A month? A year? One fantasy in a lifetime is enough. The children already believe you're St. Nicholas, and fortunately they expect you to move on after Christmas. They need permanence in their lives, not fantasy. Evan can give them the stability they deserve."

"Children need love," Nick persisted. "What do you need, sweet Jenny? When you decide, I want to be the one to fulfill that need."

"I don't need you, Nick St. Clare!" Jenny cried. "You're too much like Lucas."

"If that's how you really feel, then I reckon I'll be moving on soon," Nick said with a hint of regret.

"Perhaps that's best for all concerned," Jenny agreed, leaping to her feet. She ran into the bedroom before Nick knew what she intended. The slamming of the door sounded so final he sat in stunned silence, wanting desperately to go after her and kiss her and kiss her until she realized that he was nothing like Lucas. It wasn't as if he didn't have dreams the same as Lucas. His problem was that all his dreams revolved around Jenny and the children. And maybe one day, children of their own. But he realized that Jenny was in no mood to listen to him. Life had dealt her a bitter blow, and she was too beset by the cruel realities of life to admit that he and she had been attracted to each another from the very beginning.

"Is Mama mad at you?" a small voice behind Nick asked. "What did you do to her? She's crying."

Turning abruptly, Nick saw Annie blinking down at him, rubbing sleep from her eyes. Evidently Jenny hadn't seen her daughter slip out of the bed they'd been sharing since Nick's arrival. Annie looked so innocent and vulnerable standing in her patched flannel nightgown, her pink little toes sticking out from the bottom, that Nick wanted to protect that innocence forever.

"I didn't do anything, sweetheart."

"She cries a lot at night," Annie revealed, "but she doesn't know that we hear her. She thinks we're sleeping. I don't think she really wants to marry Mr. Gillespie."

"I won't let her marry him," Nick said with such resounding vigor that Annie was inclined to believe him.

Annie smiled and slid onto Nick's lap, resting her head against his chest. "You *must* be St. Nicholas," she sighed happily.

Nick stared into the dancing flames, thinking hard. Holding Annie close to his heart, he finally arrived at a decision. When Annie's even breathing told him that she had fallen asleep, he carried her into the room she normally shared with her brother. Pulling the blanket up to her chin and kissing the top of her blonde head, he tiptoed from the room.

When he returned to the main room of the cabin, he fed enough wood to the fire to keep it going till morning, then dressed in his warmest clothes. Before he quietly let himself out the door he picked up his pack and slung it over his shoulder. Once outside he slipped his booted feet into the snowshoes propped beside the door. The moon was a bright silver ball riding high in the sky, illuminating Nick's path as he started off toward town.

Jenny stirred restlessly, missing the slight weight of Annie's warm body beside her. She frowned, then came fully awake, aware that something was amiss. Throwing the covers aside, she leaped from bed. The cold floor beneath her feet made her toes tingle, but she paid them no heed. Going to the children's room, she dragged in a sigh of relief when she saw Annie blissfully asleep in her own bed. Nick was nowhere in sight. Returning to the main room, she found the fire burning brightly enough to see that the room was empty.

At first Jenny thought Nick had merely gone outside to relieve himself. Then her eyes fell on the empty corner made conspicuous by the absence of his pack. Abruptly she recalled Nick's last words to her tonight. He had said it was time he moved on. He must have been terribly upset with her to leave in the middle of the night without telling the children goodbye. What was she going to tell them when they awoke in the morning and found Nick gone? she wondered bleakly. Why did she feel more alone than she had ever felt in her life? Not since that day a year ago when Evan Gillespie told her Lucas was never coming back had she felt so utterly bereft.

Her feet were like two chunks of ice when she returned to bed, but she hardly felt them for the frost in her heart. In the few short days since

Nick's arrival the hard core of ice in her heart had begun to thaw. Suddenly she had the stupid notion that Nick St. Clare really *was* St. Nicholas. Looking back on it, his arrival had wrought a tremendous change in their lives. If he hadn't come when he did she would have robbed the children of the joy of celebrating Christmas. Before his arrival she had been on the road to becoming someone she no longer recognized, her zest for life buried beneath layers of bitterness and indifference. Nick St. Clare had left a legacy, one she'd remember for the rest of her days.

He had shown her that it wasn't a sin to feel again, that she deserved to live life to the fullest. So did the children. And if she never found anyone to love her, she at least had the children. Somehow they would survive. Even if she decided not to marry Evan Gillespie.

Despite logic, Jenny couldn't deny the twinge of resentment she felt at Nick's desertion. He had accused her of acting like a coward, yet he was as much a coward as she. He had left like a thief in the dead of night, thus avoiding sentimental goodbyes. Before sleep claimed Jenny, she recalled their earlier conversation. Nick had asked her to marry him, and for the life of her she didn't know why she hadn't taken him seriously.

"Where is St. Nicholas, Mama?" Luke asked as he padded into the main room the next morning. "I hope he hasn't forgotten that we're supposed to decorate the tree today."

Jenny bit her lip, aware of how Nick's desertion on Christmas Eve was going to affect the children's enjoyment of Christmas.

"This is Christmas Eve," Jenny said brightly. "There are other children expecting St. Nicholas tonight. He couldn't remain here indefinitely."

Annie emerged from the bedroom behind Luke. Her face grew thoughtful when she realized that Nick's pack was missing from its usual place. "Is St. Nicholas coming back?"

Jenny felt like crying. How could she tell the children that Nick was never coming back and it was probably her fault? They had grown to love Nick in the short time they had known him, but she didn't have enough trust to believe in him. All she could see was a man who was footloose and fancy free, one who would leave when the notion struck him, just as Lucas had done.

The children were looking at her expectantly, waiting for her reply. "I'm certain Nick won't be coming back," she said softly.

Luke's face fell and Annie looked so devastated that Jenny felt like a destroyer of dreams.

"I don't believe you!" Luke cried, pulling away as Jenny tried to comfort him. "What did you do to him? He never would have left if you hadn't sent him away." Turning abruptly, he ran into the bedroom, sobbing.

Jenny made to follow, but Annie's question stopped her dead in her tracks. "Did you want St. Nicholas to leave?" Her face was so solemn it nearly broke Jenny's heart.

"The real St. Nicholas exists only in our hearts," Jenny explained carefully. How could she make

Annie understand that Nick's leaving was for the best? "Nick St. Clare came to us at a time when we needed something to believe in. He gave us Christmas, but he couldn't do more than that. Even if I didn't want Nick to go, I knew that one day he would leave. It was inevitable."

"I knew you didn't want him to go!" Annie crowed triumphantly. "Last night St. Nicholas told me he wouldn't let you marry Mr. Gillespie."

Jenny frowned. "Last night? When exactly did he tell you that?"

"After you went to bed. I heard you crying and it woke me up. You didn't hear me get out of bed. St. Nicholas was sitting by the fire and we talked. That's when he said he wouldn't let you marry Mr. Gillespie. I must have fallen asleep in his lap and he carried me back to bed."

"Nick had no right to make such a promise. And perhaps I won't marry Evan," Jenny admitted, "but it won't be because of Nick. It will be because ultimately I must do what's best for you and Luke. Nick is gone and we just have to accept that. Now, sweet, let's go in and comfort your brother."

There was little that Jenny could do to comfort Luke. The child was truly inconsolable. It was like losing Lucas all over again for all of them. Jenny feared Christmas would be a miserable affair after all.

Later that morning when Jenny suggested that they decorate the tree, her words were met with indifference. The children seemed to have lost the lively spirit of Christmas that had prevailed from the moment Nick came into their lives. Nevertheless, Jenny carried the tree inside, set it on the stand Nick had made, and popped a huge kettle of popcorn. Then she brought in the bucket of red holly berries they had collected on their outing the day before and provided the children with thread and needles. They were sitting at the kitchen table listlessly stringing popcorn when Evan Gillespie arrived.

His arrival created a flurry of excitement, until the children saw that it was only Evan Gillespie.

"Evan, how nice of you to come," Jenny said, offering her cheek for his cool kiss.

"I wanted to make certain that you weathered the storm without difficulty," Evan said as he stepped into the house.

"Say hello to Mr. Gillespie, children," Jenny said when she noted their keen disappointment. Dutifully they responded.

"Hello, children," Evan replied shortly. "I can't stay long, Jenny, I must join my children, we're going to decorate our Christmas tree today. Their list of gifts is nearly endless and I've still got a lot to do. I thought it would be appropriate if you and your family joined us for dinner tomorrow. Cook has prepared a large turkey, and you all could get to know one another. I'll come for you in the morning."

Suddenly Luke perked up. "We can't leave, Mama. What if St. Nicholas comes back?"

Evan frowned. "What's this nonsense about St. Nicholas? All my children were told at an early age that fairy tales belong in story books."

Connie Mason

Jenny stared at Evan, comparing his slight, stooped frame with Nick's rugged strength. In his late forties, Evan Gillespie was a nondescript man with graying sandy hair and opaque blue eyes. He was an astute businessman and prosperous rancher who provided well for his five motherless children. But he didn't have a sentimental bone in his body—or a sense of humor—or compassion. Nick's compelling magnetism attracted Jenny, while Evan's cool and proper reserve left her cold. The thought of going to bed with him repelled her.

"I see no harm in believing in St. Nicholas," Jenny replied evenly. Then she said something that made the children giggle. "For a short time I believed in him myself."

"Yes, well," Evan said dismissively, "you always were rather fanciful, my dear. About tomorrow, should I come after you and the children in the sleigh? I've asked my younger children to wrap some of their castoff toys to place under the tree for Luke and Annie. We can't have them going back home empty-handed. And since they aren't accustomed to receiving costly gifts they should be quite happy."

Evan wasn't a deliberately cruel man, just a thoughtless one, Jenny thought. She could see the years stretching before them, her children existing on the crumbs of Evan's affection and his children's castoffs. It wasn't a pretty picture. She looked over at Luke and Annie, saw their bleak expressions, and realized there was only one answer she could give Evan.

"The children and I would like to spend Christmas alone, Evan, but thank you for asking us to join your family."

"You'll be a part of our family soon," he reminded her.

"I don't know how to tell you this, Evan, except to come right out and say that I don't think marriage between us will work. Though you've done me a great honor by asking, I fear I must refuse."

Evan looked thunderstruck, but he wasn't one to press an issue. Marrying Jenny would have been advantageous to both of them. She was a wonderful mother and housekeeper, but he had been without a wife for so long he was more annoyed than disappointed.

"I'm sorry to hear that, Jenny," he said, shrugging. "I proposed because I felt it was in the best interests of both our families. I hope you know what you're doing."

Jenny smiled. "You're a good man, Evan, but not the right one for me. This is the first thing I've done right since Lucas's death. The children and I will manage somehow."

Chapter Six

Somehow the Christmas tree got decorated, but the children's hearts weren't in it. The spirit of Christmas had disappeared with Nick St. Clare. The popcorn was strung, the berries were threaded, and Jenny had even baked cookies in honor of the occasion. She found it difficult to believe that until Nick had shown up to point out the error of her ways, she had actually tried to deprive the children of an important holiday like Christmas.

If for no other reason, the religious aspect of the day deserved to be celebrated by every God-fearing family. There might not be toys or new clothing to unwrap, but they still could read the story of the Nativity from the Bible. The reading had been a ritual in the family from the time the children were old enough to understand, narrated by Lucas before the fire on Christmas Eve.

By mid-afternoon heavy gray clouds hung ominously low over the mountains, threatening to unleash another storm by nightfall. Luke was restive and cranky, while Annie seemed to have drawn further into herself. Both children strayed to the window from time to time, gazing pensively at the snow-shrouded hillside. Jenny realized they were looking for Nick and couldn't bring herself to scold them for harboring hope where none existed.

But when Annie approached the window for the fifth time in an hour, Jenny's patience, which had been stretched thin, finally snapped. "Nick is not coming back, Annie. When will you learn to stop living in a dream world?"

"He'll be here, Mama." She said it with such firm conviction that Jenny nearly believed her. Beneath her breath she cursed Nick for leaving the way he did, and herself for not having the sense to admit to him that she wanted him to stay.

For the first time that day Luke's little face grew radiant. "Do you really think so, Annie? Do you know why St. Nicholas left?"

"I don't know," Annie declared resolutely, "but he must have had a good reason. He'll tell us when he comes back."

"That's enough!" Jenny cried, clapping her hands over her ears. "I don't want to hear another word about Nick St. Clare. You're both driving me crazy with your peering out the window every few minutes. Go to your room. If you must wear a path to the window, do it in your bedroom."

When the children walked out of the room, their shoulders stooped, heads hung low, Jenny hid her face in her hands and collapsed into a chair. "Oh, God," she sobbed aloud, "what have I done? What have *you* done, Nick St. Clare?" How could he have made such a lasting impression on the children in such a short time? she wondered with almost desperate yearning. He had blown into their cloistered, dreary lives with the winter storm and withdrawn so abruptly that his leaving had created a dismal void in their lives.

At least Nick had brought her out of the apathy that had settled around her after Lucas's death, she thought, mentally summing up his credits. Ultimately the children would benefit, for she now realized that before Nick's arrival she had become a mean-spirited shrew. And he had shown her that Evan Gillespie wasn't the answer to her problem. Perhaps there was no answer, she reasoned, and she'd be forced to sell the cabin, move to town, and take employment, if any existed for a young widow with two children.

Having given herself sufficient time to recover from her annoyance with the children, Jenny rearranged her face into a smile and prepared to go to them and mend fences. But they burst out of the bedroom before she could rise from the chair. Their faces were radiant, their motions more animated than she had seen them all day. Normally staid Annie was jumping up and down, while Luke was literally exploding with excitement.

"He's here, Mama! He's come back!" Luke shouted, pulling on Jenny's arm as he led her toward the window.

"I told you so!" Annie cried with smug satisfaction.

"What in the world are you two shouting about?" Jenny asked, fearing the children had lost their grip on reality.

"St. Nicholas, of course," Luke explained with the lack of patience one would expect of a five-year-old. "He returned with a sleigh, and it's loaded with packages. Do you suppose all those gifts are for us?"

"Of course they're for us, silly," Annie said with the supreme arrogance of an older sister. "He didn't know we were watching and hid them in the shed, Mama," Annie continued, regarding Jenny with shining eyes. "He's probably there right now seeing to his horse. Can we ride in the sleigh, Mama?"

Jenny groaned aloud. Not only were the children imagining things, they were seeing things too. "I've scolded you before for being fanciful," she said sternly, "but this time you've outdone yourselves. I don't want to punish you, children, but if you continue with this farce, I'll be forced to it. I've relented and agreed to celebrate Christmas for your sakes, but there is no money for gifts. What we will celebrate is the birth of the Christ Child."

Annie's eyes grew solemn. "But the Bible story Papa always read us told about three Wise Men bringing gifts to the Christ Child."

Jenny felt as if the entire world were resting on her shoulders. Explaining to her children that there would be nothing for them on Christmas taxed her emotions to the breaking point. She loved her children beyond reason, and hurting them made her more miserable than it did them. She opened her mouth to form the words that would force them into a world of cruel reality but was forestalled when the door to the cabin flew open, admitting a blast of cold air and—Nick St. Clare.

"See, Mama, we weren't lying," Luke squealed, greeting Nick exuberantly. "St. Nicholas *did* come back."

Nick scooped Luke up, lifting him high in the air. When he set him back on his feet, he greeted Annie just as heartily, hugging her tightly and planting a frosty kiss on her cheek.

"What's this?" Nick asked, his inquisitive gaze settling on Jenny. "Did you think I wasn't coming back?"

"Mama said you were gone forever," Annie complained.

"She did?" His penetrating gaze pinned Jenny to the wall. "I know I left rather abruptly, but had I waited around till morning I wouldn't have gotten back in time. It's a long walk to town. I'm sorry if I upset you." He walked over to the hearth, stomping his feet and holding out his hands to dispel the cold. "I see you've put up the tree," he said absently as he gazed about the cozy room, amazed at how much he had come to appreciate it.

Why was Jenny so quiet? he wondered, unable to turn his eyes away from her. Was she angry? He knew he should have left a note, but she had expressed no great concern over his leaving when he had mentioned that it was time to move on. Actually, he had considered leaving for good, but the image of the children's faces, so innocent, so expectant, wouldn't allow him to walk out of their lives without trying again to convince Jenny that they needed him as much as he needed them.

"Will you take us for a sleigh ride?" Luke piped up.

"You saw the sleigh?" Nick asked, unaware that the children had been looking out the window.

"We were watching for you," Annie revealed. "We didn't believe Mama. We knew you'd return."

"There's plenty of time for a sleigh ride before dark," Nick said. "Put on your wraps."

Nearly beside themselves with excitement, the children ran from the room to put on their warmest clothes. When they were gone, he turned and found Jenny staring at him, her green eyes enormous in her thin face.

"Have I disappointed you by returning?" he asked quietly.

"Why did you leave? Was it because of what I said? It was cruel of you to leave without bidding the children goodbye."

"I never intended to leave for good. I thought you knew how I felt about you and the children. I couldn't bear to see them disappointed on Christmas, so I've taken matters into my own hands. I hope you won't be angry with what I've done. I was never allowed fantasies when I was a child, and I don't want Annie and Luke suffering the same fate."

"Where did the sleigh come from? What have you done?"

"We're ready!" The children, bundled in layers of warm clothing, rushed into the room, tugging on Nick's hand as they led him out the front door.

"Wait for your mother," Nick said as he grabbed Jenny's old jacket from the hook and held it out to her. Still in a state of shock, Jenny didn't object when Nick shoved her arms into the jacket and buttoned it up to her chin. "Stay here, I'll get the sleigh from the shed and bring it around." He didn't want the children seeing what was hidden in the shed.

The sleigh ride was a huge success. In previous years Lucas had attached a pair of crude runners to their old wagon, but it was nothing like this sleek sleigh, which fairly flew over the snow. When Nick had first arrived at their door he had left his mount at the livery in town and retrieved him when he had returned today. The animal pulling the sleigh was a huge bay stallion who seemed completely at ease in the wintry landscape.

The gray sky was leaking giant snowflakes, and a murky dusk had settled over the land when Nick drove Jenny and the tired children back to the cabin. Their noses were red, their cheeks icy and their feet tingling when they trooped into the welcome warmth of the cabin. Jenny immediately began preparing supper while Nick unhitched the horse, rubbed him down, and placed feed and water within reach. When he returned to the house he thought Jenny looked strangely subdued and pensive despite her rosy cheeks and sparkling eyes. In fact, she had scarcely said two words to him since he had returned from town this afternoon.

Nick took charge of the children, helping them off with their wraps and sitting them down before the fire to dry. When Jenny had dinner on the table she announced the meal, then politely excused herself. Nick's puzzled look followed her all the way to the bedroom door. Their eyes met briefly when she turned to close the door behind her. She flashed him an ambiguous smile that sent the blood racing through his veins. To cover his confusion, he sat down at the table with the children and toyed with the food on his plate. When Jenny reentered the room a short time later, Nick leaped to his feet, unable to swallow the food he had just placed in his mouth.

She looked so damn beautiful she took his breath away. She had changed her drab black mourning attire for a rich bronze velvet gown. Though the velvet was worn thin and shiny in places, it was a magnificent creation that brought out the red highlights in her chestnut hair, enhanced the pure whiteness of her skin, and lent her green eyes a mischievous sparkle he hadn't noticed before. Before him stood a Jenny that Lucas had described many times during their association; a Jenny Nick had only imagined in his wildest dreams.

Her face no longer looked thin and drawn, but provocative and lovely with high cheekbones, lush lips, and mysterious eyes. Her high breasts were perfect, with enough weight and substance to entice a man, while her waist was tiny beyond imagination. He could only guess at the long, shapely limbs hidden beneath the fullness of her skirt.

And her hair! She had released it from its strict confinement at the nape of her neck and brushed it until it tumbled to her waist in lustrous waves of pure burnished copper.

"Jenny." Her name tasted like sweet honey on his lips.

"Look at Mama!" Luke cried as Jenny walked slowly toward the table. In his five years he had never seen his mother look as lovely as she did this minute.

"Oh, Mama, you're so beautiful," Annie sighed.

"Annie's right, you know," Nick concurred as he held Jenny's chair out for her. "But I've always known that."

For the first time in years Jenny did feel beautiful. But more than that, she felt loved. And she owed it all to Nick. The rugged cowboy had come into her life at a time when she despaired of anything good or exciting ever happening to her again. She had been prepared to sacrifice her youth and happiness to a loveless marriage, and then Nick had arrived to show her that miracles do happen. Staring at Nick from beneath lowered lids, Jenny marveled at the compassion and love concealed beneath his rough exterior. It was as if he had known from the beginning exactly how lonely she was. Could it be that he was just as lonely?

The children's excitement seemed to build during the meal. It was Christmas Eve, St. Nicholas had returned to them, and all was right with their world again. They all helped with the dishes, and afterward Annie grabbed Nick's hand and led him toward a chair by the hearth.

"It's time to read from the Bible," she said as she knelt at his feet. Luke climbed into Nick's lap, while Nick looked to Jenny for enlightenment.

"Lucas always read the story of the Nativity on Christmas Eve. The children haven't forgotten it. You can read, can't you?" she asked anxiously.

Nick smiled. He was no scholar but he could read and cipher well enough to get by. "When I was a child my uncle made me read from the Bible as punishment for misdeeds. This time it will be for pleasure."

Jenny left the room briefly and returned with the tattered family Bible. She placed it in Nick's hands. The brief contact of their flesh sent a jolt of electricity shooting up her arm. She drew back as if burned. Nick grinned at her, his potent look promising more, much more than a tantalizing glimpse of what his touch could do to her if she'd allow it. Her limbs grew weak just looking at Nick, and she sank down beside Annie on the floor as Nick found the appropriate place in the Bible.

Connie Mason

Then he began to read, the deep resonance of his voice dispelling the gloom from the snow-bound cabin and spinning a web of contentment and well-being over the occupants. For a brief time, as Nick unfolded the story of the Christ Child's birth, the children forgot the loss of their father and the poverty that threatened their very existence. They were warm, they were safe, and they felt loved.

And they owed it all to the man they had named St. Nicholas. A man who had brought Christmas back to them.

By the time Nick finished the engrossing story, Luke had fallen asleep in his lap and Annie was no longer able to stifle her yawns. When he closed the book, Nick felt like the luckiest man alive. Even if this family wasn't meant to be his permanently, he had shared a very special time with them.

When Jenny took Luke from Nick's arms so she might carry him to bed, Annie hung back. "Did you bring gifts for us, St. Nicholas?" she asked shyly.

"What do you think?" Nick grinned mischievously.

"Luke and I saw the sleigh when you arrived this afternoon. There were many packages in it."

"I reckon you and Luke will just have to wait until morning, sweetheart."

"You're teasing," Annie said with such a solemn face that Nick burst out laughing.

"Perhaps."

"Did you bring Mama something too?"

"I reckon there will be something in St. Nicholas's sack for your mother."

"Didn't Mama look beautiful tonight?" Annie asked wistfully.

"Someday you'll be beautiful like her."

Annie beamed. "I'm ever so glad you came, St. Nicholas. I hope you stay forever." Then she took Nick's hand, pulled him down, and planted a wet smack on his cheek before scampering off after Luke.

Nick sat in pensive silence until Jenny returned to the room several minutes later.

"Are they sleeping?" he asked.

"They were exhausted. I doubt they'll stir till morning."

"Good."

His dark blue eyes were compelling, magnetic, glowing with an eagerness that held her suspended.

He reached for her.

Chapter Seven

Without hesitation Jenny went to him, and he pulled her down onto his lap. Grasping her chin with a long tanned finger, he raised her mouth, at the same time lowering his. Their lips met in splendid fusion, and Jenny felt the demanding heat of his kiss sear her to the depths of her soul. When he nudged her lips apart and she tasted the sweet essence of his tongue, her bones melted. Then his lips grew hard, searching, as his hands moved boldly over her body, and Jenny knew a moment of panic. There were too many unanswered questions about this mysterious, rugged cowboy for her to succumb to his allure without first finding the answers. Breaking off the kiss and pushing his hands aside, she searched his face.

"Please, Nick, I can't think when you kiss me like that."

"You don't need to think, sweet Jenny. I want you to feel."

"Humor me, Nick. There are things we need to discuss before this goes any further."

Nick heaved an exaggerated sigh. "Very well, but I don't know if I'll be able to answer with you sitting on my lap." She made as if to rise, but Nick held her in place. "It's all right, I was only teasing. Ask me whatever you like and I'll answer to the best of my ability."

His arms tightened and she settled back against him. "Why did you leave in the middle of the night?"

"It's a long way to town and I wanted to get back before dark."

Jenny seemed to accept that. "I thought you were gone for good."

"I could never leave you and the children like that. Especially not on Christmas Eve."

"You told me it was time to move on."

"I said it in anger. After I had time to think about it, I realized you needed me even though you wouldn't admit it. I didn't believe you truly wanted me to leave and decided to stick around a little longer."

"Why *did* you leave, Nick? And where did you get the money to buy the sleigh?"

Nick flashed a mysterious grin as he lifted Jenny from his lap and set her on the chair. "Wait here. I'll be right back." Grabbing his jacket from the hook beside the door, he dashed outside. He returned within minutes, his arms full of packages, which he placed beneath the Christmas tree.

Dropping to his knees, he carefully unwrapped one of the packages.

Jenny drew in a shuddering breath when Nick drew forth a beautiful doll with bisque face and hands, glass eyes, and real hair. She was beautiful. "Nick, where did you get these things?"

"Wait," Nick said, "that's not all." He dashed outside again. When he returned, his arms were piled with more packages, and he pulled a shiny red sled behind him. "There are tin soldiers for Luke and a tea set for Annie. I also bought new clothes for each of the children. I hope I got the sizes right. If not, the man at the mercantile said you can return them. And I bought sugar, flour, tinned fruit, and milk, tea, and coffee. And candy for the children. I want them to have the best Christmas ever."

Tears of gratitude and disbelief were streaming down Jenny's cheeks. It was inconceivable that a rough drifter like Nick could return the spirit of Christmas to her family at a time when their lives were at their lowest. Perhaps the children were right. Perhaps Nick St. Clare really was St. Nicholas, sent expressly to bring them hope and faith—and love.

Nick saw her tears and dropped to his knees beside her. The pad of his thumbs felt rough but oh so gentle as he tenderly brushed away the tears. "Don't cry, sweet Jenny."

"I can't help it," Jenny sniffed. "Where did you get the money, Nick? Cowboys aren't known for being frugal with their meager wages." She managed a watery smile. "Did you rob a bank?"

"Didn't you or the children look inside my pack?"

Jenny shook her head. "The children wanted to, but I wouldn't let them. I figured if you wanted us to know what was inside you would tell us."

"Do you recall me telling you I did some trapping on my way here?" Jenny nodded. "My pack was filled with animal pelts. Beaver, mink, fox, all prime and in good condition. I took them to town and sold them. I bought the sleigh and gifts with part of the money."

"But that was your money!" Jenny cried, stunned by the extent of Nick's generosity.

"There are more where those came from. These mountains abound with wildlife. As I said before, a man could make a good living hunting and trapping here. And perhaps running cattle in the valley."

"You seem to have thought this out quite thoroughly," Jenny said.

"I've thought of nothing else since I've arrived."

"But you didn't even know us! We were virtual strangers when you walked through that door."

"You're wrong, sweet Jenny. I fell in love with you just listening to Lucas talk about you. His children became my children. When I promised him I'd look in on you if anything happened to him, I did so willingly. Had Lucas lived to return to you, you would have remained an unattainable fantasy in my memory, but Lucas's death suddenly made my dream possible."

"You had no idea what you'd find when you got here," Jenny argued. "We might have hated one another on sight."

"But we didn't. The attraction between us was there from the beginning. I want you, Jenny, not for a night, or a month or a year. I want you forever. I'll be a good father to Annie and Luke, and perhaps one day there will be children of our own. I promise to take care of you and keep you all safe and happy."

Jenny leaped to her feet. "I—I don't know, Nick, you're confusing me. Until you arrived a week ago I thought I was going to marry Evan Gillespie."

Nick rose to stand beside her. "You can't marry Gillespie. Neither you nor the children would be happy."

"Maybe not, but at least he would guarantee us a secure future."

"I can't believe you're still thinking of marrying Evan Gillespie," Nick cried, swinging her around to face him.

"I'm not."

"I know the man. He's cold and reserved and not at all the kind of husband—what? What did you say?"

"I said I'm not going to marry Evan. He was here this afternoon and I told him I wasn't going to marry him." She smiled a derisive little smile. "He didn't seem overly perturbed by my refusal. Besides, Nick St. Clare, how do you know the kind of husband I need?" Her hand rested on her hips in open defiance.

His blue eyes turned to raw flame, and the

warmth of his smile sent molten fire licking through her veins. Reaching out, he pulled her roughly against him. "Your sweet kisses hint of the passion you're capable of, sweet Jenny, and I long to unleash that passion. Marry me, my love, and you'll never regret it."

Burying her face against his shoulder, Jenny whispered, "I'm afraid. I was aware of what to expect from Evan, and knew I could count on him, but I know nothing about you. Will you become bored with me as time passes? Will wanderlust seize you one day and drive you away from us?"

"I love you, Jenny Montgomery. Nothing short of death will ever make me leave you or the children. You must have some feelings for me if you've already told Gillespie that you aren't going to marry him."

"I don't trust my feelings," Jenny said shakily. "Bitterness and resentment have been a way of life with me for so long I don't know if I'm still capable of experiencing or giving love."

"I'm willing to take that chance."

Suddenly the door to the children's bedroom opened and Annie and Luke stumbled sleepily into the room. "Is it morning yet?" Annie asked as Nick and Jenny leaped apart.

"No, children, go back to bed," Jenny said, flushing guiltily at having been caught in Nick's arms.

But it was too late to send the children back to bed. Luke had already seen the packages piled beneath the Christmas tree and was tugging on

Annie's arm. "Look, Annie, look what St. Nicholas left for us!" Nothing in the world could have prevented the children from rushing to examine the gifts beneath the tree.

Annie picked up the doll, admiring its hair and eyes before hugging it tightly to her chest. Luke was so enthralled with the shiny new sled that he began tugging it around the room by the pulling rope. When he turned toward the other gifts, Jenny put her foot down.

"Annie, Luke, the other gifts will have to wait till morning. Go back to bed, children."

"Must we, Mama?" Luke's disappointment was keen as he cast sidelong glances at the profusion of packages remaining to be unwrapped.

"Yes," Jenny said firmly.

"Can I take my sled?"

"Can I take my doll?"

"I suppose, if that's the only way I can get you two back to bed."

Luke scampered off, pulling his sled behind him. But Annie hung back, glancing up at Nick through long, feathery lashes. "Is there a gift under the tree for Mama?"

"Of course, sweetheart. You didn't think St. Nicholas would forget your mama, did you?" He reached amidst the packages and pulled out a long, flat box, handing it to Jenny with a flourish. "Open it," he urged, amused by Jenny's confusion.

"Go on, Mama," Annie said excitedly. "Open it."

Jenny paused briefly before tearing the paper

away. Inside the box was a shawl made from the finest wool Jenny had ever seen. Its color reminded her of Nick's eyes when he looked at her. Jenny held it up, admiring the thick, lush fringe edging the entire garment. "It's beautiful. I've never owned anything so fine. It must have cost you a fortune. Thank you."

"Your smile is thanks enough." He moved to take Jenny in his arms when he remembered Annie. "It's late, Annie, off to bed with you."

"I love you, St. Nicholas," Annie said before she turned and ran off to join Luke.

"I wish they'd stop calling you that," Jenny said with a hint of exasperation. "Showering them with gifts will serve only to convince them that you're some kind of miracle worker."

Nick grinned. "I know what the children think. I want to know what their mother thinks."

"I think—I think, oh God, Nick, perhaps the children are right. Perhaps you are St. Nicholas. I've never met a man like you, or received such a wonderful gift. I'm sorry I have nothing to give you in return."

"You do, sweet Jenny. You have but to utter the words to give me the greatest gift of all."

"The greatest gift of all," Jenny repeated thoughtfully. She stared at Nick curiously, searching her memory for a hint of where she'd heard those words before. "Oh." Clutching the shawl to her bosom, she turned and fled into the bedroom.

Nick's face crumpled in keen disappointment. Had he frightened Jenny off? he wondered despondently. Was he moving too fast? He hadn't meant to rush her, but he had waited his entire life for a woman like Jenny Montgomery. He already loved her children. Absently, he dropped to his knees before the hearth, feeding it wood and staring into the flames. He hadn't even had the opportunity to tell Jenny that he had ordered her a real cook stove from Denver, wanting to make her life easier.

He scowled into the flames, wondering if Jenny and the children would be better off if he quietly disappeared from their lives. He doubted it, but apparently Jenny didn't feel about him the same way he felt about her. But no matter what Jenny decided, he didn't regret one penny of the money he had spent on gifts for them. For the first time in his memory he felt a part of a real family. He sat staring into the flames, thinking, brooding, wanting to follow Jenny into the bedroom but fearing she would hate him if he did. Instead, he remained where he was, dreaming of the miracles he would work if he truly were St. Nicholas.

Jenny closed the bedroom door softly behind her. She leaned against it and hugged the shawl to her breast. Tears turned her eyes into shimmering emeralds. She wanted desperately to believe that Nick would make her happy, that he meant what he had said about loving her. She held the shawl to her face, rubbing the soft material against her cheek as she stared pensively into the purple shadows dancing on the bedroom walls. Suddenly an arrested look came over her features and the corners of her mouth lifted in a slow smile. Her eyes glowed with a dark, mysterious fire as resolutely her right hand slid upward to the neck of her dress as she moved away from the door.

Nick had been staring into the dancing flames so long he felt suspended in a world between fantasy and reality. He had no idea what made him sense that something extraordinary was about to happen. Intuition, perhaps, or the strange, compelling sensation that he wasn't alone. Slowly, so that each movement was an exaggeration of motion, he turned his head toward Jenny's bedroom.

"Dear God!"

Jenny stood in the open doorway, wrapped from neck to ankles in the Christmas shawl. Her chestnut hair rested like strands of pure copper against the blue wool mantle. Though little of her was visible, her bare ankles and white toes poking out from beneath the fringe sent a surge of raw flame racing through his blood. She looked innocent, vulnerable, yet so provocative that his need for her escalated to a threshold he'd never visited before.

"I've thought about what you said, Nick," Jenny said quietly. "I can't begin to describe what you've done for the children in the short time since your arrival. Nor can I ever repay you."

Nick swallowed convulsively. "I've never asked for payment." It was difficult speaking around the lump in his throat.

"But I was wrong. I *do* have a gift for you. The greatest gift of all—love, and I give it freely."

She opened her arms wide and the shawl fell

open. A log popped in the hearth and a flame flared to life, turning Jenny's body to pure gold. Nick stared, wondering how he could have ever considered Jenny skinny. She was perfect in every respect. Every incredible inch of her was daintily made yet lush and ripe with the promise of passion.

"Am I dreaming?" Nick asked as he rose shakily to his feet. "If I am I don't ever want to wake up." Jenny merely smiled. "Is this a commitment, sweet Jenny? I'll accept nothing less, you know. I want us to be married, with the children in attendance. As soon as possible."

"That's what I want, too, Nick. Will you accept my gift? I give it with all my heart."

Nick moved toward her like a man just coming out of a long dream. "I accept it joyously, my love, for your gift is without equal. Merry Christmas, Jenny."

Sweeping Jenny off her feet, he lifted her high in his arms and carried her into the bedroom. Kicking the door closed behind him, he set her on her feet. She shrugged her shoulders and the shawl dropped to the floor. She kicked it aside and held out her hand. Their eyes locked as he placed his large hand in hers and she led him toward the bed.

"Merry Christmas, St. Nicholas."